Dead End Drive

Ian Kirkpatrick

STEAK HOUSE
BOOKS

First publication in the USA
Steak House edition published in 2020
Copyright © 2020 by Ian Kirkpatrick

Print ISBN: 978-0-578-72576-5
Hard Cover: 978-1-7368870-8-0
ebook ISBN: 978-0-578-72577-2
LCCN: 2020914024

Our books may be purchased in bulk for promotional, educational, or business use. Please contact your local bookseller to order.

Printed in the United States of America.

13   10   20   3

CONTENTS

The author would like to thank her family for their continued encouragement and support. A special thank you to her mother for reading the novel so many times and to her writing partner, Samuel Johnson.

ONE.

Benedict Estate Conservatory, Louisiana
August 1st, 7:31 A.M. 1993

The sun was always brightest and the air sweeter on days when misfortune struck the Benedict Estate. The rising sun warmly lit the conservatory, reflecting brilliantly through the glass walls. Flowers and vines hung from the ceiling, sat potted in colorful artisan vases, and grew around the furniture. Kelly Benedict, the fourteen-year-old adopted son of Benedict Estate heiress Agatha, sat at a round, lattice table that was not only years older than him, but much more sophisticated than the boy could ever hope to be. Steel bent into angel wings and misshapen hearts held up the glass tabletop. He impatiently tapped his finger, watching the door for his mother's usual entrance that would sadly not come today. Every morning for the better part of the eight years, the hours of 7:30am to 10:00am went as follows: for the first hour, Kelly and Agatha would sample the breakfast made by chef Angus, who sometimes avoided burning the eggs, but often didn't. The next thirty minutes would be spent on a walk through the garden during which Agatha would trip on a soft, sometimes bony lump buried among the flowers. Finally, to further young Kelly's education, Agatha would take Kelly to the library where she would read to him a portion of her favorite romance novel, one where she had modeled on the cover as a young maiden with a bosom nearly exposed and a long-haired Adonis holding her to his chest. At the end of the reading hour, she would send him into the butler's care while she resigned herself to the care of her thirty-three-year-old boyfriend, Beauregard, who always seemed to look different upon the change of season.

But this morning was different. This morning, after eight years, would be the first time Agatha Benedict did not greet her son for breakfast, walk among the roses, and read him a saucy romance novel. The only company Kelly had on the morning of August 1st was the smell of bacon, eggs, and toast. Accompanying the griddles soft sizzle was the whistle of a tune Kelly recognized, but couldn't name. The kitchen door opened just as he'd become impatient enough to leave the table.

Angus McGregor, the estate's head chef, entered, whistling and knocking the door hard enough into the house that the wood cracked. There were three specific things to know about Angus McGregor:

First, he was recognized for his size, hardly able to fit through the doors of the house, with shoulders so broad he had to turn sideways to enter most rooms. Second, his accent distorted every word he spoke into unintelligible gibberish, though Agatha was fond of listening to him speak and often pretended she knew what he was saying. Third, though he had been employed as the estate's head chef for thirty years, the edibility of his meals wasn't assured. Still, for all those years, his smile and polite demeanor had kept him securely under Agatha's employment where it would not have saved him at the cheapest, moldiest bar in Parvenu.

Angus approached the table, holding a plate in one hand

and a small glass of milk in the other.

"Where's Auntie?" Kelly said. "We're supposed to go to the city today."

"Auld anes tak' time tae wake, laddie." Angus laughed. It was anyone's guess what he said. The dishes clattered as he placed them onto the table.

"What?" Kelly blinked rapidly as though it would translate the words into sense.

"Old ones," he said again, slower. "As ye get older, gettin up in the morn takes a bit more time."

Kelly turned away and crossed his arms. "She's never taken this long to come down. Mathias is usually down here by now too."

Angus placed his hand on Kelly's shoulder and urged him back to the table. "Maybe it's best not disturbin' the madam and her lad."

Kelly ducked under Angus's arm and ran to the ballroom door. "I'm going to get her."

"I don't think that's a good idea—" Angus reached to catch the boy by the arm, But Kelly was already halfway across the ballroom by the time Angus turned around. He maneuvered around the furniture to the grand staircase. Agatha's bedroom had never been far from Kelly's. Attached with a bathroom between them, the separate rooms only served to give Kelly a place to go to bed early when Agatha wanted to play well into the night.

Her bedroom door was latched closed, though streaks of light slipped beneath it. "Auntie?" Kelly rapped his knuckles against the door. Without receiving an answer, he opened the door.

Heavy emerald curtains darkened the room, the budding light of the morning snuck through the cracks. A form laid on the bed, blanket pulled over her head. Holding a pen and clipboard, Doc, Agatha's private physician, sat in a chair bedside. Mathias Lockheart, or the man Agatha currently referred to as Beauregard, and Gavin Aker, the head butler, drew the curtains open.

"What's everyone doing in here?" Kelly hurried into the room. "Auntie?" he approached the bed slowly now.

Gavin stopped Kelly before he came too close. Grabbing him by the shoulders, the butler guided the boy back to the door. "Go downstairs. Eat breakfast."

"Why's Auntie still in bed?" Kelly squirmed in Gavin's hands, but Gavin hardened his grip and pulled him back toward the door. "We're supposed to go to the city today."

"Her plans have changed," Doc said while scribbling on her clipboard. "She's not going anywhere unless it's the morgue."

Tears welled in Kelly's eyes. This time, he wiggled free of the butler only to be stopped at the bed by Mathias. Kelly pressed his hands against his sleeping mother. He rocked her in the bed as tears flowed down his cheeks. Mathias grabbed Kelly's wrists tightly. "Let go!" Kelly jerked, but he couldn't get away. Mathias was too big, too strong. A sob broke through his lips.

"If you'd still like to go, I will be going to the city today." Gavin walked across the room to the window overlooking the garden. The sky was bright and everything under it green. "There will be a storm soon. We must send the letters."

"So, the traditions are true after all," Mathias said.

"The Benedict Estate is known for a lot of things. Dishonesty is not among them." Gavin took Kelly by the shoulder and guided him toward the room's exit. "Eat your breakfast, Kelly."

Kelly glanced over his shoulder at the scene, at Mathias's stoic stance beside the bed and Doc's unresponsive nature as her pencil moved over the clipboard. The heat gathered in Kelly's eyes. He swallowed it back. "What's going to happen to me?"

"I'll tell you everything you should know if you wish to inherit the estate. Not now, but after breakfast."

Laughter came as the door closed and Kelly was locked on the other side. Without answers, without a goodbye, and with a cold breakfast waiting for him alone at the table downstairs.

TWO.

Los Angeles, California
August 9th, 9:23 P.M.

Not all of Agatha Benedict's employees lived in her rural swamp. Some preferred the urban swamps of lights, camera, and casting couches to mosquitoes, alligators, and invasive vines. Los Angeles was known as a haven for the hopeful, though as it turned out, those rich in hope were often poor in desperation and desperation was the only currency accepted in the city of fame, fortune, and manufactured reputation.

Adelaide Bellwater was such an employee. While the rest of the staff at the Benedict Estate had known of Agatha Benedict's unfortunate passing on the day of her death, it was days before the Hollywood hopeful found the hand-written letter in her mailbox.

The letter read as follows:

"Dear Madame Astra,

We regret to inform you that on August 1st, your employer, Agatha Jane Benedict, owner of the Benedict Estate, peacefully passed away in

her sleep. It is estate tradition that upon the owner's passing, family, friends, and associated employees are invited to the manor for an open Will reading. All those interested in the inheritance are welcome to attend, but we request guests familiarize themselves with estate policies and recognize invitation does not guarantee receipt of an award.
    Sincerely,"

Kelly Benedict was written across the bottom edge of the paper in large, looping cursive. The name elicited a chuckle from the Hollywood starlet. Everyone who worked at the Estate, even in a part-time capacity, was well-aware the boy couldn't read or write. Signing a letter in neat cursive was out of the question.

After receiving the letter, Adelaide was sure that her luck was about to change. Though the letter warned of unpromised rewards, she was certain that if she wasn't going to receive anything from her employer then she wouldn't have received an invitation at all. So Adelaide Bellwater of off-Hollywood boulevard began packing her bags to become the heiress of the new swamp she would call home.

"Clara! Have you seen my headscarf?" Adelaide said. Her voice went unheard, lost under Chrissy Amphlett singing, *"When I think about you, I touch myself."* The bass rocked the living room into a sultry lullaby only appropriate for putting go-go dancers to work on the Sunset Strip after ten 'o'clock.

Adelaide packed her suitcase until teal, purple, and gold clothing spilled over the edges. Pressing her weight into her palms, she beat everything down. As she stepped back, the mess of garments sprung over the zipper edges and spread across her mattress again. Adelaide growled, threw her hands in the air, and marched out of her room. "Clara!" She picked up the remote and muted MTV's top 50 countdown.

"My headscarf. Have you seen it?"

Clara was everything Adelaide was not. From her perfect blonde hair (that looked straight out of a box), to her eighteen-inch waist. She was young and fit with a boyfriend in the papers and leading roles coming through the mail what felt like every day. She was confident to an obnoxious extent, but she deserved to be. Though the music stopped playing, Clara continued swaying her hips. "Uhm…" Her bright, natural hair bounced against her shoulder as she turned around. "Did you like, check, like, under your bed?" she asked, twisting a strand around her index finger.

"Yes. I've looked everywhere for it. The last thing I remember is letting you borrow it a week ago—"

"Wow!" Clara laughed, covering her mouth. "I'm, like, super impressed you remembered that. I kinda, like, thought you'd forget on the count of—well, you… you're old. Let me go get it for you." Clara stepped out of the room and returned with a teal and gold headscarf crumpled in her hands. Clara tossed it at Adelaide as she walked by, only stopping beside her to stare at Adelaide's face, scrutinize it, and assign it a number between one and ten like the editors had done for her in her most recent teen magazine editorial. While Clara had received a ten out of ten, she assigned Adelaide a three, as in thirty-five, as in, she believed it was time for Adelaide Bellwater to retire. "Uhm, Addy…" The young girl pursed her lips. "I hate to ask, but is that a—"

"—Is that a what?" Adelaide crossed her arms and tapped her toe like her mother had every time she became an impassioned child or an impassioned teenager or an impassioned thirty-three-year-old at her last birthday party.

"Are you growing a beard?"

"What?" Adelaide gripped her headscarf and stepped back quickly.

"Like, right here." Clara caught up with Adelaide to poke

at the hair sprouting from her chin. "You have, like, a really dark, *really long* hair—it's practically a full beard. Hey! Are you getting ready for a part? Congrats!"

Adelaide ran back to her room and shoved the door open, it bounced against the wall and rattled the knob. The headscarf fell haphazardly onto her luggage pile and she slammed the door shut. A full-length mirror hung on the back of the door, the thinness of which stretched her body long like a funhouse mirror. Her shoulders appeared frail and delicate, though her neck exceedingly long. She leaned into the mirror and examined her jaw to find a coarse, brown strand standing out from the lower edge of her chin.

Keeping an eye on the enemy of her beauty, she groped around her vanity until she found her tweezers and plucked the intruder from her face. She examined herself for any other stray hairs she may have overlooked. Once satisfied with her appearance, something she never should have felt, she tossed the tweezers into her luggage with everything else. Sure, Adelaide wasn't disfigured, but she wasn't beautiful, exemplary, or memorable either. More times than she cared to remember, she'd been referred to as tragically average; people couldn't seem to remember even when they met her just a day prior. Every meeting with agents, directors, or actors she'd previously spent time with started with, "nice to meet you."

Adelaide folded the letter and slipped it into her back pocket. She checked her wallet and reviewed her plane ticket one last time. A passing glimpse in the mirror showed the dark rings under her eyes, aging her face with depth that didn't belong. Crow's feet grew from the corners of her eyes and broke off into her hairline. She pulled at her face and flattened the skin under her eyes. "God," she muttered. "I look like my mother..." She tied her bleached hair into a loose bun and dabbed her face with the concealer laying on top her vanity. The dark spots disappeared, and her face was relieved of half a decade for a couple of hours or until she worked up a sweat.

Adelaide dropped the small container into her purse and closed her luggage only after she pressed it together with her weight. She dragged her luggage to the front door while Clara danced to MTV in the living room.

"Wow, Addy," she said. "I'm like, so proud of you." She walked around the couch and gave Adelaide a hug.

"Really?" Adelaide's arms hung at her side, too surprised to hug the girl back.

"Like, I'm sorry to see you go like this, but, I can't, like, say I'm surprised. Your face just isn't cut out for this kind of work. Maybe you should try radio in Montana. Isn't that where you're from?"

Adelaide shoved Clara away. "What!"

"I'm glad to see you like, finally admit it. You seemed pretty far in, like, denial for a while, I do have like, one question though. Are you sending movers to pick up that other stuff or should I just... ya know, sell it?"

"What are you talking about?"

"Well, I kinda, like, figured you weren't cut out for LA. I mean, look at you. You're like, fifty and you barely leave the house."

"Clara..." Adelaide's fingers tightened around her luggage handle, "I'm thirty-five."

"Yeah, but, like, what's the difference though?" she quirked her head to the side. "Look, point is, I don't even know what you do to pay rent. Are you a waitress? Or like, a streetwalker? Like, no shame if you are! No shame! Julia Roberts played a streetwalker just last year and she looked so good, not that I think you're as pretty and talented as Julia Roberts, but, like, you're better off going home to work at a drug store or something, stocking shelves, bagging milk, selling condoms to pretty people with sex lives. You'll be better off there. I know, because I've been in drug stores and you look just like those cashiers. You'll fit right in! Promise! And you know the best part about all this? I already found someone to take your room over! Wanna hear something cool? She knows Matt Damon! Can you believe it? Matt-freaking-Damon! So, I need to know when the movers are coming, when you're moving out, so we can officially par-tay."

Adelaide took several deep breaths so that her first major TV appearance wouldn't be on an episode of Cops. "I'm not *quitting* L.A. My *richest* client just passed away and she invited me to the will reading. If you knew anything about dead, old, rich people, it's that if you get in at the right moment, they will spoil you like you're their child. So, I'm going to collect my inheritance."

"Wait, for real?" Clara stepped forward, clapped, and pushed Adelaide toward the door. "You mean, like, that whole *psychic thing* really worked out?"

Adelaide rubbed at her temples. Clara pulled the luggage along. "Yes, that *psychic thing* worked out. Despite what you and the directors here might think, I'm, like, a good actress." She did a valley girl laugh. "And people take their afterlife way serious."

"So, like... how much are you, like, getting...?"

Adelaide dropped her head back and smiled. She covered her hand with her lips to fake modesty. She couldn't smile about someone's death. What would that make her? But in the face of fortune, it was hard to resist glee. "I don't know. Millions, billions maybe."

"Wow! Hot stuff over here! Maybe with all that money, you can fix your face and get some real jobs!"

Adelaide went out the front door without saying anything. As she went for the elevator, she heard Clara yelling from the apartment, "So, can I like, sublet your room out at least? My new roomie is coming on Friday! What do I tell her?"

Adelaide said nothing as she left the building, hailed a cab, and made her way to the airport. Aboard the plane and taking off, she looked at the lights of L.A. as they passed her and she said, "When I come back, I'm going to buy Beverly Hills and you're going to be the first to go..."

THREE.

Benedict Estate Garden, Louisiana
August 10th, 5:03 A.M.

Wrapped around the Benedict Estate stood a cast-iron gate, mixed with flecks of gold that brought out the vibrant pink and purple from the exotic, vining flowers that climbed the length of the wall. Enormous leaves weighed down with morning dew rustled softly as a thick and humid breeze brushed over the grounds. The gate wasn't merely for decoration. It kept the healthy, bright yard separate from the dark, colorless swamp just outside the grounds. Like a predator, the swamp waited for the rain to weaken the yard before attempting to conquer it. Wherever it was able to touch, the colors of the grass became dull, the flowers shriveled and died.

The Benedict Estate consumed everything it could, including generations of Benedict children and their employees. A large dirt path, lined with leaning trees, gray and petrified, led visitors to the estate grounds. Pale iron poles with sharp, gold-dipped edges dug into the earth, protecting the property from trespassers. Green and yellow vines contorted around the bars and bore succulent salmon and white pear-shaped fruit. The main gate was situated a mile away from the nearest highway and metal spider webs held the initials 'A.B.' captive, like a trapped animal. Beyond the gates, vast untamed swamp grew into marble structures, iron bars, tidy grass, and large and perky flowers. The Estate steps glowed, rich light reflected from salt and crystals mixed into the pavement. Doric columns framed the large front door. Each groove in the marble was sanded smooth and soft to touch. Despite being miles outside of Parvenu, the mansion's rooftop could be seen between the trees anywhere the skyline was visible.

Waves of deep blue and cool purple blended seamlessly into rows of warm red and orange buds as the sun peeked over the treetops on the horizon. As usual, the estate had been awake and working for hours already.

Bertrand Lilygrove, the head gardener and groundskeeper, knew every flower by name, every blade of grass by the sound it made in the wind, and every acre of the estate by where he had buried Agatha's bevy of Beauregards. He had been Agatha's groundkeeper for forty-five years, intimately tending to it as he would have tended to her sensitivities. Without Agatha in the house, without her eyes upon the garden, there seemed little reason for him to keep up with it any longer.

Bertrand stood beside the shed, lifting his head, he inhaled the morning air. The garden smelt sour and moldy. The humidity of the coming storm hadn't hit yet, but the decay of the household had already begun. His bones ached with familiar anticipation. The last will reading he went through with Agatha weighed his shoulders. He hadn't intended to make it to a second will reading; he hadn't intended to outlive her.

Bertrand reached up to pull his weathered cap off his head and ran a hand through what remains of his thinning hair. Once black strands had long since become peppered gray. Deep creases aged his face, his dark, mono-lid eyes sullen, somber, as he stood before his crew, hands in his pockets.

Bertrand called for everyone to gather at the shed, and after he took attendance, he spoke: "The *will reading* is tonight." He dug into his deep overall pockets. Dirt-stained fingers stroked the smooth surface of his lighter. His thumb ran over the carved indentations AB and HY. Her gift to him. "I beg you: any *decent* person, don't stay. If you think passivity will bring you anything, stay away. Do not come to the reading." His voice was stern. "The only people who should come are those who want to meet their monsters. No one is spared. Whatever you think might be worth it, you will find the sacrifice too great. This godforsaken house will promise you the world, then take everything you have." He stroked the lighter again. Tomorrow, the manor will be in disarray; some of your family, friends, or coworkers may be missing. Don't go inside. Don't ask questions. Keep your head down. Keep to yourself. Accept that things have changed. Accept what they tell you has happened. Do your work and go home to your families. Be happy you're alive."

Studying his employees, they wouldn't look at him. Some grimaced, others coughed as an excuse to look away, and a few whispered to one another with tense shoulders. None of them were old enough to remember the last *will reading*, and none would attend the reading tonight. They would live out their lives to old age, watching people they may have loved or hated disappear and willing the rumors true because they would rather not believe them.

"Please, enjoy your day off and show Peter the respect he deserves as he takes over for me. He's been here for many years and the garden enjoys his company almost as much as it enjoys mine." Bertrand turned to his garden to tuck in his plants one last time.

FOUR.

Kelly's Bedroom, Benedict Estate
August 10th, 8:03 A.M.

Gavin drew back the amethyst bedroom curtains with strong, gloved hands and masterfully tied them back using hanging golden tassels. Matching carpets devoured the morning light, softening the wake of the sleeping young master. Kelly pulled the covers over his head at first exposure to light. He groaned. The blankets shifted around him as he burrowed further, becoming a lump under the heavy bedding.

"They'll be arriving soon. Dress and come downstairs," Gavin said.

Kelly grumbled through the blankets.

Gavin turned away from the window and regrouped with Anna, the head maid and his loyal assistant. She, like him, was the caricature of a classical maid wearing a black dress and a lacy white apron. She had long hair, almost black, tied up in a neat, top bun and the complexion and face of someone mixed race. Her slim, modest figure was another statement to her efficiency as a maid, slipping in and out of rooms discretely. They had worked together for so long and so closely, their morning routine was predictable and comfortable, they didn't often need words. A glance could be a question or a command, a nod was confirmation, and anything Gavin left Anna to do, he could trust it would get done. With a couple towels folded over her arms, Anna slipped into the attached bathroom.

Gavin approached the bed and removed the blankets with a strong yank, exposing Kelly's slim, teenage form. Shoulder-length, curly brown hair covered his face. Gavin continued to reel the blankets to the end of the bed. "You should have been up ten minutes ago."

"I don't feel like it today." Kelly burrowed his face into his pillow and blindly reached for the blanket.

Gavin tossed the comforter on the floor at the foot of the bed. "The guests will gather whether you greet them or not." Gavin walked around to the side of the bed. "And the reading will take place."

Kelly's legs prickled from the cold. "We could say screw tradition and lock them all out." Kelly picked up his pillow and put it over his head. "Lock the gate. Lock everything. Don't let anyone in."

"You won't inherit the estate if you act like this."

Kelly snorted. "What are you talking about? It's already mine. Auntie's gone and..." Kelly sighed. "everything's already mine."

"I've already told you: the tradition doesn't work like that, Kelly. If you wish to inherit the estate, you must survive. The guests are coming whether you like it or not. We will gather in the dining room and read the will. Alliances have already been made and if you are not part of those alliances, you will be killed. There are many in this house who will have no issue killing you for the money, Kelly. Whatever you think you know about anyone in this house, forget it. There will be blood; monsters are not only things of fairytales and bad dreams. If you don't prepare accordingly, you will die—"

"Shut up!" Kelly sat up instantly, jaw clenched and face flushed. He threw one of the pillows at Gavin then reached for another. "You're a liar! You're lying! Like Mathias and Johnny and the rest of them!" He rolled onto his back and laid flat, staring at the ceiling. His hair fell away from his face, exposing his long boyish eye lashes and dark brown eyes. His petite figure gave the appearance that he was younger than he really was. "And even if you weren't lying to me, no one cares about traditions anyway. I'm in charge now. I get whatever I want, and I say we don't care about what some old, dead people said."

"That's not how it works." Gavin folded the comforter and set it on a nearby armchair. "You must fulfill your obligations and follow the rules already set in place. You may not like them, but the traditions are there for a reason and you do yourself no favors by ignoring them. Ignorance will not spare you from consequence. Anna and I will take care of you as best we can, as we always have, but you will have to trust us. Understand, we will not be able to do everything for you tonight, Kelly. You may have to do something uncomfortable."

"What are you talking about?" Kelly sat up.

"Actively rejecting the truth does not spare you of responsibility or fault." Gavin came to Kelly's bedside.

Kelly slouched and rubbed his eyes. He sat with his head down turned. His heart throbbed. "It doesn't matter..." He rubbed his eyes again. His fingers curled in the bed cover. "Auntie's gone and she left everything to me. Nothing can change that."

"Absolutes are a dangerous thing to rely on," Gavin said.

Kelly looked at the empty armchair where the blanket sat, taking Agatha's place in weighing the cushion down. "I don't want to take her place." His lips curled tightly. "I want her to come back..."

"It isn't what one wants that one gets."

The water ran in the connected bathroom. Anna re-entered the bedroom.

"Take your bath before the water turns cold. Your suit will be laid out when you're done," Gavin said.

Kelly climbed out of bed and drug his feet as he walked. When he was done bathing, he exited to find the bed made and his suit with shorts and a red bow tie laid out. Once dressed, Kelly scowled at himself: shorts with socks that ran up his legs just below the knee made him feel small. He slipped his feet into polished shoes and held the untied bow tie. He watched himself, but never tried to put on the tie. His hand tightened around the fabric, his lips straightened, and his face grew hot. "Gavin!"

The butler entered the room and without any further prompting, took the tie and pulled it around Kelly's neck. "We'll have to get you a new suit after tonight." He folds the collar of Kelly's shirt over the tie and adjusts the bow. "This one makes you look like a child."

FIVE.

Tennis Courts, Benedict Estate
August 10th, 8:35 A.M.

Ex-tennis pro Johnny Green stood center court in the Benedict Estate's private tennis court. He took to the courts ten times a day, honing skills he would never use in the pro circuit again. Three years into forced retirement and the thirty-two-year-old athlete hadn't yet accepted his fate. He swung his most powerful backhand and, after hitting the face of his designer racket, the ball echoed through the court and off the clay. Three years into forced retirement and his backhand was as good as it had ever been.

The tennis pro favored wearing his signature tennis uniform even outside of a tournament. A too-small white polo clung to Johnny's chest, immodestly outlining his muscles and threatening to pop at the stitches every time he flexed. White shorts encased his lower half, thinly stretching up his thigh, they left a quarter moon uncovered in the back and little left to the imagination in the front. When he ran, the fabric disappeared into his sun-kissed skin.

Johnny returned to the rack to grab another set of balls

and dumped all but one of them into the ball launcher. He took his place across from it, bounced the singular ball he held against the clay a couple times, then served it with a powerful, unrestrained swing. The ball hit the fence that circled the court, and ricocheted off the terrain into the short, white net.

The throwing machine quickly shot another ball at Johnny, and this one he hit harder than the last. The chain-link fence rattled on impact. The throwing machine growled, sending another at him. He swung, he flexed, he growled, his polo struggled to stay in one piece. He wiped the sweat from his forehead with the back of his hand and smiled toothily as his racket pressed into the clay court. The pose should've been considered unnatural; the smile too large, the angle of his arm, his back, his head twisted just right, would have seemed only appropriate for the toothpaste commercial he had starred in fourteen years ago. However, Johnny Green lived his life as if the cameras were always watching and thus, there was little more natural than a pose meant to tickle the wallet out of one's back pocket.

Johnny closed his eyes and listened for the machine, swinging only once he heard the bump and swoosh of a fired ball. The blood rush blotted his eyes with red around the edges. His lips curled further into a sneer and crinkles gathered on his nose. He swung again and again, smacking harder with each ball until the racket flung out of his sweaty palms and into the fence. The racket's neck snapped and Johnny opened his eyes to examine the instrument's damaged corpse, cracked at the handle and its face partially detached. Broken rackets weren't so much a crime scene as a display of passion, given to observers by the player. "Whoops." He laughed.

Yet Johnny had made a mistake to stop and admire the results of his passion. He had neglected to count how many he dumped in the machine and how many he had received. The machine never shot out of malice, but out of duty. Johnny had been shot one too many times by these machines, and as the ball came at him, he jumped outside of the ball's path. A gold-plated dog tag hung from his neck, bearing his copyrighted catchphrase, "Only Losers Lose." The same phrase could be found written in gold on the ivory grip of his designer rackets, but signed with his thick, masculine signature, 'Jonathan B. Green.'

"Don't worry, racket. Yours isn't the only neck snapping tonight." Johnny picked the racket up but allowed the face to hang. He stroked his name with his thumb. The throwing machine shot another ball. It bounced off the fence and hit him in the back of the head. Johnny stumbled forward then turned around swinging the broken racket. He growled, tossed the racket to the ground, and stomped on it until the neck broke completely through, then he crossed the court to do the same to the throwing machine.

SIX.

Doc's Office, Benedict Estate
August 10th, 10:41 A.M.

Doc's morning was unremarkable like any other. She sat at her desk in her office, alone, with a decade-old historical romance novel as her only company, *In the Cabin Behind the Colonel's House*. She didn't enjoy reading them so much as laughing at what she determined were pathetic portrayals of business relationships. You see, Doc recognized every interaction to be something of a transaction. One should only enter an interaction if they plan to get something out of the other. However, more than half a book would be spent on the emotional manipulation of a woman in order to get the dowry her father placed over her in a desperate bid to be rid of her for good. Doc licked her finger and turned the page with a snicker.

The late Agatha Benedict's medical report laid open on the desk. A three-ring binder filled with twenty years of information Doc had gathered on Agatha's body through testing, analysis, and observation, including the final analysis and the closing of Agatha's life. A second copy of the health file had been sent to the proper authorities for verification in New Orleans.

Doc set her novel aside and picked the binder up. Reviewing the notes on her police report, the physician had assured the authorities that Agatha Jane Benedict was healthy until the very last moment she existed on this earth. Her death had been an event of natural causes in her sleep at and there was no reason to suspect foul play. Sure, Agatha was a bit young to struggle for survival when the lights were out, however, at the Benedict estate, previous owners had a tendency to check out a little early. Rather than suspect loving household employees or relatives of malicious action, all chose to believe it was the stress that took them home early.

Before the will reading could begin, a full autopsy was required by the Benedict Estate's legal team. Without it, no dinner and no distribution of the heiress's belongings could take place. After the initial autopsy was completed, a second autopsy was required from a doctor in Parvenu and then a final review from a team of doctor's in New Orleans. Once the health, medical records, and cadaver were confirmed, all legal changes would be considered official in the morning light. It wasn't that Doc had a particularly bad record; none of the previous in-home doctors were trusted at their word for the sake of the inheritance. However, of all the doctors previous, Doc would take the honor of being the most accurate.

After all, Doc had been at the top of her class in medical school. She'd been named the most desired doctor in New Orleans up until her practice closed just six years out of medical school. No one could argue the skill and attention she brought to work, however her losing feature would always be her lack of compassion. Unfortunately, as a doctor short of a soft touch, she had no place in the private sector. And though she would have fit perfectly into government healthcare, she found the private practice for one Agatha J. Benedict to be far more lucrative and respectful than being another black woman at the mercy of the government's dollar.

Up until she moved to Parvenu for this job, Doc avoided the city at all costs. Her parents never ignored an opportunity to tell her the people of Parvenu were nothing better than thieves and madmen. As a child, she contested this. As an adult, she realized her parents were right. The streets of Parvenu were filled with actors and artists, and what were artists, but thieves and madmen who had convinced themselves that someday they would be of value to society?

After reading her report for the thirteenth time, Doc closed the binder and slipped it into her desk drawer. Not a typo out of place nor a diagnosis forgotten. She took the key from around her neck, locked the drawer, and opened the one above it. Inside: an oxygen mask and scalpel among other medical knickknacks. She picked up the scalpel and ran her finger gently along the edge of the blade. Her skin peeled apart even at the mildest contact and a drop of blood trickled down her thumb, staining her sleeve. She smiled, replaced the cap over the blade, and slid the instrument into her pocket.

SEVEN.

For the last two and a half years, Mathias Reginald Lockheart had lived in the room immediately attached to Agatha Jane's and had tentatively been known as Beauregard. It was the affectionate name she gave every boyfriend when they came to live in her house, mostly for simplicity's sake. Most of her boyfriends only lasted a couple of months, few lived longer than a year. Thus, Agatha had found it too much trouble to learn their names and so provided all of them with one.

She may have been old, but everyone who knew her would say she was sporty, energetic, and very much alive. On his bedside lay a small green service bell to match the emerald blankets, shades, bed canopy, curtains, and anything else with color in his room. The bell had a wire that ran along the floor, beneath the door and into Agatha's room to a small buzzer at her bed side. Whenever Agatha felt frisky, she would press this button and any time Mathias was in earshot, he was required to attend to her. Unfortunately, the bell was fixed with an extremely loud buzz that echoed across the entire second story, the ceiling, and the floor. So, if ever Mathias was not in the attic or in the yard, he, and everyone else in Benedict Estate could hear when Agatha wanted her sheets freshened.

For more than a week now, the buzzer had been silent and the residents of the Benedict Estate breathed easy not having to imagine the old skeleton of a woman intimately writhing beneath a man less than half her age. Most relieved of all, was of course, Mathias, who on many occasions explored means to silence the bell without causing alarm to the old mistress.

Now, in his quiet bedroom, Mathias tugged his collar into place. Running his fingers through his hair, he pushed the strands into place with just enough care to look inconsequentially handsome. He was a classic kind of good-looking; the type to walk into a bar in the 1920s and demand attention and respect for the strong, geometrical shape of his jaw, straight nose, broad shoulders, and slim waist. Built like a Persian tower blessed by God Himself, there wasn't anything Mathias couldn't get with a smile and the word, "please." He wore three-piece suits religiously, perhaps by belief that if he died today, or any day, he wanted to be found wearing nothing but the best. A small mole dotted his left cheek beneath his eye, marking him with the most perfect imperfection nature could use to make the man appear flawless. The smell of refined passion marinated his bed sheets in a noticeable fashion and mixed with something much younger, a soft, honeysuckle scent.

Mathias adjusted his blue silk tie. He patted down the front of his jacket, looking for any parts of it that stuck out unnaturally. Only once he deemed himself presentable did Mathias leave his room.

Downstairs, Kelly sat in the observatory eating breakfast. Gavin milled about looking busy, but more so moving things around to keep an eye on what he deemed important. He slipped in and out of the pantry that connected the kitchen to the dining room and often peered through the window from the kitchen to the green observatory.

"Good morning." Mathias entered the room and sat down at the table.

Kelly barely shrugged without looking up from his plate.

Angus came from the kitchen and placed a cup of coffee down before the man. "Can I make ye anything?" Angus said.

"Coffee is fine for now, thanks."

"Aye." Angus nodded; a wide smile buried in his peppered, red beard. "Holler if ye need me." And he returned to his place in the kitchen to continue preparations.

Mathias sipped at black coffee, watching the field workers through the glass.

"What are you staring at?" Kelly's fork knocked against the edge of his plate.

"Not staring. Thinking." The cup edges warmed his fingers and drew the boyfriend into the warm yard. "What an exciting night it will be."

EIGHT.

Stylist Salon, Benedict Estate
August 10th, 1:14 P.M.

His name was Alexandre Ashley Lamont. It never could have been Alexander because the *er* was too plain. When people thought of him, the young, personal stylist wanted them to think of show business, to think Broadway, to associate him with the stars and the red carpet and Antonio Banderas. Since he hadn't been able to accomplish any of that yet using skill and virtue, he accomplished it with the façade of a legal name change from Alexander with an *er* to Alexandre with an *re*.

He stood behind a makeover chair in his beauty studio. In quick yanks, he sharpened a pair of hair shears on a thick leather strip. This was his third pair today, but he figured, there was no telling when such a fashion emergency would arise that he'd need four pairs of dangerously sharp clippers.

Elizabeth Benedict sat in a salon chair across from Alexandre knowing she had the advantage of being the only one of Agatha's children to pay her a visit on any occasion. While Agatha's reputation for hospitality was famous across Louisiana, her eccentricity was a pesticide that killed any closeness to the family tree. While Agatha thought it was fun to send her children, grandchildren, nieces, and nephews pieces of her art, the extended Benedict family did not enjoy explaining why Aunt Agatha's bosom was always coming undone on the romance novels she posed for or what came after the stockings fell down her thin, rouged knees.

Running her fingers through her long, red hair, Elizabeth pulled it straight only for the thick curls to bounce back up. She wore a peach sundress that fitted around her bust and waist but hung freely around her hips and draped over her knees. Her form was an hourglass so perfect, nature couldn't have sculpted it. She patted her cheeks softly and bit down on her bright, red lip. "Who do you think will go first?"

"Girl, please. That much's obvious." Alex rolled his eyes, pursing his lips. The blade snapped over the leather strip.

"What about number two?" Ellie cocked her head to the side.

"Anyone in the first third to go will be low-wage nobodies who underestimated the game. They'll think this is just a lottery or some shit, they probably don't do any actual work, and nothing of value will be lost when they die. It's gonna be a shit show for freaking hours. Just a lot of screaming if they don't die immediately. God, I'm gonna get such a headache."

"Don't worry, hun. I brought Tylenol."

"Thanks, bitch."

"But I don't think there'll be as many wage slaves as you think. Bertrand is trying his hardest to keep the carpets clean this time. I'm sure Gavin gave the same speech to his staff."

"Leave it to Daddy Pansy to ruin the fun for the rest of us."

"Still, it's not that unusual. Very few low-wage workers

have ever stayed for the reading. If they even believe in the rumors, they aren't willing to take the risks associated to win."

"Few are."

"But isn't that how it is in life? So many complain about their positions on the totem pole, but won't take the risks necessary for success."

"God, I hate plebs." Alex slid a thin pair of glasses down his nose. Turning the scissors over, he carefully inspected the edges. "I'm dying to see Gavin reenact those cat stories though." Alex laughed.

"Ugh… No, that was disgusting…" Ellie leaned back and buried her eyes in her palm. "You have no idea what it's like to stumble across that when you're nine."

"Aw, don't lie. You loved it, though," Alex said.

Ellie looked up, targeting Alex through one of the salon mirrors. "I know this might be hard for you to believe, Alex, sweetie, but us girls are delicate creatures who don't find mangled, dead cats cute."

"Oh my god, you're so right." Alex slid the glasses off his face. "I do find it hard to believe you're delicate. What was that thing dear old Aggie always said about you? Oh— That's right! When you were a kid, weren't you, like—"

"I'll cut you."

Alex gasped overdramatically. "So, it's *not* just a rumor?"

"The past is the past for a reason; don't bring it up again. I'm nothing like when I was a child."

"So… you'd be into that whole cat-thing now, if you like, found Gavin doing it again?"

"That's not what I'm saying at all, stupid." Ellie turned her chair to face Alex.

"Watch it," Alex pointed his sharpened scissors at her, "I'm armed."

Ellie chuckled, shaking her head gently. "You're not

gonna sully those before dinner…"

"Sure, but you could be first. My styling hand is getting itchy, you know?"

Turning around again, Ellie admired herself in the mirror. She straightened her posture and her smile. When her eyes met Alex's in the mirror, she licked her lips. "We both know that's not going to happen. I've been under the knife so many times, I'm practically immune to it."

Then they laughed together.

NINE.

I-90, Louisiana
August 10th, 3:05 P.M.

Clint Anderson believed the name chose the job. Clint was the sound when metal tapped against metal when sitting at a green light in traffic because the driver ahead of him wasn't moving, so he had to urge him with a minor tap to the acceleration pedal. Clint was the sound of rocks tapping against the windshield when he was racing down the highway, leaving cracks in the glass. Clint was the sound of deteriorating police sirens for when he saw them in his rearview mirror, he pressed gas to the floor until he couldn't see them in the rear-view mirror any longer. Clint Anderson's job was truly destiny.

He had been Agatha's chauffeur for eight years. He drove a 1964 Lincoln Continental any time he went into the city. In his mind, a car should make an appearance, and for the last eight years he'd lived like royalty. Soon, he would be promoted from guest of the queen to the king himself.

Clint slipped the keys into the ignition, starting his journey to the New Orleans airport. His only job this evening was to retrieve Madame Astra and return to the estate before the storm started. The blue morning sky had been devoured by a nightmare of gray that had grown larger and darker with each passing hour. The air was thick and humid, it justified how much faster he drove. A bright flash of lightning and illuminated shadows reflected in the pregnant clouds every couple of moments. The clouds threatened New Orleans and Clint prayed Madame Astra's flight hadn't been delayed.

Clint wore a black scally cap and a matching suit. He turned on his cassette player and the electricity of Boston's music started to play. He cranked the volume up until the sound escaped the car, even through closed windows. He stepped on the gas, the engine growled, and he shot down the highway. New Orleans was just over an hour away. Singing off-key and bobbing his head to the music, perhaps Clint would make it in record time tonight.

TEN.

Front Yard, Benedict Estate
August 10th, 5:15 P.M.

Sitting in the back of Clint's Lincoln Continental, Madame Astra powdered her nose and curled her lips down into what she thought was a most believable, dispirited frown. "Can you turn that noise down? It's breaking my concentration." Her voice was lost in the sound of Clint and Eric Clapton singing together, "in the sunshine of your love!" Madame Astra grabbed Clint's seat and shook it, growing more and more vicious until the music's volume went down.

"You doin' alright back there?" Clint glanced in the rearview mirror. "Not sure if yer dancin' or havin' a seizure."

Madame Astra took a deep breath, allowing herself a moment to gather herself. "I'm trying to focus, and I can't do it with that noise on."

"'ey," Clint said. "That ain't noise. It's Cream."

"I don't care what it is. Can we just keep it at a reasonable level?"

"Yeah, but… that was the only reasonable level there is to listen to Cream at."

"Then I guess be unreasonable for a little bit." The volume started to go up again. "Please!"

"Alright, alright. Don't get your knickers twisted." Clint laughed. He lowered the radio volume and it became a soft whisper in the background, his own singing turned to intimate murmurs he shared with Eric Clapton in the front seat.

Madame Astra returned to her compact mirror, watching herself as she carefully tipped her head forward, then back, making her forehead look much larger than it was. She watched her reflection in the tinted window beside her. Clenching her teeth, she stretched her lips into a tight smile, second thoughts told her it might have been distasteful to appear at a funeral with a smile on one's face. She twisted her lips down, softening the smile. Ripples and creases spread across her cheeks and forehead, but it looked more natural and sorry. She relaxed her face and made the smile again, then slowly sank into a miserable scowl. "I'm so sorry for your loss!" she said, looking herself in the eye. "It's so sad! I was so sad when I heard the news!"

The tin band sounds of Parvenu began to envelop the car and override Clint's music. She looked up from her compact and out the front window. The massive white body of the Benedict Estate rose from the mud ahead. Her heart skipped with glee. Her lips curled up into the largest smile. She cleared her throat and forced scowling misery back onto her features.

Staring into her mirror, Madame Astra quivered her bottom lip. She stiffened as she breathed in. She held the breath for a time, then released. In, she sucked, and slow release again. "At least I know her passing was peaceful." Short breaths through the nose, she snorted, coughed, and tried to create enough mucus to sniffle. "At least I know her passing was peaceful."

The car jerked to a stop. Madame Astra shot forward, her head slammed into the driver's seat. Her compact bounced off the seat and flipped onto the floor between her feet. She placed one hand against the car roof and held onto the door handle with the other. "What the hell do you think you're doing?"

"Sorry. I think I saw a possum crossin' the road," Clint said. "You got those in L.A.?"

"There are no possums out here," Madame Astra blew stray strands of loose hair from her lips, but they clung to her bright pink lip gloss. She tucked the hair behind her ear. Plucking her compact off the floor, she checked herself in its mirror. "You ruined my makeup."

Clint glanced over his shoulder and looked at her face in the dim lighting. "I don't see a difference. Your face always looks pretty beat." His muddy brown eyes scrutinized her. "I guess I shoulda warned you though. My bad." He laughed.

Madame Astra rolled her eyes. She lifted her free hand to prod at her face and examine the pink splotches forming by her cheekbone.

Just as soon as the vehicle started moving again, it jerked to a stop again. Madame Astra smacked her head into the headrest and her compact mashed into her eye socket.

"Oh my god!" She jerked back into the seat.

"Sorry—sorry. I thought I saw a gator that time," Clint said. "Damn things everywhere out here. Hey, you got gators in L.A.?"

She saw him looking at her in the rear-view mirror. A crooked smile on his thin lips, his chipped front teeth showing. "No, we don't have 'gators' in L.A., and I doubt there are any out here." She picked up her compact, snapped it shut, and slipped it into her purse.

"You kiddin'? There are so many of 'em out here, guy

could get rich makin' everythin' outta 'em. Shoes, hats, suits, wallets, seat covers, soup, stew, gumbo, steak. Anything. Almost lost my arm one time movin' the car outta the yard. Big thing comes chargin' out of a puddle. Swear to God."

"Still, Clint, can you do me a favor? Next time you think you see something in the road, please save my face some trauma and just run it over."

"That's pretty dramatic, but I guess you got it if you want it," Clint said.

"You can make gator-opossum soup out of it or something," she muttered.

"That's a great idea!" Clint said, "You know it's actually been a while since I've had either uh those things. Sounds real good."

"Wait, what?" Madame Astra said. "You were for real about—"

"Kiddin'! You don't gotta look so horrified," Clint laughed again. "Not everythin' you hear about the south is true."

Madame Astra pinched her lips together. Based on Clint alone, she was partial to believe everything they said about the south was true.

She watched the trees, vines, and water zoom past. The closer they came to the house, the duller the plants grew: grayer in color, sagging limbs, and fewer leaves. Her own eyes in the window startled her, like seeing a ghost in the swamp. She barely recognized herself and turned away. Every inch of skin attempted to wrinkle. If she allowed the shapes to carve themselves into her skin, her eventual biographical TV movie would describe her as the nutty, bogus fortuneteller of an eccentric old woman in the middle of a Louisiana quagmire.

Passing through the Estate gates, Madame Astra breathed deep with relief. Like a trip through a television, the plants regained their color and soon they'd be at the door's steps.

The car stopped and the engine died in the same moment. Clint stepped out of the car and pulled open Madame Astra's door. He lowered his head, and tipping his hat, he jauntily said, "Welcome back to the Estates, Madame." His crooked smile was far more charming outside the car than it was inside.

Madame Astra's four-inch blue heels clicked against the pavement. Bedazzled along the straps, Clara had helped her pick them out, and back in Hollywood they were referred to as the height of fashion. In a place like this, she doubted they'd receive the recognition they deserved. She believed it wasn't just the lack of insight that held the farmhands back, but a disassociation with presentation, hard work, and what work truly mattered that ended with continual failure, but she believed some had to fail for others to succeed and she was okay with this tradeoff.

She slipped the handles of her blue and green tribal-embroidered purse over her shoulder and made her way up the bright marble steps. Her fingers glided along the columns as she passed them, luxury at her fingertips relaxed every tense muscle she had. She would never get over how expensive everything in the Benedict Estate felt.

She grabbed the door knocker and hit it against the plate three times. While she waited, she found the window by the door and watched herself, checking her expression and makeup one last time.

Metal clattered as the dark oak door swung open. "Good Evening, Madame Astra. You look well," said Gavin. His pale blond hair was so tightly gelled to his scalp the humidity couldn't move it, but stressful fingers had displaced a few strands throughout the day. He had a sharp nose and long jaw, yet his head appeared too cherubic for a man a few years short of thirty. The combination made his face look as though it had not grown with his adult body. His eyes were a cold blue that resembled the iron bars of the front gate. Madame Astra had never discerned whether the butler uniform was a requirement of Agatha's or a charade Gavin put on to feel he belonged in his position. The Benedict Estate had been understaffed for some time, so while Gavin spent his time filling in the holes to keep the estate running, the chores kept his body slim and firm. "The coat was a good idea," he said, gesturing to the dark clouds creeping over the Estate gates.

Madame Astra followed Gavin's gesture and turned back around. "Looks like the fence can't keep everything out."

"Unfortunately," Gavin said, looking at her. "I hope you didn't plan your return for tonight."

"Even if I had, it doesn't look like I have much of a choice anymore, does it?" Madame Astra said.

"I don't believe there ever was a choice," Gavin said. He stepped aside and she entered the home. She slid her gypsy shawl from her shoulders and folded it over her left arm for Gavin to take and hang, but instead, he stood at the door, holding it open.

"I'm gonna put my car in the garage. Don't want the ground to eat it once the rain hits, ya know?" Clint said from the bottom of the porch.

Madame Astra cleared her throat and waved her left arm a little less than subtly.

"I'll leave the door open for you, but please remember to lock up when you come in."

Clint waved his fingers in a half salute then walked down the drive, back to his car.

Gavin closed the door.

"Does it really get that bad out here?" Madame Astra said.

"Sometimes. We've lost equipment to the swamp: mowers, tractors, field sprinklers. Sometimes we've lost worse." Their eyes lock, and for a moment, Madame Astra held her breath. Gavin's calloused hand brushed her bare arm as he took the shawl and hung it in the entryway closet.

Wide and decorated with a pair of century-old tapestries and hand-carved frames, the foyer contained padded armchairs sheltered within the shadow of a line of columns. The floors were made of bright marble, patterned in a checkerboard of white and gray diamonds. Twelve feet from the door stood another line of columns separating the foyer from the grand ballroom. Windows stretched from floor to ceiling and decorated all sides of the house. These usually flooded the house with light, but the incoming dark gray clouds left the house under a curtain of heavy darkness. To the left of the foyer was the door to the guest waiting room where Madame Astra spent most of her time waiting for Agatha when she came for a visit.

Madame Astra moved through the archways and into the grand ballroom. The ceiling was immaculate, designed with large colored windows in the center to allow natural light to flood the house. Eight honeycombs made of gold, silver, or copper decorated the ceiling and within them were eight original Renaissance-style paintings. At first glance, the images appeared as innocent flirtation between man and woman, sometimes in a crowd, sometimes in a field, sometimes in a home or library, but upon closer examination, the true debauchery became clear.

Also, in the room: an antique grand piano, a handful of eastern European couches and tables, Asian and European-looking knickknacks, and an old photograph of a suited man riding a large tricycle. From the main ballroom, every other area of the house could be reached; the main hallway led to the grand staircase, library, music room, service area, and the resident doctor's office and living quarters. In the opposite direction were the kitchen, formal dining room, tap room, breakfast area, conservatory, and servant's staircase.

"Please follow me," Gavin said, leading the way through the ballroom and down the corridor. The soft pitter-patter of raindrops began against the windows; their soft echoes sounded like the footsteps of ghosts following behind them.

ELEVEN.

Entryway, Benedict Estate
August 10th, 5:33 P.M.

At the end of the hallway stood a pair of opened dark oak doors, boasting matched carvings of intricate Celtic knotwork featuring what looked like dogs or dragons. The dining room had two entrances: one through the large, decorative guest doors and the other through the servants' pantry. A large gold-plated fireplace sat at the head of the room, lit, and dozens of electric candlesticks mounted to the wall filled in the dark spots the fire missed. The sweet burn of firewood spilled into the air, creating a cozy atmosphere against the delicious chill of the mansion's overworked air conditioner. Sporadic rumbles of thunder didn't seem to interrupt, but rather, faded into the background of contentment.

The expansive table stretched across most of the room and contained place settings for twelve: five chairs on both of its long sides, one chair at the head, and one chair at the end. Above the fireplace, the mantel was filled with trinkets; a jade lion statue from China, a silver lucky cat from Japan, a golden elephant wearing a blanket of precious gems from

India, and an English romance novel entitled *The First Body*. Above the shelf was a recent painting of Agatha and her house pet, Kelly, wrapped in a gold frame.

Agatha, being a woman of tradition, had a portrait painted of herself every year. The mantel image was never to be photographed. Accompanying her in every portrait was her most darling pet, a white Persian cat wearing a diamond-studded collar and a nametag that read *Poopsie*. However, a decade ago, the white cats ceased being featured in her images, and instead, a young boy with curly brown hair appeared at her side, and with each year, the boy grew just a bit bigger. The current portrait displayed Agatha with straight silver hair piled on the top of her head in coiling loops, none of it touching her neck. Her face looked bright, long, slim, and a bit cartoony. Wrapped around her neck was an excess of pearls, complementing the red mink coat hanging from her shoulders. To her right stood fourteen-year-old Kelly. He was too skinny underneath the traditional navy blazer, white button-up, and striped, blue bow tie. Long waves of messy brown curls hung over his face, too long to gel back, but too short to tie up. Around his wrist, he wore a diamond-studded bracelet with the odd aesthetic of a cat's collar. Engraved on a connecting gold plate was the name, *Poopsie*.

Now, Kelly sat at the head of the table, underneath the painting with his hair just as messy as it ever was. His tailored blazer outlined his slim body, making him appear delicate and powerless. The rest of the table was filled with Agatha's closest staff. Mathias sat to Kelly's right. Across from him, an empty seat waited for Madame Astra. Beside the empty seat was Johnny, then Doc, then Clint, and then Anna. Down Mathias's side was Ellie, then Alex, then Angus, then Bertrand. At the furthest end of the table was an empty seat set for Gavin.

Of everyone at the table, Bertrand looked the worst. He had a small build and tight skin that appeared to stretch over his skeleton. His clothes hung off his frame, attempting to give him more body than he had. He hadn't always been like this, but since Agatha's death, it was as if his body had given up and he was slowly vanishing to join her. Faint brown fingerprints stained even his nicest blue-gray shirt. Decades of work could be found on every article of clothing he owned.

Madame Astra walked the length of the table and sat down beside Kelly. Her chair screeched against the floor as she dragged it back in, drawing Kelly's attention. "Hey," she said.

He defiantly looked opposite to her direction.

Madame Astra clenched her jaw.

"Nice to see you again, Madame Astra," Mathias said. He walked around the table, took her hand, and placed a gentle kiss on her fingers.

Heat rushed to Madame Astra's cheeks. She jerked her hand away, and to recover, waved her fingers like a southern belle fanning off a fainting spell. "Ditto," stumbled from her lips.

Mathias chuckled, returning to his seat across the table. "I'm glad you were able to make it here safely. I was afraid your flight may have been delayed and you wouldn't make it. The clouds don't seem too inviting this evening, do they?" he said.

"Let's just say if Gavin looked as unappealing as the weather, no one would visit this house again," she snorted when she laughed. She straightened herself, lacing her fingers together on top of the table. "I'm glad the rain held off until I got inside. I don't know what I would've done if I'd been stuck in the car with Clint for much longer."

"I can think of a few things…" Mathias said with a husky

laugh. His smile was perfect, straight, and white.

Madame Astra's fingers pressed into the cool tabletop. "Oh, no, no, no! I would never." Madame Astra cleared her throat. "Not that. Not with him."

"You may surprise yourself with the things you'll do in desperate times."

"Maybe," she said, "but I hope I'm never quite that desperate... People do some crazy, messed-up stuff in life or death situations, but him?" She glanced down to the end of the table where Clint slapped his hands together in Doc's face in some retelling of a car accident he may or may not have been involved in while Johnny leaned back, rocking in his wooden chair. "There is someone else at this table I'd rather be stuck in a car with."

"I'm sure you've heard the stories," the low drum of his voice purred. Mathias folded his arms and leaned forward. "Were you surprised to hear Agatha wrote you into the will?"

"Not really. I mean, how could I be? First of all, I'm psychic, but more than that, I've been her faithful spirit guide for almost a year now. The work we did was so intimate. We connected with her lost relatives. It was easily some of the most spiritually and emotionally draining work I've ever done, but I'd say it was well worth it to give her a better idea of, you know, where she was going and who was waiting for her. I believe she saw the benefit of looking forward like that as her lifeline grew shorter. Building relationships with her family of the future. If you think about it, I probably know her better than anyone else at this table." Madame Astra laughed, stroking the polished tabletop absently.

"You're such a liar," Kelly muttered.

Madame Astra's head turned sharply, her right eye twitching. "What?"

"Sounds like the kid wants a fight," Alexandre said from across the table. "Not saying I agree with him, but you know, once someone hits a cultured age, such as yourself, understanding the kids can be some kinda task, huh?"

"I'd like to point out that my service was much more valuable to the dearly departed than yours," Madame Astra said. "Considering all her hair was someone else's at this point, all you did was plop a wig on her head and paint her like a queen."

"Wow, hold up," Alex said. "First off, all that hair was real, bitch. The Bennies have like, crazy good hair in their family. Example." Alex gestured to Ellie who sat beside him. She flicked her long locks over her shoulder and combed her fingers through the curls. "Second, styling isn't just about making the hair look fly, it's about the entire ensemble, okay? And if you had, like, hired me to fix you, I could have told you where your outfit went wrong and how you needed to beat your face. Here's a freebie though: all of it's wrong. Oh—and that color on your lips? What the frick is it? Hubba bubba gum? Yeah, all it says is 'trying too hard.' You're not a teenage girl, sweetie."

Madame Astra resisted the sudden urge to pick up her table napkin and wipe off her newly applied lip gloss. "...Even if that was true, it's still nothing compared to providing a communication vessel to the extraterrestrial gods."

"Good god, girl! You sound like you've been talkin' to aliens!" Alex threw his head back with laughter so hard his thick, black-framed glasses slipped down his face. He swiveled his head, tilting it down to allow the glasses to fall off his nose and into his hand. He reached for the baby blue handkerchief tucked into his vest pocket. "Seriously though, relax hunny. I'm playin' with you."

Madame Astra bit her tongue. Her mouth was dry. She

picked up her glass of water and took a sip. "Sure," she smacked her lips. "Me, too."

"You don't even know what that means." Kelly shifted to sit up right. His seat squeaked against the floor as it moved. "When are we going to do this thing? I'm tired of sitting here."

"I dunno, are you gonna read it for us, sweetie?" Alex said.

"No—"

"Aw, still haven't learned how to read?" Alex said.

"Sad!" Ellie said.

"You should get daddy on that shit right away. You have one of those, don't you?" Alex said.

"Wait—we're doing the will reading now?" Madame Astra said, looking from Alex to Mathias. "Where's the lawyer? You need a lawyer present for this kind of thing, right?"

"Sure," Ellie said, "but there isn't one."

"Not tonight anyway," Alex added.

"The lawyer is coming out Saturday afternoon to make everything official. Clearly, nothing will be official until he gets here, but we're all impatient bastards, so why wait?" Ellie said.

"Saturday is only two days from now. You can't wait until then?" Madame Astra said.

"I mean, we could, but then there's tradition which says party now, officiate later and I don't see the problem with that," Alex said.

Mathias stood after a moment. The firewood crackled and the storm, once a soft pattering of feet had now become stomping against the glass. The echoes of its throes ricocheted around the dining hall. "We will begin in a moment," he finally said. "Let me first take a moment to thank you all for being here, particularly those who do not live on-site like the rest of us. It wasn't required that any of you be here, but I believe those of us who are present tonight possess certain traits that Agatha was attracted to. There's a reason why we are here now; it takes a kind of courage, determination, and drive to follow through and find success in the Benedict Estate, and for that, I'm honored to share the room with all of you."

"Oh my god! This isn't Miss Universe!" Alex cupped his mouth with his hands to make his voice louder. Ellie jabbed him with her elbow.

"Presently Angus is working on supper and it should be ready by the reading's conclusion for anyone who is both hungry and daring." Mathias laughed. "Agatha was known as an incredible storyteller, but by the size of the envelope, I don't imagine this is something she wanted to drag on." He retrieved a dinner knife from the table and sliced the envelope open in one quick movement. "I'm actually surprised how short it appears to be." He removed a pair of folded white pages from the envelope, then set it down on the table.

"Wait a minute," Madame Astra said, examining the papers in Mathias's hands. "So that... that's real?"

Alex snorted. "Yes, it's real." He covered his face, rubbing his eyes. "God help me."

Again, Madame Astra's face twitched, this time, her eyebrow. Tilting her head down, she rubbed her brows. "I just thought the real thing would have been with the lawyers, in their office, you know, to make sure no one tampered with it. That's all. I think it's weird that it's here, you have it, and there's no lawyer present. How are we supposed to trust that?"

"It says relatively the same thing every time a master passes on," Mathias said. "And of course, nothing will be made official until the lawyer makes it out here Saturday afternoon at which point, he will confirm all awards. The lawyer will bring verified copies of the house rules along with the property contracts, and a matching version of this letter. Before anything is finalized, you will be able to verify all the information presented tonight until you are satisfied."

Madame Astra looked around her for other signs of resistance or discomfort, but no one seemed put-off by the situation. "I guess if we get to compare the copies..." she trailed off. A loud whip of thunder crackled through the room. The wall lights flickered and shut off. Another strike illuminated bodies moving around the dark end of the table.

"Is everyone alright?" Mathias said.

"Who's moving?" Madame Astra said.

Wooden doors creaked.

"Who's moving!" Madame Astra said again.

Gavin and Anna appeared from the pantry carrying a pair of lit candlesticks and a dozen more unlit candles in their hands. They split down both sides of the table and began placing unlit candles in candle holders across the table. As they were lit, the table gained a soft glow of heat, linking one end to the other.

The candlelight wasn't enough to illuminate the faces gathered around the table. Individual features obscured and the silhouettes of familiar people appeared vague and bizarre. All at once, everyone began to chatter. Their voices mixed together until they were an unrecognizable chorus of indiscriminate words. Lightning filled the dining hall with a few strikes, creating snapshots of familiarity.

The lights flickered back on, inducing a moment of silence.

"Looks like the storm is here in full force now," Mathias said.

"Wonderful..." Madame Astra muttered.

"Shall we begin before the lights become opportunistic

and shut off again?" He glanced down the table, waiting for objections and when there were none, he began:

"To the dearest residents, employees, and friends of the Benedict Estate, if you're reading this, it means that I, the head of household, have passed away from natural causes. If you have reason to believe that there was any foul play, I request that you immediately contact the authorities and have them conduct a thorough investigation. If you are reading this, and I have not yet passed away, I suggest you return it to the novel from whence you found it. My favorite story by my favorite author, *The Importance of Being Earnest*. If you're bored, I suggest you read that instead. It's much more exciting than an old set of rules and goodbyes.

"It's difficult for me to write this, as I remember hearing the rules for the first time. It's not easy to be told you must fight for your future or suffer to someone else's hands, but it's something I had to process as a young girl and I hope my boy, Kelly, should never face this tragedy in the same way. Though I was never very religious, I've prayed that perhaps the next generation may be kinder than my own, however, I'm not hopeful. If Kelly is faced with the same fate as I had, I hope he learns the value in selfishness quickly for, at that time, he must.

"I hope this message isn't a surprise to any of you. If you're not sure what you're hearing, I feel sorry for you, dear, but I wish you the best all the same.

"Death is unkind, but I believe life is a sadist. I know tonight will not be easy for any of you, and the morning will be the hardest in your life. Everything will come at you so quickly; you may be disgusted by your choices; you may have to discard your values; you may not recognize yourself anymore. Determination is key and you must not dwell on the decisions you make in times of desperation. You can't hesitate to defend your life. You cannot evade the danger.

You will have the rest of your lives to reflect on what you will go through and what you have done. I pray that your night is kinder than mine, and you are able to endure the guilt you feel. If these feelings sound unfamiliar to you, then you will have a good time tonight. This house tends to attract that sort of person. It always has, and I believe it always will.

"I know who will be in attendance; I can't imagine there being more than a dozen of you. There rarely is; too much of a mess. As I write this, I struggle to press the pen across the paper, knowing what must happen and the many ways it may end, but I must push onward. Tradition is... Tradition is… This is not tradition; this is simply the way of the world." Her handwriting trailed off into tiny, illegible scribbles that appeared semi-melted into the stationary.

"I hate to do this, and seem like I'm playing favorites, but my dear Kelly, you had such a spirit as a boy. Sleeping in a box, your ribs stuck out your shirt, and your small face covered in dirt… It hurt me to see you raw and bleeding where the vermin had eaten you. I never stopped thinking about it, about you and everything I would do to protect you from pain. You deserved better. It was fate that caused my poor Poopsie to pass away days before finding you or else there may not have been room in the house! Some might consider your adoption to have been a bit unconventional, but my promise to you is that you have always been my son as much as any of the children I bore myself.

"I love you all dearly, but I do not love you all the same."

Another powerful strike caused the lights to flicker. Thunder rolled down the hall, stampeding feet growing more intense the closer it came until abruptly stopping at the closed dining room doors. The lights came back on.

"I have only a few regrets: Johnny, I wish I'd spent less

time collecting your balls and grabbing your shaft and spent more time learning the rules of tennis. Dr. Charity, I wish I'd heeded your warning about my diet and Angus, I wish I tried more of your excellent cuisine. Beauregard, there've been so many of you, I wish I could remember your face, and Elizabeth, my sweetest, young daughter, I wish I could leave my beloved boyfriend to you in my will so you wouldn't feel so alone. Mr. Aker, I wish I could have done more for your family. Maid… I wish I could remember your name. I'm not sure where you came from or whether you were on my payroll; I hope you were being paid. And Bertrand… I wish a lot of things had been different.

"I hope once tonight is over, whoever the new master is, you will continue to maintain this beautiful and bountiful home. Perhaps you cnd inspire the workers in ways I was never able to. I cannot overstate: nothing you ever did went unnoticed. I know who you are, I know how hard you've worked, and I know the things you've done to get to where you are today. Because of those things, this task has become more difficult than it should have been.

"Upon my lawful, natural death, I award the fortune and responsibilities of the Benedict Estate to my young darling, Kelly Benedict. Should he be beneath legal adult age at the time of my passing, I would like my darling and his inheritance to be left in the care of my personal medium and good friend, Madame Astra, until the boy is of legal age and able to claim it properly. If he and his guardian are unable to care for the property, the house rules will be applied and the individual who is able to care for it will receive it all—"

"Um, like, what the hell," Alex said. "Agatha's daughter is sitting right here! *You* weren't even mentioned by name anywhere in there!"

Mathias lowered the letter, though the words read on past what he'd said. A gentle smile came to his lips, though one of his eyebrows lifted with intrigue. He glanced at the psychic across the table.

"I was mentioned in there—once—at the only point where it matters," Madame Astra's lips curled in a sharp smile. Her fingers hovered over her cheeks, then her lips in an impossible attempt to erase the delight. "Who cares if she says your name in the same sentence as 'I regret?' Final goodbyes are nice, but not what any of us wanted to hear tonight. And unfortunately for you, I'm the winner."

"Bullshit!" Kelly slammed his hands on the table. Standing up instantly, his chair screeched. "Why her?!"

Mathias flattened his lips, turning stern eyes on Kelly, stiff with parental threat. He set the papers down and walked behind Kelly. He grasped Kelly's shoulders and pressured him back into his chair, petting him calmly once there. "I believe what Kelly meant to say is, he's a bit confused by the choice of guardianship. There are quite a few options here at the table that may be a bit more fitting for a parental role than an actress with a few parlor tricks. No offense."

"None taken," Madame Astra said. "I'm not fit to play a mother on TV—I'm too young—but if this is what Agatha wants, I don't know how we can even dispute it."

"You got one thing right," Alex said. "You're not even fit to bag groceries." He snorted.

"I meant I look too young," Madame Astra snapped.

"Oh, right," Alex said, pulling his bottom lips back in a strained look. "But first chance you get," he lowered his voice to a fake whisper still loud enough for everyone at the table to hear. He leaned in close, "you might want to check your makeup. Your crow's feet are showing. That's freebie number two. Next one I'm charging for."

Madame Astra stood up; her chair fell back against the floor. "I do not have crow's feet!"

"Just tryin' to help you out, sweetheart," Alex leaned back with conceit. He slipped off his glasses and wiped them with his pocket square.

"When she was alive, Agatha told me I offered her *the* most important service in this house. It wasn't *bed-making*; it wasn't *hair-doing*; it wasn't *companionship*. I gave her peace-of-mind. I was her friend, her confidante, her laughter. She told me flat out I deserved the best, so I can't even say I'm surprised by this outcome," Madame Astra said, crossing her arms.

"Oh, c'mon, you're not even a real fortuneteller," Alex said, rolling his eyes.

"Whether she liked me for my acting abilities or she actually believed I had spiritual powers is irrelevant," Madame Astra said. "By admission in the letter, I'm the one she trusted the most with the things she cared about. The money is mine—"

"That's not quite what the letter said—" Mathias said.

"It's mine—" Kelly said.

"—and I'd appreciate if you showed me a little more respect when you're visiting my house," Madame Astra said.

"It's my house!" Kelly yelled louder. Mathias held him to the chair.

"C'mon nae," Angus's voice vibrated off the walls, dominating the room over the crackling fire and the purring thunder. His voice carried, effortlessly boisterous as though he stood in the highlands, a bagpipe calling to the flock. "I know we're all sad. We're all gonna miss 'er. Me ma once said, 'loss can turn into anger, Angie.' She also said, 'tempers get cuttie when bellies get empty.'" He patted Alex's shoulder with his large left hand and the gardener with his right.

"Your ma talks a lot, doesn't she?" Alex said, looking up Angus's thick, hairy arm.

"All the time. How'd ye know?" Angus said, giving Alex a slap on the back so hard it caused Alex to bump against the table. "Feast's been cookin' in the scullery. Let me brin' it in and let's have a good time, eh?" The house rocked beneath Angus's eager feet.

"Food sounds wonderful, Angus. At least someone hasn't forgotten how to do their job around here." Madame Astra's words were lost as Angus had already slipped into the kitchen through the pantry door.

Gavin stood from the table and made his way to the pantry. "I'll make sure everything is presentable." He left through the pantry.

"Thank God. I'm famished—though it's kind of incredible the food continued to cook even through the power outages, isn't it?" Madame Astra said.

"Ovens don't go insta-cold when the power cuts out," Alex said.

"I might cry if they bring something inedible out." Madame Astra laughed to herself. She reached for her purse, hanging on the back of her chair and fished around for her compact. She flicked her wrist, popping it open to examine her face. The redness her face had shown in the car was now missing. She checked for wrinkles, but she saw no crow's feet.

Mathias sat down, slipping one leg over the other. He leaned back and folded his hands in his lap. "Have any plans for the house? I can't speak for anyone else here tonight, but I'll admit I've done my share of *planning*."

Madame Astra's lips parted in a toothy smile she couldn't contain. "I haven't decided anything yet," she said, "but I have been thinking about staff: who I want to keep, who I don't. Maybe do some renovations on some things..." she trailed off.

"*Some things?*" Mathias tilted his head to the side, and

smooth air slid through the wave of blond bangs. The firelight reflected off his cheeks. He looked sharp, strong, and dangerous.

Madame Astra tried not to bite her lip. "Well, you know—"

"Her face," Alex said, circling his face with his hand.

"I was actually thinking, there's plenty of room around here for a private movie studio. I could start my own company, star in some movies, and hire some big talent, like Matt Damon or Brad Pitt. I'll need a babysitter." Madame Astra laced her fingers together and leaned forward, as far over the table as she could. "Do you have any references?"

Mathias chuckled, leaning in. "Unfortunately, my previous employer recently passed away."

"Bummer," Madame Astra said, "but maybe I can make an exception if you interview well."

"When are you available?" Mathias said.

Kelly smacked the table. His chair screeched as he stood again, nostrils flaring. "You're not doing anything to *my* house and it *is* my house! She named me! She said it was mine. 'Kelly' the letter said, not whatever your actual name is. You're not doing anything with it!" His fingers shrunk into the ends of his blazer and his thumbs toyed with the fabric. His breathing matched the speed he stroked the fabric with, and every so often he would catch the end of his sleeve between his index and middle fingers instead.

Mathias leaned back. "It'll be alright, Kelly." He reached for Kelly's hand and drew the boy toward him. Kelly tried to yank his hand away, but Mathias wouldn't let go. "Change is difficult. It always is, but your age makes it seem a little worse than normal. Everything will work itself out."

"I don't want it to work itself out, I want her to get out now!" Kelly pulled his hand away from Mathias and made way for the exit.

The pantry door folded open. Gavin then stepped in front of Kelly without looking at him. In Gavin's hand was a shining silver tray set with ten clear crystal glasses, half full of sparkling pink champagne. "Angus is plating dinner as we speak but said we should toast without him." Gavin slipped his freehand around Kelly's shoulders. Kelly stiffened up, refusing to move from where he stood. "Please stay for this final toast. The master should show respect to his guests." Kelly's tension drained slightly and he didn't go running for the door. Gavin continued toward the table with the tray. "It would be lovely if you'd join us at the table," Gavin said.

Kelly dragged his feet back to his spot then fell into it and crossed his arms.

Gavin moved around the table, presenting a glass to each guest, but skipping Kelly. He saved the final glass for himself then tucked the tray under his arm.

"Doesn't it feel a bit inappropriate to toast someone's death?" Madame Astra said, looking between her bubbling glass and Gavin.

Bertrand placed his glass on the table and pushed it away. He slid his chair out and stood. Tugging down his newsboy cap, he lowered his head. His body appeared much smaller when he slipped his hands into his dropping pockets. His feet dragged across the floor with weak, shuffling steps. "Excuse me," he muttered beneath the soft crack of the fireplace. The crescendo of wrinkles on his face grew deeper. He had a limp in his step, making his shuffling sound uneven and painful. Bertrand left the dining room; the wooden doors rumbled, returning to place.

"Are you sure it's okay?" Madame Astra finally said, looking around at the other guests. She tightened the grip on the glass and allowed whatever she might have been feeling to be relieved when smiles and tilted glasses answered her question.

"Don't think of it as an end to Agatha's life. Think of it as the beginning of someone else's," Mathias said.

"Then, to Agatha!" Vigor filled Madame Astra's words. Her fingers were dry and tingled with a feeling like she'd already spent hours counting her newly inherited wealth. Glasses clinked, champagne became excited and fizzled, bubbling over the sides, Madame Astra brought the glass to her lips.

It tasted like billions of dollars and it was sweet.

"Congratz, hon." Alex swished the drink around in his glass but didn't drink from it.

"You really deserved it," Ellie said.

Glass shattered, champagne flooded the marble floor and dampened the rug. Something caught in Madame Astra's throat, it choked her, it burned. She grabbed her throat; foam began to seep from the corners of her mouth. Dizziness struck her and she fell to the ground. Wheezing, hacking, frothing, and shivering, she moaned.

Kelly jumped to his feet. "Astra!" He leaned toward her, then away as nausea and fear struck him next. "Somebody— do something!" He looked to Mathias, then Doc who smiled and looked away disinterested. "Someone!" He looked to Gavin, but no one moved. "She's—"

Madame Astra struggled to wipe the foam from her lips with the back of her arm. She pushed herself up weakly and collapsed again. Her body locked and seized. Her back slammed into the floor. She knocked her head into the table leg. She groaned; it was supposed to be words. She reached out for something, anything close enough to grab.

It was Kelly's leg. In surprise, Kelly kicked her hand off and stumbled backwards. His vision blurred. "Help her!" his voice broke. "Someone help her!"

Red foam absorbed a gargle and trickled down her neck.

It wet her hair and the top of her blouse, which now clung to her sweaty skin. She kicked her chair over; the contents of her purse spilled. Her compact popped open. Pointing back at her, the mirror filled with her horror. Her eyelids became heavy.

Kelly stepped back until he couldn't see Madame Astra over the table anymore. Heat rushed his face, and fear clouded his eyes with water. His back hit a wall; he clutched at his shirt. "She's dying!" His voice cracked.

"We know," Ellie said.

"That's kinda the point," Alex said.

The others stood and watched the energy release from Madame Astra's body until flailing turned to twitching turned to gurgling turned to nothing.

Kelly clutched his mouth and squeezed his eyes shut, but he couldn't block the growing smell. The roaring thunder tricked him into thinking Madame Astra still flailed against the floor.

Alex wrapped his arm around Ellie's waist and pulled her close. "Congratz again, Madame." A puddle of saliva, foam, and blood pooled beneath Madame Astra's head.

Straightening her white lab coat, Doc stood. She wore a stethoscope hung around her neck like jewelry, black slacks, and sweaters, always in a shade of purple. This evening she wore lavender. "She's dead," Doc pronounced without examining the body.

Clint opened the ice bucket at the bar, and prepared a bourbon on the rocks. "Whata relief," he said. "On the way back, it was like she was beatin' her own face with that powdery thing." He dabbed his fingers at his face, a messy attempt to imitate her. He shrugged then poured the bourbon. "I don't think she liked herself much."

"Probably depressed and suicidal. Everyone in Hollywood is…" Alex said.

"Then at least we had one thing in common," Ellie said.

Doc adjusted her stethoscope, making it even on both sides. "Should anyone need me, I will be in my office." She left the dining hall. Strong, constant airflow caused the air to whistle beneath the door. The door opened and gusts flew past her as though frightened by the storm. "Please don't need me," she said. The door closed behind her.

"If there's nothing else to say, I suppose this meeting is adjourned. Anyone is free to eat supper, if you feel so daring." Mathias slipped the letter back into the manila envelope and placed it on the fireplace mantel. "In case we need this again later," he said, slipping it inside the book on the mantel.

Kelly crept toward the door with his back against the wall, afraid to move, afraid to be seen. Opening his eyes, he saw the tipped chair, red gashes, flashes of her skin, broken glass beneath the table. His shirt stuck to his sweaty chest. Vomit burned the back of his throat, but he swallowed it down. He focused on the door. If he could just get to the door.

A hand wrapped around his bicep. Kelly broke away with a gasp.

"Kelly." It was Gavin.

"Stay away from me!" Kelly yelled, stepping back.

"Listen to me," Gavin said, his voice low and even.

"Don't—" Kelly's voice broke. His cheeks were pink, hot, and wet. "Don't talk to me. Don't touch me! Don't come near me!" Kelly ran out the door. Rain splattering against the window and the shutters bouncing in the wind covered the sounds of his steps. Gavin glanced at Mathias, who was already watching him. Their eyes met, Mathias smiled, nodded, and left the dining hall.

"Anna, let's clean up before the room starts to reek of ammonia," Gavin said.

Anna nodded, already waiting for the command. Gavin aligned himself at Madame Astra's legs while Anna took her by the shoulders. Their hands wrapped around her limbs, distributing her weight evenly. They carried her from the table to the large fireplace a few feet away. Swing, swing, and they tossed her in; the flames engulfed her. The wicked smell of burning flesh hit Gavin immediately. He opened the kitchen door, hoping the aroma of dinner would devour it.

"Dinner's here! I hope everyone is hungry!" Entering through the pantry door, Angus held serving plates on both of his arms. The folded wooden doors smacked against the wall and cracked. He looked around the room. Steam rose from the plates on his trays, carrying the scent of spicy gumbo. He brought the trays to the table, they landed with a loud clatter, porcelain plates threatened to break. "Who wants it first?" he said. Then he looked up at the table, and empty chair, empty chair, empty chair. They were all empty. His large smile grew smaller. He looked to Anna and Gavin. He noticed Clint at the island bar against the wall, pouring himself another drink.

"Where'd everybody go?" Angus said. "Hunger don't just go away."

Clint made a crooked-lipped face. He leaned against the bar and took a sip of his drink. "Sometimes it does, but I'll take onna those. You wanna drink, chef?"

"What kinda scotch ye got?"

"Only the best," Clint said.

"And I'll have some of that." Angus picked up a pair of plates from the large service trays and laid them out where he and Clint would sit. "What about ye?" He said to Anna and Gavin.

"One moment," Gavin said. He picked up the fire pick. He hooked it underneath Madame Astra's arm and pushed her further into the fireplace, keeping her out of Angus's view. Her skin sizzled. Gavin pushed at the wood. He hung the fire pick back on the fireplace tool rack. He and Anna turned around together. "We'll take a plate. Thank you."

Anna followed Gavin to the table.

"It's gonna be a long night," Clint said. He spun his seat around, sitting down in it backwards. He picked up a fork and dipped it in rice.

"Aye, it is," Angus said.

The lights flickered off and on, but the room stayed colored by the fireplace and wax candles spread across the table. Silverware clinked against white plates. Hot gumbo and cooked shrimp replaced the scent of Madame Astra's bile and perfume. The food looked too good to waste. The next round could wait an hour.

TWELVE.

Ballroom, Benedict Estate
August 10th, 6:31 P.M.

The fireplace illuminated every corner of the grand ballroom. It was constructed of bright red and orange bricks from around the world; some of them marked with seals from Florida, others London, and others Russia. They used to be railroads, schools, homes, streets, orphanages, wells, universities, and brothels. Every brick displayed its story with some origin: a person's name or a place, carved or printed in black.

An ebony grand piano sat beneath a large picture window near the back corner of the room, the lid propped open and copper-bound strings exposed. Beside it was a bookshelf filled with Agatha's favorite books. The lamps flickered, but the fire made sure the room never went dark. The phonograph warped Frank Sinatra's voice as he sang, *That's Life*.

Plush red curtains hung open beside the picture windows, but it was impossible to see much of the yard. Rain poured, thick, heavy, and black. It shrouded the outdoors in a murky blanket. The yard flooded and the swamp started to close in.

Mathias and Ellie sat on the couch. She leaned on his shoulder, her arms around his, and her head on him. Her leg bounced absent-mindedly.

Bertrand sat in a large armchair, his head down and his pipe in his hand. Despite the company, he didn't seem particularly engaged.

"I had a feeling she'd go first, but I was hoping for a surprise," Ellie said, pursing her lips in a disappointed pout.

"It's my understanding that outsiders have never lasted long," Mathias said. In his hands was a paperback book, the title hidden. "The ones who don't live here, I mean. They never seem to learn the traditions, the rules, the efficient behavior. They walk in here and assume they can have everything they've ever wanted without working for it. Outsiders rarely respect established tradition."

"I think it's kinda cute," Clint said, walking up to the window. He pressed his hand to the glass, creating a visor for his eyes before leaning forward and attempting to peer into the darkness. "In a 'how can ya be such a freakin' tard' kinda way."

The grandfather clock's pendulum was loud, intrusive with every tick, as though it were counting down to the next big event. It acted more as a reminder that the night was passing by, and come morning, their opportunity to ascend from servitude would be gone. Every room had a clock of some kind in it; they could be large, antique grandfather clocks or small radio clocks with red numbers and loud beeps. The room fell silent to Sinatra.

Clint turned from the window, crossing his arms. He leaned against the sill. "Ya know… I was wonderin', who owned this place before Agatha?"

"Her father," Bertrand said weakly.

"Well I know, 'her father,' and later on we'll say whoever

comes next got the place from mama Agatha, but who was he really?" Clint said.

"Her father," Bertrand said again in the same tone. He stared at the wall, unblinking. The flickers of firelight darken the wrinkles in his face, or perhaps it was the sorrow etching deeper moats in his features. His face didn't move, his body was stiff, though his shoulders fell forward. He looked tired, the bags under his eyes heavy. He stroked the wooden pipe with his thumb.

"Huh. Isn't that weird? For the house to stay in the family?" Clint said, but when no one answered, he asked: "What about before *him*?"

Bertrand said nothing. He reached into his pockets for his lighter. He thumbed tobacco leaves down into the barrel of the pipe, flicked the zippo, and lit the end. The bill of his cap acted a fence to separate him from the others and provide him a sense of solitude. He brought the pipe to his lips, inhaled, and held it.

"Why's it matter?" Elizabeth said sitting up, though her hand continued to pet Mathias's thigh.

"Just wonderin'," Clint said. "I've looked at the pictures upstairs, but hell if I know who any of them are or where they came from, ya know? They coulda been anything; they coulda been related for all the hell we know, but we ain't got much of a story, yeah? S'not like this house is known for truth-tellin', right?"

"I guess, but you could tell relationship at least. Agatha looked like her dad, but neither of them looked like great granddad," Elizabeth said. "And clearly Kelly doesn't look like Agatha if that was to happen."

"I heard you used to have a big nose," Clint said.

"You heard wrong," Ellie snapped.

Mathias turned the page of his book.

Bertrand rubbed his eyes and exhaled.

"Y'all seem pretty chill for what's at stake," Clint said.

"You may rush into battle first, if you wish, you may feel honored in doing so, but you may also have your head blown off in the process," Mathias said.

"There are worse ways to go," Clint said.

"You think so?"

"Even if ya don't see the bennies yourself, goin' out big is the only way to go. Who wants to die layin' in bed at night? If I die, when I die, I want something big. Explosions, a car chase maybe, blood everywhere. I don't want something' simple like a heart attack or old age. What the hell is that? Go out like everyone else? No thanks."

"Be careful what you wish for," Mathias said.

"Isn't that why we're all here?" Clint smiled wide. "I'm either gonna become a king or go out like one. Ain't no one doomed to failure. You fail cause you ain't tryin' hard enough. Put it in the right light, look at more than one outcome. Settin' up more than one avenue to win is probably the best thing you can do for yourself. Other people suck. They teach you to be a chump in kindergarten."

"If there's a limited quantity of something available, then some reaching for it must fail for others to obtain it," Mathias said. "Take Agatha, for instance. If Bertrand hadn't failed to court her, I wouldn't be here. Because of his failure, we were able to succeed."

"And by 'we' you mean every bottom-feeding dimwit with a pretty face and a hard cock, right?" Clint said.

"I prefer the term 'Beauregard,' but yes," Mathias said.

"I never failed her," Bertrand said.

Mathias glanced up from his book.

Clint laughed into his hand. "Sure thing. And Matty's here outta pure coinky-dink; the Madame was never real lonely or let down or nothin'."

"When you speak, you sound like a fool," Bertrand said.

"That's okay," Clint said. "I don't know how it matters if I sound dumb to you. I know what I see; I know what I'm talking about, and you sound like a senile old bastard every time you open your trap. Am I right? Are you right? Who the hell knows?" Clint winked.

A powerful gust pelted thick rain against the side of the house like bullets: hard, soft, hard, soft.

Ellie's hands invaded Mathias, slipping into his jacket, feeling his ribs, up his sides, his pecs, then something hard strapped beneath his arm. She groped around it and understood the shape: a gun. She leaned her lips to his ear with a smirk on them. "You're not supposed to have that, Matty."

Mathias leaned his head onto her. "Sweetheart, no bargains hold. Only fools know any restraint." He kissed her hair.

"I love it when you talk dirty."

Mathias cupped the side of her head and pressed his lips into her ear. "And I love you."

"Why don't I believe you?"

"Because the truth is an evasive mistress of yours." He leaned back.

Ellie hit Mathias in the arm, smiling. She let him go and slipped her hands from his jacket.

Something rumbled in the back of Bertrand's throat. He took a couple short, sharp puffs from the pipe, held his breath, blew out. "She was a charitable woman, a good woman."

"Clearly," Clint said, gesturing toward the gardener. "She kept you around, didn't she?"

Again, Bertrand didn't say anything. He had been witness to everything Agatha was capable of firsthand. He experienced her father's will reading not because he wanted the house, but because he didn't want to lose her. Despite his attendance, he believed he still lost her that night. The reading was one of the most powerful events Bertrand had experienced in his life; it had the ability to transform people, shaving them down to their most basic of desires. It had the ability to corrupt the pure and innocent, to break the mind. Bertrand was always of the belief that once something was shattered, it could only ever be reconstructed into a crude imitation of the integrity it once had.

Bertrand's stomach turned as he recalled her image; a pale, cream dress hanging shredded from her body, the hem of her bell skirt torn and dragged against the floor, leaving a red trail, catching beneath her foot, her body exposed in ways it shouldn't have been and blood staining her hands. Her hair was frayed, a mess not mischievous, but a disaster, pink lipstick smudged, and black streaks painted down her face, the shadow of tears she already cried without him. Her dress was tainted with the unholy union of someone else's body mixed with hers. The inheritance excused anything. The strongest got whatever they wanted, no exception. Mercy was a myth. She slipped when she walked, shaking, her legs too weak to hold her. "Hiro," she whispered. She couldn't smile, but she tried anyway. He ran to her and she reached for him, exchanging the wall for his body. She clung to him and cried into his shirt. "Hiro…" The distress in her voice haunted him still. Every time she laughed; he still heard the shaking sounds of her nightmares. "I didn't want to do it," she said. "I wanted things to be different this time."

Ellie's cream dress reminded him so much of that night. A girl so beautiful didn't belong here. None of them belonged here.

"You doin' okay?" Clint said. "Don't have a stroke." He laughed, then paused abruptly. "Or do. If you went, ya know, it'd be better for all of us." Clint's posture was casual, shoulders relaxed. He sat in one of the plush armchairs, his legs spread wide. He rested his elbows on his knees and leaned forward, focusing hard on Bertrand.

"She was a very good woman, but she could not forget the times when she wasn't," Bertrand's voice was nothing more than a mumble. He brought the pipe to his mouth, closed his eyes, and breathed. The heat warmed his chest. The nicotine was a nice distraction. He clutched the lighter and traced the inscriptions with his thumb. When he opened his eyes, they wandered; the colors and images in the hand-painted ceiling bled together. What should have been portraits of desire and death looked like little more than blots of pale lines. The house he had known for fifty-five years was foreign, strange, and empty. He couldn't recognize the unchanged furniture, the voices, the embedded perfume. The last time he felt this way was over forty years ago and he prayed to God he'd never feel it again.

"You can't think you're gonna see the sunrise," Clint said, noticing Bertrand's moving eyes. "What the hell you even doin' here?"

"Saying goodnight," Bertrand said, though part of him wasn't sure why he even bothered to answer. He stood up and limped toward the conservatory. His shoulders slumped, though he attempted to straighten it with every couple of steps, but couldn't. He groaned in pain, sighed, stopped, shuffled. The conservatory door squeaked open and clapped shut behind him.

"I ain't got what his problem is," Clint said, sitting back.

"Some people are more sensitive than others when it comes to death," Mathias said.

"I wouldn't have expected him to be the type," Ellie said.

"She ever notice you weren't her first?" Clint said.

Mathias's face twisted into one of confused amusement

before he began to laugh. "Of course, she knew I wasn't her first. She knew each man before me wasn't her first husband. I believe it was more of a moral thing," Mathias said. He placed the book in his hands onto the end table beside his chair. "We never spoke about it. I don't think she had an interest in discussing her short-comings or the mistakes she believes she made, but from what I learned about her in the three years I've been here, is that she never loved her first husband. She likely never wanted to marry Beauregard, but it was something she had to do for appearances and somewhat for legal reasons. Despite how it all seems, she was a very old-fashioned woman and didn't want multiple partners, marriages, or to divorce."

"But she never divorced," Clint said.

"She never had to. The person she wished she had married has always lived here and saved her from *that* cardinal Christian sin," Mathias said. "Still, seeing people after her first husband never felt right and seeing the man she wanted was out of the question. It's mostly unfortunate her first husband had the outdated name, 'Beauregard.' Every man after him has been doomed to keep up the illusion. Call it delusion if you want, but she was very aware of what she was doing."

"If she felt so bad about shit like that, why not shack up with the guy she actually liked?" Clint said. "Think it's because he's a Jap?"

"Desire is a strong thing," Mathias said. The warmth from the fireplace caressed his cheeks. "But social pressure is worse." He closed his eyes, relaxing with the exhale.

"You ever feel… bad or gross for what you're doing?" Clint said.

"World's oldest occupation. What's there to feel bad about?" Mathias said.

"I meant doing the hag and her baby daughter at the

same time," Clint said.

Ellie snort-laughed abruptly.

"It was a business deal. So long as I was there when she called me, little else mattered." Mathias said.

When Agatha inherited the estate, she was eager to begin her father's work. Many believed she threw herself into hospitality and business to distract herself from what had happened at the will reading. The summer storm around the time of her father's death had caused the fruits to grow plentiful, juicy, and quicker than normal. She was unlike her predecessors, bringing not only trade goods to Parvenu, but bountiful gifts as well. Though no one lived around her, she considered the entire city to be her neighbors. She threw constant parties in town, celebrating the staff, the citizens, and the harvest, but rarely would she invite people to her home directly. There was a fear that the gold fixtures in the home would corrupt even the most easygoing of minds that entered. She brought in no more people than she needed to run the estate and she rarely let people go if she didn't have to. There were some exceptions to this with the stylists or when she felt charitable and wanted to offer someone down on their luck an opportunity to prosper, such as the tennis pro she never used. She wanted to give them the basics to help them up, then send them back into the world, but by the time their confidence was restored, they didn't want to leave.

Despite her popularity in Parvenu, her neighbors didn't trust her and she was not oblivious to it. She disappeared from parties without a word, slipping away to her home, her room, her quiet, her books, alone. The legacy of her ownership was built upon her welcoming nature, yet the thing she was remembered for was the number of people who went missing under her leadership. Tens of men were drawn through the gate by her long legs, bright eyes, and bubbly personality. They were promised hospitality, southern manners, and fine dining. They got what they expected, but lost something in return.

Ellie wasn't half as adored as her mother. Though she was sweet, there was something about the way she carried herself or spoke to others that always seemed fake. When they first met, Mathias's first instinct was repulsion. He couldn't understand the reaction; Ellie was the most beautiful woman he had ever seen. Large breasts, wide hips, and a tiny waist, her proportions were perfect. Her long, red hair was bouncy, vibrant, and silky. Her eyes were large emeralds that brought out the delicate coloring of her pale cheeks. He should have been uncontrollably drawn to her. He witnessed the hesitation of those in Parvenu moving away from her or holding back their own twitching repulsion when they interacted with her and it took him years to learn why.

"The rumors are true?" Clint said.

"Of course, the rumors are true. To what extent? I can't say, but there is no doubt in Parvenu or the families of Beauregards past," Mathias said. He slipped his arm around Ellie and pulled her back to him, close.

Clint stroked his bristly chin with his index finger. A curious, but entertained smile sat on his lips "Whatta trip," he said. "I knew she was some kinda crazy, but I never could pin it down."

"Crazy runs in the family," Mathias said.

"You can thank my mother," Ellie said.

Thunder rumbled around the house in modest roars. The rain softened against the picture windows, making them no louder than the clicking of the second hand on a clock. "Now that she's gone, you think he'll go mad?" Clint said.

"I don't believe so," Mathias said.

"Think he's got a gun out there in the shed?"

Mathias chuckled. "No." He stood. "I don't think he's anything I need to worry about." He stood up, extended his hand to Ellie, and helped her up when she took it. Walking away, Mathias waved his index and middle finger in a lazy salute.

Clint watched the boyfriend and his girl disappear down the servant's hallway. He turned to the window and looked out into the gray screen of heavy rain. Puddles devoured the lawn and began climbing the patio. "I wonder if my car can drive through that." He licked his lips.

THIRTEEN.

Conservatory, Benedict Estate
August 10th, 6:58 P.M.

Branching off from the ballroom and kitchen, the conservatory sat on the east side of the house; glass walls allowed the plants to soak up the sun and occupants to observe the sunrise. However beautiful it was during the morning, during a storm it often felt only slightly better than being water boarded. Gusts of wind slammed into the glass panes, shaking them in the frames. The rain alternated between violent pounding and timid, almost playful taps.

Bertrand's thumb pressed a new bundle of tobacco into his pipe's bowl. He flicked the silver Zippo open and produced a flame. He held the flame over the bowl, lighting the leaves, then held it there longer, allowing the warmth to tickle his nose. He snapped the lighter closed. Piquant air snuck into his nostrils and crawled down his throat. The tobacco worked its way into his muscles; it had always been a dirty pleasure after a long day of work. There was little he looked forward to more when his muscles ached and his bones clicked against each other than the bitter breath of tobacco.

His small, frail frame curled into the shape of the couch. His vision filled with pink and orange impatiens and green donkey tails hanging above. They reached around their pots, wanting to reunite with the earth. He closed his eyes. The wrinkles in his face grew lighter. Sorrow overtook his features.

Bertrand heard faint, girlish giggles. She didn't often come into the conservatory when she was younger. It was boring, and she never seemed interested in plants. On the rare occasion, she appeared in a white, or yellow, or robin's egg sundress.

"You shouldn't smoke in the house," she laughed. She combed her hair back with her fingers, but it was too lively to be contained; stray hairs stuck out in rebellion. Her long legs made her skirt seem too short for modesty, though Bertrand never minded. Delicate fingers wrapped around the back of the red Victorian couch. "My dad would kill you." Carnelian lips pursed and dimples dotted her cheeks.

"There are worse fates," Bertrand murmured. Her breasts distracted him. He was still a boy, nineteen, and kept his eyes on the potted plants as a shield from Agatha's boldness.

"Like what?" She giggled, shifting her hips from side to side, coaxing him for attention. Loose hair fell over her pale, freckled face.

Bertrand's gloved finger sunk deep into the potted soil as he struggled to find the right words.

He opened his eyes and returned to the empty room, surrounded by a soft pitter-patter trying to make him feel less lonely. He knew no woman could live forever, but he thought if anyone could defy the laws of man, it would have been her.

He stroked the smooth bowl of his pipe. The content smelled of earth mixed with Agatha's honeysuckle perfume still embedded in the couch cushions. He breathed greedily; soon her smell would fade and this home would lose every trace of her being.

The Wandering Jews, Peace Lilies, and Yuccas whispered to him, old friends he had kept alive for the last fifty years. They were in much better condition than him. Unlike people, plants grew stronger with age. Trees thickened, flowers and weeds dominated and became more resilient to predators. Plants adapted to their surroundings, yet people became brittle, bitter, and cynical with age. The downfall of humanity was in time's ability to rip humans apart by their curiosity and trust. But one thing they had in common, both were required to work with their surroundings or risk perish.

Bertrand's family immigrated to the United States shortly after World War II ended. In school, the animosity between the Americans and Japanese hadn't been obvious to him at first. His appearance and fractured English created a barrier between him and the community he wanted to be a part of. In an attempt to assimilate, he first removed his birth name. He eagerly adopted the name Bertrand at his classmates' recommendation. It was only later he learned it was the name of a boat that sank in Louisiana less than fifty years prior. Still, he believed it would help him fit in better than his birth name, Hiroshi Yamamoto, which his classmates often slurred into 'Hiroshima.'

"Bertrand?" was the first word Agatha spoke to him and up until she said his new name, he'd thought about changing it back. "Your English is pretty good for a foreigner. You might even speak it better than me!" Her Louisiana drawl colored familiar words in a way that almost made them foreign and poetic.

"Thank you. I am trying." He bowed to her with a flushed face he didn't want her to see.

"You don't have to do that here. We're all the same." She took his hands and squeezed them. His attention drew to her radiant smile. Her cherry-shaped face was decorated with defiant strands of curly hair, slipping free from her bun. He held onto her hands, then let go, afraid he had done something he shouldn't.

"Did you just move here? I don't recognize you," she said.

"A little while—"

"Ah, that's why," Agatha squeezed his hands again, tugging him in closer. "Ya see, I know everyone here. So, if I don't know you, I know you're not from here." She winked and laughed. It was the first time he heard her laugh and instantly he knew he didn't want it to be the last.

Their first conversation wasn't long, but he heard she liked flowers.

He took up gardening and brought his work to her. He saw her beauty reflected in every petal. He became addicted to seeing her face light up when he brought her a bouquet. There was rarely a day he didn't bring her something. After graduation, she offered him a job as groundskeeper at the Benedict Estate and without hesitation he took it. He thought that maybe by tending to her garden, then someday, she might allow him to tend to her as well.

She allowed him to see her in her nightgown or sometimes, a little less than that, but she never stopped dating. Her boyfriends came through the gates with eyes reflecting gold; each name was nothing more than a bad flavor left in his mouth.

His right hand dropped beside his lap. Brittle-boned calloused fingers pressed into the cushion beside his leg, curling against the fabric. He wanted to feel her hand upon his shoulders, in his hand, hear her encouraging words, terrible complaints, laughter and sobs, one more time.

Taking the pipe from his mouth, he opened his eyes. His pipe had gone out some time ago, but he continued to breathe through it. He was cold.

Sorrow made the wrinkles in his face their home and the darkness engulfing his eyes made him inhuman. His body was too heavy to move, to walk to his home even one more time. He closed his eyes and imagined it instead. He knew what every room looked like, he had found all the tunnels and secrets, and remembered the unique scent of each room as he took the mental tour. The ballroom was empty when he walked through it. Going down the servant's hallway, the silence was savage. He remembered taking speaking lessons from the maids as they folded laundry, their gossip so loud it ventured up the stairs.

Agatha's ascension to womanhood was displayed down the halls, and for the last several years only a portrait at the turn of the century was hung simply because there wasn't enough room for sixty paintings of her. Beside the library was Agatha as a child, a face full of untamable hair and freckles. Beside it, she was a young woman and the way Bertrand always saw her. In the portrait, her hair was a loose bun, and her face was complimented by a dark shade of lipstick to accent her complexion. Fur wrapped around her shoulders above her chest, displaying her collarbone and her mother's favorite jewelry: a gold and pearl necklace she lost ten years later during a trip to London. In her arms she held a fluffy white cat, large, and wearing a diamond-studded collar with a bell and hanging tag. There wasn't a portrait where she wasn't holding a cat until eight years ago when the cat turned into a six-year-old boy with brown curly hair and a diamond-studded bracelet.

A flash of lightning illuminated the glass room. The hanging leaves created claws across the furniture and Bertrand's lone shadow projected against the wall. A bad flavor filled his mouth. He scraped his tongue against his teeth. He pressed fresh tobacco into the end of his pipe, lit it up, and washed over the flavor with smoke and weed. He used the armchair to steady himself. His eyes flickered to shed some of their weight, but they were too dry.

"Don't you have something you should be doing?" He heard her voice again. His fingers curled into the armrest. He slumped against the couch. The pressure hurt his knuckles, but he preferred it to the pain in his chest. "By the way, have you met Beauregard yet?" She tugged on the arm of some man Bertrand had never seen before. Her husband had been dead for less than a month, and already she wore new jewelry on her arm. "Tell him how we met," she giggled.

It didn't matter what he looked like; their faces became a blur after a while. "What could it be this time?" Bertrand's teeth grinded together. "Chemistry? Movies? The supermarket?" he spat. "The doctor's office, waiting to be cured of gonorrhea? Did you find him at a charity event? Because he looks like your last charity case." Bertrand looked him up and down, nothing about him was memorable. "Did he ask you to dance? I bet he can't foxtrot."

"Oh hush. You sound like a jealous lover." She brushed her hand along his jaw. Her fingers curled under his chin and lifted his face so their eyes met.

"Because I am." Bertrand's lips twitched. Her smile met his scowl, but when she gave him the attention he craved, he couldn't help but smile back.

Her eyes would go wide and innocent as a gentle smile replaced the mischief that was once there. She bit her lip with thick front teeth and her face melted into adoration. The boys wouldn't last long, and once they were gone, Agatha and Bertrand would consummate their affections, before she came home with another boyfriend and the cycle would start again. He looked forward to her new boyfriends because he never felt closer to Agatha than after one of them disappeared.

Bertrand hadn't realized he was gripping his chest. He forced his hand to let go and got off the couch. His body had grown stiffer; his joints were stubborn and unmoving. He stumbled back, then reached for a small round table in the center of the room, praying the strength returned to him soon. He waited for a bout of dizziness to pass. Something about the room was off; strange and unfamiliar, it didn't feel real. He closed his eyes and reopened them to the same mixture of being a stranger in a place he'd always called home.

A spray of rain assaulted the glass room. The yard lights were on, but barely visible through the heavy sheet of water pouring over the yard. Bertrand slipped his pipe into his pocket and limped toward the back door. He pressed his hand to the chilled glass and a mild sense of relief connected with the beating life of rain. The panes around him shook in their place. He listened to the wave of water, waiting for the gusts to lighten, then he pulled the deadbolt and opened the door.

The weather assaulted him immediately, water splattered under every step. In seconds, he was soggy and drenched. A few more steps and he was in the grass. His feet sank into the soft, muddy ground and, in some spots, water pooled halfway up to his knees. Every step, the yard threatened to devour his shoes. His fingers dug around in his left pocket, feeling around his lighter for a small set of keys. He couldn't see anything. He lifted his arm to shield his eyes from the rain, but couldn't see through the night and storm. He let his memory guide him instead. He walked through the yard, continuing in the direction of the shed, his shed, a place he called his second home. A gust wanted to take his hat, but the added weight of rain stuck it to his head.

Bertrand's hands shook as he reached for the shed lock. He inserted the key and twisted it off, desperate to enter as though it were a sanctuary and he was a sinner. The lock fell to the ground, splashing in the mud. The wind shoved the door open, causing it to crack and splinter, bounding against the shed. He stepped in the door; his clothing clung to his thin, wispy body like a saggy layer of skin. He pulled a hanging chain beside the door, and the shed illuminated in dim amber. The scent of dirt, flowers, and gasoline tickled his nose. Lined against the walls were a dozen metal and wooden shelves filled with tools, milk crates, and organized seed bins. He took a mental inventory of what he saw and stopped when he settled on what he wanted. He came to his flower shelf, neighbor of the fruit and vegetable shelves. He fingered through alphabetized packets of seeds until he came upon G. Flicking a little further, he found a white paper envelope with "Globe Amaranth" printed on it. He slipped the small envelope into his wet breast pocket.

Bertrand left the shed. The doors rattled in the wind and vigorous rain. His feet stirred the yard and a patch of petunias squelched beneath him. This was Beauregard. He was messy. Prior to the marriage of Beauregard, Agatha's boyfriends were perceptive to the hints that they didn't belong. The face of a dirty shovel etched into their clothing and pillowcases. Manure in their shoes. Biting into a ripe, red apple to find the inside, dark, rotten, and riddled with worms. The hunger usually got to them first; never certain when the meal on their plate would be rotten, though it looked the same as the meals of everyone else at the table. Beauregard had been much more resilient. He had a wedding, he had a feast not made from local produce. He had drunk too much at his wedding; celebrated and when they returned from their honeymoon, Bertrand was filled with such hatred and disgust at the sight of the new husband, he sought the nearest blunt object and bashed the young man's head in until it was unrecognizable. Blood stained the century-old entryway wallpaper and carpet; it speckled the ceiling and his jumper; there was so much blood, it seemed comically unreal. "This is why I don't see movies," he wiped his forearm across his head.

He removed the body and buried it in the yard. He was hasty, the grave was much shallower than anything he'd dig later, but it was there and he didn't want Agatha to see. He returned to the messy hallway and rolled up the rug. She came around the corner and stopped. Blood and brain fluid dripped from the ends of the rolled mattress like a half-eaten pastry oozing with marmalade. "Isn't that a job for the maid?" She laughed.

Bertrand's inexperienced hands made few mistakes, but over time, they disappeared completely while Agatha's new relationships became routine.

Underneath the morning glories rested Arthur, Bartholomew, Christian, and Daniel.

Under the carnations rested Eugene, Frederick, Gregory, and Harold.

Under the bleeding hearts, some of the more recent gentlemen from the last decade. They hadn't been around long enough for him to learn any of their names.

Bertrand's form illuminated, his long shadow cast across the ground, the image of a body waiting to join the others. It wasn't a flash; it couldn't be lightning. It was a static light field penetrating the rain. Accompanying it, a calm, purring engine. The square headlights of Clint's Lincoln flashed off, then on again. A sharp guitar solo screeched through the car, deep vocals spat out muffled lyrics of a rock song.

Bertrand turned to face the beast. His button-up was

thin, see-through, and looked like a cover on a scarecrow hanging off his body. Water rinsed his dirty hands in an effort to cleanse him of the crimes he prayed God understood.

The Lincoln's engine revved.

Bertrand's lips curled into a thin line and pulled down at both corners. His fingers wound into tight fists. Thin skin stretched painfully over his knuckles.

The engine growled again, short, then long. The long rev was cut off by the splattering sound of tires digging into mud. Deeper and deeper they went into the garden, uprooting as many flowers as they could reach, trying to gain traction. They found their grip. Screeching wheels mixed with erratic drums and the vehicle shot toward Bertrand. His body cracked against the hood. He rolled up the windshield and flew over the top of the car. Dropping to the yard, mud splashed around the body. Bertrand coughed, gasping for breath. A sharp strike shot through his ribs. Red eyes seared into the darkness, staring at the motionless gardener. The engine roared and the distant red eyes charged back toward Bertrand. The car bounced, rolling over his body with back tires, and bouncing again once the front cleared the spot.

"Wait, wait, wait!" A muffled voice yelled, barely louder than the bass.

The car switched into drive, screeching, punching it. The Lincoln ran over Bertrand once more for a much smoother ride, the gardener now planted in the garden.

A few feet away, the car went into park. The red taillights disappeared in the darkness and noisy music, obscene words spoke over the storm. Clint wore a thick, wool trench coat. Drops of water splashed off his navy-blue hat and dripped in his face. "Old man—y'alright?" It wasn't clear whether he was yelling over the music or the aggressive rain. He gripped the edge of his visor and, standing beside the sunken body, he squinted and looked around. "Bee? Where'd you go?" He moved forward. Stepping on Bertrand felt a bit like walking on gravel. Brittle, old bones lodged into the treads of his shoes. A smile crept onto his lips. "Oh my god!" He tried to sound surprised. "Can you hear me?" He pressed his foot harder into Bertrand before stepping back. Blood washed rapidly into the garden. Torn out and bent flowers curved around Bertrand's body, trying to hold and protect him.

"Hold on, ya hear?" Clint said. "I'll get Doc. She'll know what to do." Rain and mud poured around Bertrand's body, covering him in the shallowest grave on the Benedict property.

Clint returned to his car and he climbed in. "If you're gone, who's gonna take care of the garden?" He yanked the door shut.

He shifted the car into gear and drove it back to the garage. Soon even the deafening bass was drowned beneath the thickening shower.

FOURTEEN.

Kitchen, Benedict Estate
August 10th, 7:27 P.M.

Walking in the front door, Clint whistled and jingled his car keys. Familiar excitement tickled his fingertips. He wanted to move around quickly, laugh, brag, tell some jokes, talk about himself, someone needed to hear him. He flexed his fingers in a continuous wave with the familiar itch to flip through a wallet. He hadn't run someone over in quite some time. There wasn't a lot of thanks in being a city taxi driver, and it wasn't a job that he had ever wanted. His backseat filled with more scandal than one might imagine. CEOs, lonely burger flippers, teenagers making their clumsy ways to adulthood, and the hooker going to piss on a man she'd never met before. People treated cab drivers one of two ways: as therapists or as ghosts. Those who treated him like therapists were better tippers than those who ignored him. The latter often tried to skip out on their bill.

Everyone who took taxis thought of the drivers the same way: some random person behind the wheel, someone they'd never see again. One of them Clint knew better than others. Randall was a recent high school graduate, an ex-football player with nontransferable skills, and someone Clint had gone to high school with. Randall skipped out on his bill so many times that Clint wasn't sure why he even bothered to stop whenever he saw Randall waving him down, but he always did with the hope that Randall would uphold his end of the bargain and pay for his services. Clint was taught to believe in the best of people. If you do what you're supposed to do, everyone else will too. He was taught not to hold ill-will for anyone and to give people as many chances as they needed to get it right. His patience waned some time ago, but he still couldn't quite shake free of his mother's lessons.

Like usual, Clint picked up Randall outside one of the city's bars and dropped him at his downtown apartment. Randall stumbled out of the cab, tripping over his feet, thinking the smell of alcohol coming from him was a fresh brew coming from somewhere else.

Clint put the car into park and got out with him. "That'll be $25.41," he said, placing a hand on the hood.

The man laughed. "I don't owe you anything. I know how this works. Don't you?"

Clint went around the car and grabbed the man by his shirt. "I'm sorry man, but the meter says $25.41. That's what you owe," he repeated. "That's how this works."

Randall shoved Clint away and stumbled back off balance. "I don't owe you shit!" He threw an off-balance punch. It connected to Clint's jaw and knocked him to the ground. "Got that? You got that?"

Clint clutched his throbbing jaw and probed it for any immediate signs of swelling. His hands stung, scraped against the asphalt. Randall's shoulders seemed ridiculously broad, yet something about him made him seem insignificant. His perfectly muscular figure bulged out at the stomach, giving him love handles Clint never remembered him having in high school.

"Can you believe this guy?" Randall said to himself.

Clint got to his feet and climbed in his car. The radio ran softly and the engine purred beneath him. He stared out the windshield, at Randall's retreating back. The taxi company was going to penalize him for the money, time, and payment lost. It would screw with the check he used to pay rent on his mobile home; Randall wouldn't just cost him $25.41. He would cost him the late fee Clint would receive in the mail assuming he wasn't kicked out of his home completely. He'd have to live in his taxi and then he'd get ticketed for it and be even more behind than he already was. His fingers tightened around the steering wheel; black leather gloves stretched over his knuckles. He switched his car into reverse and stepped on the gas. He flew back, switched to drive. His tires screeched against the pavement. The lights streamed past Randall, flooding the ground beyond where he stood. Randall turned around and placed his hand over his eyes to see what was staring him down.

"Hey! Anderson? What are you—"

Hood met gut. A thud, a tumbling roll, and the body landed on the other side. Clint shifted into park and climbed out of the car. "Hey, hey, Randy?" Clint ran to the back of his car. Randall curled over, holding himself. His forehead bled, his skin raw in places, and his shoulder looked dislocated. "You okay, man?" Clint knelt. "Sorry, I don't know what came over me." He rolled Randall onto his back.

"What—what did you do to me?" Randall said.

"I think I hit ya," Clint said. He noticed his hand was shaking. A burst of energy spread in his chest and infected the rest of his body. His fingers tingled with a sense of eagerness.

"Why'd you—you little punk—" Randall gulped, struggling to speak through painful breaths. "Wait until I get my hands on—"

"Well, I mean, you kinda owed me for the ride," Clint said.

"I told you, I don't owe anything to shits like you."

Something snapped in Clint. He stood, drew his leg back, and kicked Randall as hard as he could. The agonizing groan Randall released was satisfying, but still not enough. Clint knelt and reached into Randall's back pocket. He pulled it open and took whatever money he could find, though it wasn't as much as Clint needed. He took a couple of coupons he found crumpled in the second wallet pocket. Standing up, he tossed the wallet down. "Pay yer bill next time, yeah? Then we can avoid another one of *these*." He didn't wait for an answer and returned to his taxi. Sitting behind the wheel, his heart raced. He looked at the mixture of cash and coupon in his hand, then in the rearview mirror to check on Randall laying on the road. He noticed his own face instead, a smile on his thin lips. When did that happen?

He slipped the bills into the cash box and slid it back under his seat. His mind was still racing from what he had done. He stepped on the gas and left the scene; afraid Randall might find the ability to get up and bust in his cab's windows. That was an expense he didn't need.

Clint's night went on as normal, but as it progressed, he realized he had never loved his job more than he had earlier that evening. All this time, he'd been doing his job wrong. His mother had taught him all the wrong lessons when he was a boy.

It wasn't about killing people with kindness until they treated you well. The only time someone cared about someone else was if the well-being of the someone else was proportional to the well-being of themselves.

And he found a surprising amount of enjoyment in the sound spines and skulls made when they smacked into his windshield.

Clint slipped his hat off and tossed it into a nearby chair in the ballroom. He unbuttoned his jacket and tossed it over his hat. Water dripped down his neck and dampened the collar of his shirt. His index finger hooked on his keyring and he jingled it again, this time louder than the last. He looked past the pillars into the ballroom, the only thing occupying it was the fire's warmth. Muffled laughter trickled in from the kitchen down the hall. Clint headed that way, still jingling his keys.

In the kitchen, he found Ellie leaned against the kitchen bar with a glass of red wine in one hand and a thin slice of white cheese in the other. Alex stood beside her, his elbows rested on the countertop, his chin in his hands.

Clint stepped in, swinging the keys in a lazy circle. He tapped them on the counter and continued toward the liquor cabinet, whistling now.

"Going somewhere?" Ellie said, looking from the keys to Clint.

Clint was smiling too much; he couldn't hold the whistle. He tucked the keys into his pants pocket and picked up an empty shot glass. "Nah, I was tryin' to catch Bee though." Mud splashed more than halfway up to his knees and a trail of dark footprints followed him; a puddle began to form under him. "Saw him runnin' out into the storm, sayin' some kinda crazy shit about Agatha. Senile or suicidal? I dunno, but I thought I'd check on him, ya know?" He stuck his mud-crusted hand into the icebox and dropped a handful of cubes into his cup.

Alex pressed his lips to the edge of his wine glass but didn't take a sip. "You find him?"

"My car did," Clint said, "three times." He poured bourbon over the ice. He turned from the bar, a crooked grin pulling at his lips.

Laughter snuck up on Alex like an unwanted sneeze. A loud, "HA" echoed through the room before he was prepared. He cleared his throat. "Is he alright?"

"I told him I'd get Doc, but he was bein' kinda impatient," Clint said.

"Shame," Ellie said. "The garden will miss him." She sipped her red wine.

"But what can you do with old folks? It feels like when one goes, a bunch of 'em go," Clint said.

"Sounds like a good enough reason for Astra!" Alex said, "What was she? Sixty? Seventy-nine?"

"I think she was thirty-four," Ellie said.

"And with one foot already in the grave," Alex said, "the poor thing."

Alex clicked his glass against Ellie's. Laughter echoed off the kitchen surfaces, the glasses, hanging pots and pans, and across the smooth floor. The walls, thunder, alcohol—something distorted the sound, causing it to seem deeper, melted, and less human. It crept under the kitchen pantry door. What should have sounded like friends laughing about simple jokes instead sounded like hyenas gagging on self-indulgence. Kelly stood in the dark pantry, clutching his ears and keeping his eyes shut like it would all disappear if he couldn't sense any of it. His heart throbbed so loudly, he couldn't hear the voices on the other side of the door anymore, despite standing against it. His shirt clung to his chest from perspiration. He lowered his hands from his ears and gripped the doorknob. He pressed his ear to the wall, trying to gauge how many of them were in the kitchen. Paranoia brushed his skin like fingers creeping over his arms. He pulled away from the door and looked around behind him; shadows flickered from the fire outside the sliding pantry door to the dining room. He saw nothing.

He steadied his shaking hand on the doorknob and

twisted it open, cracking open the kitchen-side pantry door. The overflow of light created a slash down the right side of his face. His dilated pupil struggled to stay open. His heart sounded louder than before, and now his chest violently revolted. He couldn't feel his hands anymore.

"Who ya think will go next?" Clint said.

"I'll tell you who I'd like to go next!" Alex laughed. He picked up the wine bottle and emptied it into his glass. "Frankly, if Beau or Gav were gone, I could die happy."

"I woulda thought you'd say the kid," Clint said.

"I mean yeah, it'd be fun, but I'm not worried about an illiterate brat. Threats first, we can have fun later," Alex said. "Gotta be at least a little responsible, ya know?"

"I bet whoever gets to Kelly could make him yowl like a puss in heat," Clint said.

"So not an image I want to associate with a child," Ellie said.

"He's legal in some states," Clint said.

"Can does not mean should," Ellie said.

"Since when do you have a conscience?" Alex laughed. "Going soft in your old age?"

"Shut up." Ellie snorted.

Lightheadedness struck Kelly. He clutched the shelf beside him for balance. Pulling the pantry door shut, it seemed much darker than before; the voices muffled, becoming indistinguishable from each other. Kelly couldn't tell if he had his eyes closed or open. Holding onto the shelf, he used it to guide himself back toward the dining room. His movements were careful and calculated, his hands traced the edges of the shelves. The back of his hand ran into something, he anticipated the clatter of a box, but instead, the pantry remained so quiet, his ears started to ring.

The kitchen burst into laughter again. Something heavy hit the ground; glasses clicked together.

Kelly stood frozen. The feeling was familiar and something he hadn't felt since the alley. At six-years-old, he imagined the monsters that accompanied the growls he heard behind dumpsters, how long their claws were, what they'd say before they ate him. He shook his head, blinked rapidly, wishing for the blocks of dark pantry shapes to form in his vision and bring him back. If he got out of the pantry, the fireplace was still going.

Glass shattered against the kitchen floor.

More laughter.

Kelly couldn't move. He panted, breathing heavily, trying not to pass out. "It's nothing, it's nothing, they are drunk, it's nothing," he said to himself. "Keep going. You have to keep going."

He reached for the pantry handle, but it wasn't there. Soft linen and warm muscles heated his fingertips.

Fingers curled into Kelly's biceps, tight. A scream lodged in his throat, scalding it like bile. Lips parted, terror rallied to escape. A dishcloth crammed into his mouth, deadening the sounds before they could make it out. He pulled away, arms flailing for any kind of advantage he could get; the shelves clattered around him. The hand wrapped around his bicep controlled him, tightening harder, causing pain he couldn't fight off. He was pulled back, his legs stumbled over themselves. The folding pantry door to the dining room rattled open, amber light crowded the small room, and a shadow much longer than his own took over the wall. His struggle for escape became weaker, while the dish cloth was pushed harder into his mouth. Instead of trying to scream, he was trying to breathe.

Kelly's eyes watered, his throat tightened, and the vomit burned him. He slammed his heel into a foot beneath his. It was absorbed by the thick leather shoes and went unnoticed.

The shoes' detail came to Kelly; the familiar shine, the

rounded point accented by circular shapes at the toe; the way the lace was tied.

"Be quiet."

The words sent a chill down Kelly's spine. He drew his elbow back, trying to break free, desperate for breath. His fingers curled around the ends of his sleeves. He held the fabric between his fingers. His eyes watered and vision became blurry. He squeezed them shut to stop the tears, to stop himself from seeing what he knew. His jaw hurt from the grip around the towel. He relaxed his jaw, and the towel loosened, no longer held in place. The hand around his bicep loosened then disappeared. Kelly threw his arms back to smack the person behind him. He stumbled away, removed the towel from his mouth, and tossed it to the ground.

An awful, acrid odor surrounded him within an instant. He picked the towel back up and pressed it to his face in hopes of cutting the scent off, but it was too late. The smell imprinted inside his nostrils. Strong, putrid copper mixed with burnt liver and a sweet, musky cerebrospinal incense. A charcoal-like smell, Madame Astra's burning skin, glided through the warmth of the fireplace accompanied by the sulfuric scent of burnt hair.

Kelly walked to the head of the table in long strides to put distance between himself and Gavin. "Why would you do that?!" His voice cracked. His normal embarrassment was replaced with rage. "I couldn't breathe. I couldn't breathe, Gavin!"

"Quiet," Gavin said, still standing by the pantry door.

Kelly turned around the closer he came to the head of the table. Shadows in the pantry moved behind Gavin like ghosts. He swallowed saliva flavored with burnt blood vessels. "You're crazy. Everyone's gone crazy, and you've gone crazy too!" He tripped over himself. "What is wrong with you?!"

"You had your back to the door," Gavin said. Kelly backed up until his rear hit the edge of the table. "You can't make mistakes like that tonight."

Kelly jumped at the touch and glanced over his shoulder, paranoid that someone stood behind him. He moved along the table's edge, and now Gavin walked toward him. Kelly shuffled away faster, but Gavin gained on him. "What were you doing in my pantry?" Kelly snapped.

"As the butler, it's my pantry," Gavin said.

"It's my house. It's my pantry!" Kelly reached behind him for something forgotten: silverware, glasses, even a napkin, but the table was clear of even the candlesticks Gavin had brought out during the reading.

"Were you hungry?" Gavin said.

"Why would I be hungry?"

"You were in the pantry. You didn't have supper. It's a fair assumption."

"I—" A strong gust slammed against the window. Kelly moved around the curved table edge at the front of the room. His freehand clutched the back of the master chair. He stepped past it and used it as a barrier between him and Gavin. Flickering, eager flames caught his eyes, then a body, and a melted head, shrunken and split off. White globs of fat nursed the fire like wax. Madame Astra's muscles dried out and contracted. The fire made them throb and tremble, a mirage that she was still alive. The flames released sharp hisses that held for seconds at a time. Madame Astra's hairless head dropped back showing her empty eye sockets. What was left of her face was stained by evaporated cerebral juices.

Kelly tried to hold it in, turn away, and run, but the sickness forced itself out and splattered on the floor. He doubled over, hands pressed against his knees for stability.

His stomach emptied little more than acid and tiny chunks of lunch. Still compelled to vomit, he dry heaved. Strings of sticky saliva hung from his lips. Her smell wrapped around him and strangled him.

Gavin slipped into the pantry, returning with a pair of white towels. He made his way to the head of the table. Kelly maintained the space between them, stepping back and running his sleeve against his wet mouth. Gavin dropped the towels on the floor where Kelly had vomited and, with his foot, pressed them into the floor to mop up the mess. "Rotting bodies smell much worse when they burn."

"Why is she dead?" Kelly stuttered.

"I should have given you a warning."

"Why is she dead?!" Kelly's throat was raw and a dry heave shook his body. He covered his mouth and nose with his sleeve. Tears ran down his cheeks and darkened his blazer.

"Human nature," Gavin said.

"What is that even supposed to mean?" Kelly sucked in a sob.

"All people have urges and the urge to kill is no different than the urge to eat or sleep or urinate. To kill for personal reasons, feelings, or achieve personal goals is an inherently human trait. She's dead because she was a moron; because she was unprepared; because she got in the way of what everyone else wanted." Gavin stepped over the towels.

"That's not an excuse to kill somebody!" A sob interrupted him. "It was all given to me. What was she even going to do?"

Gavin's pace quickened to close the gap between him and Kelly. He tucked his thumb beneath Kelly's chin. "So trusting you still are—"

"Don't touch me!" Kelly slapped Gavin's hands away.

He tripped over himself, stepping back.

"And so—" Gavin said.

"I'm not—!"

"That's fine."

Kelly's throbbing heart caused his body to tremble. He couldn't feel the ground beneath his feet.

"This situation is much larger than you realize. It's not about what's said. It's never about what's said; it's about what people want and what they'll do to make it happen."

"I don't understand."

"She wanted the money."

"She wasn't going to hurt me."

"There are more kinds of harm beyond physical."

Kelly hesitated. "What would she gain?"

"She wanted the money," Gavin said again.

"If she wanted it that bad, I could have given her some so she'd back off."

"And if that wasn't enough?"

Kelly backed up, glanced over his shoulder, he quickened. "I don't know—I'd give her some more."

"And if that wasn't enough?" Gavin said. "What if whatever you gave her wasn't enough until she had all of it?"

"She didn't need all of it." Kelly's jaw clenched.

"It's not about need. It's about want." Gavin towered over Kelly. His shadow enveloped Kelly's much smaller one. "No one's goal here is to have 'just enough' or to be taken care of. No one fights for equality. They fight and kill for superiority, status, kingdom. Anyone who says otherwise is a liar."

"No one thinks like that, Gavin!"

"Everyone thinks like that, Kelly."

"People aren't animals who just—take and take and hurt people because they can."

Gavin stared at Kelly with a distant, scrutinizing eye. "That's exactly what people do. You think anyone wants to see you succeed? They'd sooner throw you in the fireplace."

"No, Gavin. That's just you!" A lump formed in Kelly's throat. His back hit the wall and he yelped in surprise. He glanced back, then at Gavin. "I don't want to die!"

"If you don't play the game like everyone else, you will."

In the pantry door, Ellie, Clint, and Alex emerged from the shadows. Ellie leaned against the door frame, Alex stood beside her crossing his arms, and Clint stood behind them both.

"Charity, mercy, and goodwill are nothing but disadvantages. If you let them dictate the way you act, you will lose," Gavin said. "To enter the ring but abstain from playing is suicidal. Your virtue makes you nothing but a liability."

"Oy vey," Alex said. "And here I thought Astra couldn't stink worse than that god-awful perfume." He pinched his nose, though the playful smile spreading across his lips said he wasn't too bothered. "What was it called? *Ode to the middle-aged spinster?*"

Kelly's eyes darted between Gavin and the group, unsure of whom to watch. The slightest movement captured his attention. The fire stole it a few times, the lightning caused shadows of people who weren't there to appear in his peripheral vision. His chest grew tight; he couldn't breathe, and the dining room air became thinner.

Alex entered the dining room, taking a couple of steps toward the fireplace, he stopped short and glanced over it. "Looks like there might be just enough room in there for a cat," Alex said, eyes now fixated on the boy.

Kelly bolted out of the dining room. His arms smacked into the doors he didn't bother to open fully. They closed behind him with a muted thud.

Gavin returned to the set of towels on the floor, and once more, pressed his shoe into them, moving the fabric around until it dampened all the way through. He rolled the towels up with as much moisture to the center of the ball as possible.

Ellie took a deep breath. She sighed and relaxed against the wall as she released it. "Nothing quite like the stench of desecrated human life, is there?"

"Sure," Alex said, "But you've gotta be a saint for that. Instead, we have Astra."

"So, what we're smelling is an exorcism, really," Ellie said.

Alex choked on laughter then said, "but for real, this smell—I can't deal anymore." Ducking back into the pantry, he escaped to the kitchen.

Ellie rolled her eyes. Her weight switched hips. "Prima donnas, right?" She turned on her toes and followed Alex's wake.

Clint moved aside, giving Ellie room to pass, then stepped out from the pantry. He leaned against the wall beside the folding door and watched Gavin fold the damp towels, hiding the vomit. He picked at single, short beard hairs and wore a calculating smile that only twisted up wider the more he turned his head to the side. "I never listened to my mom either," he said.

"I'm not surprised," Gavin said. He returned to the pantry door.

"I got plenty of manners," Clint said. "That's why I'm here."

Uninterested, Gavin said, "what are you talking about?" He opened the dining room door.

"Bee had a ritual of buryin' people with flowers, right? We were talkin' about it in the kitchen, ya know, what would be the best flower to bury him with. We couldn't think of it.

None of us talked to him much. Pretty sure he didn't like us—that's fine. We decided we didn't like him neither, but you hung out with him a lot. You'd know what kinda seeds to bury him with, yeah?"

"There was meaning behind his methods. Flowers represent character for some—" Gavin said.

"So, you got a suggestion?"

"Of course," Gavin said.

A priceless Indian vase shattered against Clint's head; he dropped to the ground with a thud. Clattering around him were finely painted pieces of gold, tan, and brown clay.

Gavin's blue eyes trailed down the curtains to the new mess on the floor, then the short, black heels and stockings behind it. "There were many less fragile items to choose from. That was the one you went with?"

Anna slipped into the pantry. Reaching against the wall, she retrieved a handheld broom and dustpan. She knelt beside the shattered vase. Her slim legs were completely covered by the bell curve of her black maid uniform. Her hair was black, straight, and restrained in a tidy bun on the back of her head. "I never liked that pot." She swept the pieces into the dustpan.

"They were making a mess in the kitchen not long ago."

"I've taken care of it." Anna discarded the glass shards in the pantry garbage can and hung the broom and dustpan on the wall. When she returned, she knelt beside Clint, careful to keep her legs together. Clint's shirt came untucked in some places despite his belt. She nimbly reached into his pockets and withdrew his keys. "Did you want to run him over?" She held the keys out to Gavin, wearing the key ring around the tip of her index finger.

"He may enjoy that too much," Gavin said, taking the keys and slipping them into his pocket. He would hang them up with the other house keys when he had a spare moment.

"What shall we do then?"

"He decided his own fate when he left Bertrand to drown in the garden." Gavin positioned himself at the heavier side of Clint's body. Anna lined herself up with the chauffeur's legs. A pattern formed on the fabric below Clint's knees: dried mud cracked around the creases and folds. Gavin threaded his arms underneath Clint's and lifted the weighty torso with a soft grunt. Gavin dragged Clint back far enough to unfold his legs and when he nodded at her, Anna threaded her arms around Clint's legs. The dry mud smudged into her clean white apron but disappeared on the black parts of her uniform.

Together, they carried the body out of the dining room and toward the nearest back door. The rain's violence became more obvious in the ballroom. Where the dining room was designed to quiet the outside to assist the atmosphere for easy conversation, the large and numerous windows in the ballroom amplified the weather's aggression.

"Would you like your jacket?" Anna said.

"We'll be soaked either way."

Anna dropped Clint's legs. His heels clicked against the floor. She held the back door open for Gavin who pulled the body out. Clint's feet dragged along the floor in defiance.

The covered patio should have offered some level of cover, but the rain breached the area with help from the wind. If not for the rain, the Louisiana humidity would have caused his dress shirt to turn transparent and cling to his pale skin.

The wind blew Anna's knee-length skirt between her legs, making it look like a lopsided pair of shorts. Anna closed the house door.

"Help me get him onto my shoulders," Gavin said.

Clint wasn't heavy, but he was bony with a mild gut that stretched larger when it hung. Anna wasn't strong enough to hold Clint on her own, but she could relieve enough of the weight from Gavin to allow him to reposition himself. He bent over and connected his shoulder with Clint's waist. Anna leveraged Clint's weight while Gavin wrapped his arms around the driver's body.

The tricky part was only beginning. The patio stairs were slippery. Changes in the weather turned the beautiful marble into nothing more than a device for breaking necks. Anna stood close behind Gavin, offering him stability, ready to become cushioning should he slip. The full wrath of the rain was hard to gauge until they'd stepped into it. Neither could see much of anything. Water darkened their clothing, dripping from their bodies as though they stood underneath a running tap. The smooth surface of Gavin's leather soles slid in the squishy earth. Though the yard appeared to be sinking, it was much more soft and yielding than the patio. A couple of the yard lights were barely visible in the distance. The shed's normally blinding light was reduced to a timid flicker.

Water weighted Gavin's clothing. If not for his belt, the rain surely would have stripped him like a lustful woman. Water flooded through the sides of his shoes and filled them. Anna scouted ahead, guiding Gavin toward the shed. Tire tracks carved furrows through flowers, grass, and the walking path; they were small, overflowing ravines. Petunias, roses, and tulips ripped out by the roots bobbed like casualties leading the way to Bertrand's half-buried body. His skin had become pale and clammy. The large gashes left by Clint's grill were mute in color.

They moved past the body without stopping and soon arrived at the shed. The doors flapped against the side of the building,

Once inside, Gavin dropped Clint to the ground. Everything was clean and organized. Gardening tools hung on poles, mower, and gasoline covered in a tarp kept the dust from slipping into the engine. Extra pots, soil, seeds, labeled shelves, crosshatch fencing left over from the wine garden completed twenty years ago leaned against the far wall.

Gavin pushed his wet hair back; it flattened against his skull. Water dripped down his chin. He sucked a breath through his now stuffy nose. His body was twice as heavy as before.

Gavin searched the workbench against the wall farthest from the door. A medical kit stuck to the wall beside it. On top, a toolbox and Bertrand's keys, keys for the mower and the old barn. Gavin pocketed the keys then went through the toolbox. He searched the cabinets until he found a coil of sapling wire and wire cutters. He dropped the sapling wire beside Clint. Heaving the man onto his stomach, Gavin brought Clint's hands together and bound them with the wire, then did the same to his ankles. Gavin returned the supplies to their place.

Anna stood over Clint, one shovel in each hand.

"We'll take care of Bertrand first," Gavin said.

Anna nodded and gave him one of the shovels.

Gavin knew how to dig holes. When his father had died, Bertrand taught him how and where to do it. However, he had never dug a hole in a storm.

In the center of the yard, the flower beds appeared raised from the rest. They pushed their shovels into the sodden earth. The ground moved like quicksand. Whatever hole they started was quickly filled in with over-saturated soil that may as well have been dirty water. Because of that, Bertrand's grave wasn't deep. It likely wasn't even three feet deep, but it was enough to conceal his small form. Anna continued digging, keeping something of a hole in the ground while Gavin retrieved the old man's body. He patted down Bertrand's pockets and withdrew the package of Globe Amaranths from his shirt. Anna took the engraved lighter from his pants pocket, but the carved pipe from Agatha remained with him. They placed him into the shallow hole, and the earth began the burial process immediately. Brown covers tenderly tucked him in for the rest of his life, first his arms, then his chest, then his face disappeared. Gavin tore the package of flowers open and spread the seed across where Bertrand lay. Would they grow? Would they be washed away? The ritual may not have grown all the flowers over the years, but it seemed to grow most of them. If the Benedict Estate was grateful at all for Bertrand's care, then he would blossom within six weeks.

Their muscles ached. Anna and Gavin wanted to give up and go inside, but they weren't finished yet. Two bodies, two holes. The second hole was far from Bertrand's. Instead of being in the flower garden, Clint deserved a place in the ground reserved for cowards, an undecorated spot beside Gavin's father.

The digging strategy wasn't working. Their arms were too tired and the water was too rapid. They tried peeling back the mud in shallow shovelfuls to make room for a person. The tougher dirt didn't melt back into the hole quite like the soft flowerbed had, but digging even one foot into the ground was difficult and time-consuming.

Tired of its soggy weight, Gavin unbuttoned his jacket and tossed it to the ground. If it's gone in the morning, so be it. "Keep digging," he said, driving his shovel in the ground. "Keep the hole open." Gavin returned to the shed and picked up an oil rag from the workbench. He splattered it with gasoline from a red canister beside the lawnmower. The smallest dribble filled the area with the stench of petroleum, leaving him faintly dizzy.

Clint still laid in the shed doorway. Gavin pressed the cloth to his face. Clint cough, before yelling, "my baby, my baby! Is Rosaline on fire?!" The smell stuck to his nose. He continued to cough.

Gavin tossed the rag to the side, grabbed Clint by the legs, and dragged him out of the shed.

The coughing was replaced with burbling, water replacing air. Clint wiggled against the wet ground. "The hell...!" he gasped. His legs writhed against the restraints. He jerked his arms and felt nothing but the sharp edge of the wire cutting into his skin. "What's goin' on?" The silence made Clint want to say more, but the rain became a gag, and his yelling turned to a mere gurgle.

Gavin tossed Clint into the hole the moment they reached it. Mud slipped in around his body but didn't cascade the same way it had around Bertrand in the softer soil. The rock-mixed dirt held better against the rain.

Clint turned his head to the side, to stop the mud from drowning him. "She dig your hole for ya?" Clint said. "How sad ya can't do the work yourself. Ya gotta have a woman do everything for ya." His wrists pulled at the wire. His body flopped around a bit.

Gavin and Anna pushed mud into the hole. It pooled around the underside of Clint's body.

"You wanna go at it? Then do it like a man. Not with your girl. Not this cheap—"

"You struck him with your car," Gavin said.

"Yeah... but I wouldn't call it a cheap shot—the ride's expensive," Clint said.

Anna shoveled more mud into the hole; it rolled off Clint's chest and contoured around his body.

"He was gonna die anyway. Least I did it fast." The words rushed out of Clint. "Get it? Fast?" He laughed at himself. Panicked eyes tried to stay open, to watch them, but the rain blinded him.

Gavin and Anna shoveled more dirt into the hole. It rolled off Clint's head and settled beneath his face. Clint struggled to laugh as the weight pressing down on his chest and lungs strangled him. Water forced its way into his throat. Gavin shoveled faster, Anna mirrored him. Clint's voice became louder, yet shallower with jokes that turned to pleas that turned to muffles that turned to thunder.

Mud seeped into the hole. Gavin stepped on it a few times, patting it down with a heavy foot.

He looked at Anna. Her black hair, once a tight bun, hung flaccid. A few wet strands stuck to her neck like black tentacles.

They returned their shovels to the shed, locked it, and returned to the patio.

Though they no longer stood in the rain, they continued to drip. Anna released the bun and dropped her hair tie into her apron pocket. Slim fingers wrung water from the dark locks.

Gavin's white shirt clung to his body everywhere it could, now flesh-toned. Excessive water pulled Anna's dress down her slim figure.

Gavin's hand scraped his hair back. Every time he pressed his hair tighter against his head, more water oozed out. He headed for the house door first. His foot slipped along the marble. Instinctively, he reached out. Anna caught him.

Everything was coated in mud. Everything was uncomfortable and messy. Underneath each step, mud squished in his socks. He slid his shoes off and kicked them against the house. Anna took hers off and set them gently beside Gavin's, arranging his just as neatly. Bracing himself with the wall, he pulled his socks off. Each sock smacked the ground, heavy and wet. He wiped his feet against the waterlogged mat, then entered the house. Anna followed suit.

Gavin's tongue clicked against his teeth. His chest and shoulders rose calmly with every hot, urgent breath. The warm ballroom fire tingled his freezing skin. He wished it would follow them down the hall. He glanced through each corridor they passed on their way to the laundry room without slowing down. He pulled his shirt loose from his pants and unbuttoned it. The water trail they left bothered him, but he had to ignore it for now.

Gavin pushed the laundry door open. A soft click and Anna closed it behind them.

Gavin opened the washing machine and tossed his soggy shirt in; Anna locked the door.

He dropped his trousers and underwear; she unzipped her dress and pushed it to the floor with her pantyhose.

They emptied their pockets and tossed everything they wore into the washing machine. Detergent on top.

She began the wash cycle; he wrapped callous hands around her bare thighs.

She closed the lid; he pressed himself against her, pushed her against the washing machine, and lifted her off the ground. Her legs wrapped around him and every muscle contracted and relaxed. Their lips mashed together in lustful desperation.

Gavin pressed himself against her, eager, anticipating, and greedy. His responsibilities tried to distract him. The threat of the reading lingered in his thoughts, but were somehow insignificant in comparison to what he needed now. Their bodies rocked together. The washing machine shifted beneath them.

In that moment, there was nothing more important than filling his desire. All other responsibilities could wait.

FIFTEEN.

Kelly's Bedroom, Benedict Estate
August 10th, 8:15 P.M.

Stuttering rain tapped against the windows and echoed down the long, empty hallways. The furniture and fabrics in Agatha's bedroom exuded her honeysuckle perfume, but it wasn't strong enough to remove the smell of burning flesh from Kelly's nose. He closed his eyes and saw blank, empty eye sockets staring at him. The twitching muscles possessed corpse and a bare jaw dropped open.

He held a copy of Agatha's favorite book splayed across his lap. He leafed through the pages, but the words were foreign symbols he couldn't understand. Line after line of nothing. He'd seen Agatha disappear into this world for countless hours, the symbols painting people, park benches, trees, and conflicts she relayed to him. "They're lying," he muttered. He followed each curve into the next one, willing it to make sense. "There's nothing here." Anger bubbled in his stomach until his temper flared hot. He tossed the book from his lap with a growl. It smacked into the wall and fell to the floor, pages spread and paper bending against itself.

Heavy, even beats throbbed behind the closed bedroom

door. Kelly sat up and stared at it. After a moment, he slid off the bed and checked the deadbolt. He never questioned it being there; they were in almost all the rooms and always had been. Now he knew why. He double checked that the door was locked tight then took hold of the doorknob and rattled it gently to check that lock as well.

The thumps outside the door became louder. Something was hitting a wall somewhere.

He leaned against the door and pressed his ear to it. The balls of his feet dug into the floor. He held his breath.

Kelly looked over his shoulder, surveying the bed, the dresser, the bookcase, the vanity, the window, the bookcase, and the bed again. The shadows cast by lightning ignited anxiety inside of him every time it flashed. His childhood home was now a foreign labyrinth guarded by monsters.

He crept back to bed and pulled the covers back; a job Gavin normally did for him once the bed was warm and ready. He slid between the sheets, and the cool fabric chilled his legs. He laid down, closed his eyes, rolled onto his side, and then onto the other. If he fell asleep, he was sure he would wake up to normalcy in the morning and this would turn out to be a nightmare. He opened his eyes and yanked the dangling chain on his beside lamp. The room fell into a darkness he'd hoped he would recognize, but it was just as distorted as the rest of the house.

He pulled the comforter over his head and let the familiar smells surround him. Detergent, Agatha's lotion, his shampoo.

The rolling sound in the walls picked up again. It started to his left, then it came to his right. It multiplied, surrounding him within seconds. Waving branches scratched against the window, each new gust reinvigorating them.

Kelly tensed and pulled the covers down from his eyes.

Ornate, purple silk curtains drawn back by the golden tassel ropes remained unattended to by Gavin. An antique rocking chair and Agatha's box of crochet projects sat a few feet beneath the window. Long shadows, like fingers, vaguely came in through the glass. They scratched at his legs and reached for his face. Something climbed his leg, moving higher and stroking the outside of his calf, then his thigh, then back down his calf. He pulled his legs closer. The finger-like branches continued to bounce against him.

Kelly tossed the blankets back and climbed out of bed. The window overlooked the courtyard and flower gardens. The gray curtain of rain had become much lighter, but the yard was still veiled in darkness. What could be seen looked like a washed-out swamp: plants with the color drained out of them, standing water, bubbling pools. He pulled at the drawstrings, clumsy in undoing the knots. He never tied them back, he never tied his shoes. His face grew hot, and the knot only got worse until it wasn't there anymore. The second tassel he couldn't break free, and instead, tangled it within itself.

Kelly threw the curtain away with a huff. He crawled back into bed and checked the sheets. The fingers that teased his legs were no longer visible, and what was making it through the window spilled onto the floor at the end of the bed. His heart raced and he couldn't sit still. He climbed out of bed again to pick up Agatha's book from where it laid on the floor. He returned to bed and turned the bedside lamp on. He traced over the soft pages, pushing the new creases down and twisting the pages back into place. He caught the edge of the bent page between his index and middle fingers and kept it there. Flipping it between his fingers made him think of the way Agatha ran her hands through his hair as she read to him. The soft sound of her voice played in his head, telling him a story he'd never hear again.

Three powerful knocks shifted the bedroom door in its frame. The knob twisted, rattled, first quizzically, then aggressively. It resisted.

Kelly sat up and watched the door with alarm. The light around the frame wasn't there, the shadow of what was on the other side appeared invisible.

For a moment, there was nothing, then there was knocking, louder this time. "Hey, kid, you in there?" Johnny's voice came through the door so loudly, it was almost as if he was standing in the bedroom.

Kelly slid off the far side of the bed. Keeping the sheets in his hand, he backed away. In the silence, his heart sounded like a drum, overpowering the wind. He released the blanket and ran to the door, throwing himself against it as if his body would provide some level of reinforcement.

The door rocked in its frame; the hinges clattered against the wall, and the knob twisted and caught, clicking as it ran into the lock and couldn't move.

Kelly ran to the bedside and clicked the lamp off.

Deep amusement resonated shamelessly in the hallway. "Sure!" Johnny said. "Turn the light out and I'll totally forget you're in there. Like I'm really that dumb!" Johnny circled his hips and picked his feet up, high knee. He reached across his chest and grabbed beneath his left bicep, stretching. He plucked at the back of his tennis shorts, pulling them loose from his crack only to have them sink back in immediately. Cut high, his cheeks hung out the bottom. The white shorts hugged his muscular thighs like cellophane wrap.

Johnny had always enjoyed the way tight clothing showed off his hard work. White clothing brought out his tan and made his brown hair appear royal. In his right hand, he gripped his signature, designer tennis racket, a limited edition from his competition days in the National Tennis League of America.

Even when he wasn't playing a game, Johnny made a habit of carrying a racket with him in the same way a woman might carry a purse or a miniature dog. It was a professional tool, yes, but more importantly, it was a fashion accessory.

Johnny leaned his racket against the wall and ran thick fingers through a well-endowed pompadour. He leaned his forehead against the door and twisted the knob again. "Really kid? Still locked?" He jiggled it again. "Coach always said behind every locked door is a scandal. Cheating wives, blowjobs, kiddy diddlers—real PR nightmares. The guy was terrified of opening locked doors, I swear. Don't think he even locked his own house." He released the doorknob but pressed his ear to the door. Indecisive wind knocked against trees, rattling them against the house and creating an echo of wind from the ballroom balcony down the hall. Johnny couldn't hear into the room. He hated the acoustics of the house sometimes. Made it sound like there were ghosts everywhere. Johnny stepped back, picking up his racket. He surveyed the thick door frame and carved panels. He cocked a brow. "You're not gonna open up, are you kid? C'mon. You know me. We've been on the court before. Maybe we never played together; maybe that's the problem. I'll teach you about ball chasing like your daddy never did. They say real bonding happens over sports, so how about a round of tennis, champ?" He flipped the racket around; the grip rolled over the backside of his hand before he clutched it again. He repeated the action, then knocked the butt cap into the door.

Johnny waited, grunted, and rammed the butt cap into the door again. This time harder. His arm bounced back, nearly smacking him in the nose with his own fist. Johnny staggered back a couple of steps and stared at the door. One hundred and fifty years of hard work had created a sturdier home than he had thought. Time was supposed to eat away at structural integrity, but it appeared to only make the Benedict Estate more stubborn. He licked his upper lip; his soft white tennis heels bounced against the floor, shifting weight. Blood circulated faster, his body warmed up. Johnny, half squatting, held his racket, preparing to serve. He always did his best thinking when in that position. He tossed his racket between his hands, stepped back and forth, and swung it around the empty hallway.

Standing in serving position usually gave him numerous ideas to solve problems. The thunder had other plans, rumbling to clear his head of thought. He clenched his jaw; muscular body going rigid and trembling. Knuckles matched his shirt until he threw his tennis racket against the door as hard as he could. It snapped and bounced right back at him, smacking into his chest and threatening to smack his face with its own. His racket clattered to the ground. Growling profanities, Johnny kicked the racket across the floor. "The longer you make me wait, the more this is gonna suck for you. You know that, don'tcha kid?"

More silence.

He bit back a growl and licked his lips. Long strides covered large lengths of the hallway all at once. He retrieved his racket and carried it back with him. He sped up, his steps becoming heavier and more deranged. He set the racket against the wall across from the door.

A new idea formed.

He backed up to the opposite side of the hallway. With every step, his body built in anticipation. His pectoral muscles twitched, alternating. Then, once situated as far down the straight-line hall as possible, he ran. He slammed his shoulder into the door. It rattled and splintered catching his weight.

He stepped back. Again and again, he charged down the hall, ramming the door. With every tackle, the door cracked until the lock handle tore from the notch in the wall and the door swung open. Johnny's shoulder throbbed, but the adrenaline rush nullified everything and allowed him to focus. It was like he had blinders on, he couldn't see anything he wasn't staring at. Red flooded his vision. He scanned the room through the open door, breathing in and out like a bull waiting to charge again. He ran a hand through his pompadour three or four times, brushing it back into place compulsively. "With moves like that, you'd almost think I played football." He laughed to himself. He picked up his tennis racket from beside the door and walked into the room.

The window across from him hung open. The satin curtains blew against the frame and the thin tree branches reached into the opening. On the floor, steel fireplace tools laid scattered. Johnny turned on the overhead light and scanned the room from one side to the other. Agatha's bedroom furniture was some of the finest in the house: a hand-carved dark wood bed set from seventeenth-century Ireland.

Surveying the room, Johnny spun his racket by its open throat. He swung his hips in circles again and muttered a song to himself. Every couple of words it would grow quieter, but harsher pronunciation as he came upon a threat or curse. "If I were a pussy, where would I hide? Where would I hide? Where would I hide?" he sang, walking toward the window. He dipped his racket behind the edge of the curtains and drew them back. "I don't think you're dumb enough to get yourself stuck in a tree." He leaned out the window. The nearby branches were too slim for anyone to climb on. Light specks of rain splashed him in the face. He grabbed the handles on the window and pulled it shut, locking it. Turning around, he caught sight of the knotted tassel rope. "Looks like your motor skills are right up there with your cognitive ones, kid." He laughed. Johnny opened the closet next. Inside: a couple baskets of yarn in mixed colors, unfinished knitting projects, and board games like Monopoly, Go For It!, Sorry, and Grape Escape.

Something squeaked against the floor.

Johnny closed the cabinet and spun on his toes. He glanced sidelong at the vanity, watching for movement in the mirrors. Disheveled comforters hung halfway off the bed. The nightstand on the far right clattered. Johnny tilted his head down, watching the bed as if it were a small animal. He grabbed a handful of the blankets and tossed them onto the bed, revealing the bare floor beneath. Johnny set his tennis racket on top the bed and squatted. Thin white shorts slid up his thighs and squeezed his buttocks. His calves clenched then he dropped to his hands and knees to peer beneath the bed.

A flash of white fabric and a skinny leg slipped out from the other side of the bed.

Johnny stood up.

Staring through messy brown locks, Kelly met Johnny's eyes. The boy gripped the coal shovel from the fireplace.

"Stay back," Kelly said.

"Really? Under the bed?" Johnny said. "That's such a predictable hiding place."

"But you didn't check it first?" Kelly's gaze darted to the broken door hanging open. Johnny stood between the bed and the window. His escape route was clear.

"Think I don't see what you're doing?" Johnny said.

Kelly dashed for the door. Johnny vaulted over the bed and slid off the edge. The door slammed shut and bounced against the frame, the broken latch unable to keep it shut. Johnny yanked the door open and entered the hall then stopped, breathing hard.

Somewhere down the hall, another door slammed. Johnny cursed under his breath and stomped down the hallway toward the new door: the guest room of the late Madame Astra.

Johnny rolled his shoulders, hopped, and loosened up his body. Like before, he rammed into the door with all his weight. The crack of the door yielding to his strength excited him. It reminded dear Johnny of the sound bones made when he pummeled them with his racket, again and again and again and again.

The door flung open and he stumbled in. He flicked the light on and walked over to the bed. "Not gonna get me this time, kid," he said, kneeling at the edge of the bed. He pulled the skirt up and saw nothing.

The door closed behind him, slapping against the frames and rebounding open again. His brow twitched. His fingers curled into the shag emerald rug. Getting up, he pushed his hair back while fingers gripped his racket's shaft.

In the hall, another door snapped shut.

"Keep going, kid! I can do this all night!" Johnny walked with anger, but laughter thrust through his lips; the snicker of a bad call by the ref; the guttural chuckle that said if the ref made that call one more time, he'd be calling 911 instead of out of bounds. Then, standing before the door, he laughed again. "Great! Perfect! Pick the door I have a key for!" Muscular fingers dug into the tight pockets and withdrew a small brass key. He slipped it into the lock and opened the door. "Getting sloppy, kid." He flicked the light on. "And my agent said that marks the end of a career." Johnny stopped in the doorway, though ritualistically he wanted to check the bed. He looked over the bureau, the bathroom, his own closet. He looked back at the bed, then the closet again, then the bathroom. Eyes narrowed. He stepped further in but hesitated. He tapped his racket's butt cap against the floor. Another step toward the bed.

The floorboards creaked.

Kelly stood in the doorway.

Rapidly tapping his racket against the floor, Johnny turned around to face the boy. The moment their eyes connected, Kelly dashed out the door, but this time, Johnny was fast to follow. The door wasn't slammed in his face, and Kelly couldn't get away from him.

Five doors down, Kelly ran out onto the second-floor balcony, which circled the upper level of the grand ballroom. It branched off to the servant's quarters to the left or a staircase beside the barroom to the right. With his shorter legs, Kelly couldn't outrun the athlete. Johnny drew his racket into the air and smashed it into the boy's back. The beam cracked; Kelly was thrown to the ground with a yelp. Johnny swung the racket again, bringing it down on Kelly full force. The boy curled into the fetal position, covering his face with his arms. The racket snapped; the beam separated in a few places. Johnny quickly disposed of the broken tool and switched to kick Kelly instead. His toes dug deep into the small of Kelly's back, eliciting high-pitched whimpers. Johnny hadn't planned on breaking the kid apart yet. Baiting some of the other players with him would be easy enough and if the kid turned too blue and bloody, some might assume he was dead. But, when drawing his leg back, he couldn't stop himself from kicking again. There was a reason Johnny was an ex-tennis pro. They called him a prodigy when he was a child and a rising star as a teenager. He was not only fast, but he had an inimitable swing. Leading athletes and coaches in the league bid to become his trainer, sharpen his skills, and make money off him as he moved to the top of the league. There was one small caveat they had to deal with.

Johnny Green had always had something his parents carefully described as 'major anger issues.'

Johnny stepped back after another kick. He eyed the small ball Kelly had become on the floor then panned to the broken racket lying beside him. "You busted my racket, kid," Johnny said. "How you plan to fix that?" He grabbed Kelly by the shirt.

Kelly gripped the coal shovel, and with one powerful swing, smacked Johnny in the shins.

Johnny stumbled back, growling.

Kelly rolled away and used the wall to help pull him to his feet. He didn't waste time checking on Johnny. He hobbled down the hall, using the wall to keep him upright while he clutched the shovel in his other hand. Kelly passed through the archway to the ballroom and moved along the edge of the balcony. He looked over the edge, hoping there was someone to call out to, but even if there was, he didn't know if he dared trust any of them anymore. He continued down the service wing. Johnny's stomping grew louder behind him. A couple of doors laid ahead, doors he didn't often go into.

Johnny ran around the balcony, behind the corner.

Between a couple of the doors was a small dumbwaiter box with a metal crosshatch cage covering the opening. He remembered playing in it when he was smaller. Kelly pressed the button to call the dumbwaiter and pulled the small gate open. It beeped upon reaching the floor. Kelly climbed in and as his back hit the wall, Johnny rounded the archway. Kelly pushed the button sending the dumbwaiter down then closed the metal gate. Charging like a machine, Johnny made it to the dumbwaiter just as it sunk below the small window. He pressed the button aggressively in an attempt to stop its process, but the thing wasn't coming back up.

Rage rattled the dumbwaiter gate above. The metal screeching echoed down the shaft. Kelly wrapped his arms around his legs and buried his face. He tried to ignore the sounds and breathe, but his chest throbbed and grew too tight for anything outside of shallow breaths and Johnny's snarls carried like a hungry animal, dark, deep, and lusting for blood.

Most of the time, Johnny's fury ended in broken rackets and an exuberant amount of cursing. That changed the first time he lost a game due to bad calls made by a referee. The ball barely hit the net once. Called a let, it happened a second time, then a third. The flags piled up and points were unfairly assigned to his opponent. Johnny's solution to the foul play by the court's ruler was to break his racket across the back of the referee's head. The game was called, he lost, but he rested easy knowing it wasn't because he was the worse player.

He built a reputation by having the most peculiar temperament in the league. Referees became hesitant to flag breaks in the rules or messy plays, and other players became wary of calling Johnny out on inappropriate form, or backing up the ref. He soared to the top of the league, entered the international championship, and was supposed to be awarded second. They met for the handshake and his opponent met God. Johnny wasn't kicked out of the league immediately. His career brought in too much money. Tennis viewership and ticket sales were up. It wasn't just Johnny and his coaches who had something to lose if Johnny were to 'retire' early. The league excused the single act of aggression and labeled the incident a freak tennis accident; the racket had slipped out of sweaty hands. It happens all the time, but it's not usually fatal.

The league could cover up one event, but the aggression spread worse when Johnny realized he could get away with it. Referees, players, and fans became casualties in his crusade to be the number one tennis player on the planet. Lawsuit after lawsuit was filed until it was costlier for Johnny to remain in the league than to have him retire and lose the income he added to the sport.

His place in the Benedict Estate wasn't the same as being at the top of the league, but Agatha's attention reminded him of how his fans used to adore him from outside the court. With the money he'd make from the reading, he could buy his way back into the league.

Kelly was not going to escape.

SIXTEEN.

The dumbwaiter reached the first-floor laundry room, scented with apple-cinnamon and warmed by the working dryer. Kelly removed the gate and climbed out quickly. The soft tumble of drying clothes gave Kelly a feeling of normalcy for the first time that night. Tears pooled in his eyes. He stumbled across the room for the door. His legs were stiff and caused him to limp. He opened the door and peered out, careful and quick. If Johnny followed him, he could come down the grand staircase and the first place he'd look if he had any mind at all was the laundry room. Kelly's options were outside, the library, or Doc's office.

Her door was solid dark oak with a foggy glass window panel in the top half and brown crosshatching painted across. The glass was textured like unsettled water and plastered over the decorative crosshatch were the words, *Dr. Charity*, a nickname Agatha had given her the day they met.

Doc had never told anyone what name they should call her by, but Agatha thought it was too impersonal to always refer to her as Doc. Doc, on the other hand, refused to disclose her name, and when met with protestation, often stressed how difficult it was for her to receive her MD. "It's not just something people can do, you know," she said. She was so proud of her accomplishment that once the degree was in her hand, she renounced her given names and told even her relatives to refer to her as Doc. Anyone to refuse was swiftly ignored out of existence and there was no way to recover a relationship with Doc once it was lost.

Doc never pictured herself as a private physician with one patient. Generally, she hated people and getting to know anyone too well only affirmed her prejudices. She often questioned why she became a doctor in the first place, but she enjoyed the feeling of power that came with the tools she knew how to wield and the complete control of emotions her words had. "You're dying," could shift a mood or change the course of a life. "You need this surgery or you will die," was all she needed to convince her patients to line her pockets.

However, her private practice was closed more than two decades ago due to an abundance of malpractice lawsuits she couldn't settle out of court. Most of the suits were connected to patients who suffered from "Inordinate Discursive Disorder," or what most referred to as talking too much. When Doc was faced with a problematic client who couldn't bother to treat Doc with the respect she so deserved, within months they'd find themselves victims of this deadly diagnosis. Doc's only recommendation for patients with IDD was immediate surgery; and the only cure: death.

Doc won a handful of the malpractice cases, but the lawsuits became too much for her private clinic to absolve. Her degrees became worthless; her time was wasted, and her talents disappeared into obscurity. With nothing better to do, she joined a book club where she met Agatha.

Kelly slunk down the hall, hoping Doc's door was unlocked when he tried it, and it was. He slipped in and closed the door behind him. The sterile fluorescent lights lit up half the small office. They bounced off Doc's desk, the chrome examination chair, clean black cabinets, and instruments for human examination. Like an invader, warm, amber-colored light bled in from the cracked door of the adjacent bedroom suite.

Kelly surveyed the room with attentive eyes. Though Doc had lived in this house longer than he, he'd never been in her office before. When he was sick or needed checkups, she'd come to his room per Agatha's request.

He ran to a cupboard, checking Doc's door constantly. He feared she heard him come in, but she didn't come out of her room. He pulled open a couple of cupboards, looking for a place he might fit, and after three or four, he squeezed between a box of bandages and needles and a couple of white, folded towels.

Then there was a knock on the door.

"Doc?" A curious, high-pitch voice inquired, pushing the door open. Alex didn't wait for a response before he entered. "Doctor Charity?" he sang.

Doc came out of her bedroom suite with heaviness clouding her face, pulling down on her shoulders, her eyes were bloodshot. She clutched and old-looking book at her side and did a thorough job of blocking the cover with her fingers. "What?" she said, continuing to her desk. She acted as if she were about to see a regular patient. She pulled out the large leather chair; the casters rattled, and she sat. She slipped a key out from her pocket, unlocked a desk drawer, and slipped her book into it. On the edge of her desk sat a small golden nameplate that read, Doctor Charity. A gift from Agatha.

Alex's eyebrows perked and a friendly smile spread across his face. He tapped the door shut with his foot before strolling across the room. Doc grimaced at the sound, but said nothing.

"Ya know, I was thinking, tonight's events so far have been horrendous at best and I could use something to take the edge off. Would you happen to have anything?" His glasses fell down his round nose when he tilted his head. He pushed them back up.

Doc reclined, crossing her arms. She looked disappointed and unbelieving with her bottom lip protruding.

Alex pursed his lips and mirrored her posture. "Maybe a Prozac?"

"I don't have Prozac." Her voice was deeper than his.

"Shame. You look like you could use one," Alex said.

Doc's shoulders stiffened and she sat up straight again. She glanced toward the examination chair. Alex's glance couldn't help but follow. Thin, white paper lined the blue-cushioned bed. Its stirrups stuck out like skeletal arms, though they hadn't been used in some time. Doc swiveled. Her hands dipped below the surface of her desk and she pulled open a bottom drawer. It roared against the rails. "What do you want, Alex?"

"I really don't feel like I should have to want anything to be here," Alex said. "With all the mischief going on, I know I can always count on it to be dead in your office. I mean, it's practically a morgue."

The pale office walls were boring, empty aside from Doc's framed degrees and the generic plastic clock that now filled the silence with soft ticking. There were a couple of medical posters around the examination chair, all sporting a grotesque amount of detail when it came to liver decay, sexually transmitted diseases, and punctured, deflating lungs. The sterility of the room reflected Doc's personality.

Alex crossed his arms and groaned. "Okay, fine." He squeezed his lips tight and rubbed his eyes. He stood up and swerved toward the desk. Hands placed on the edge of the desk, he couldn't help but lean over a little more, trying to see inside of the drawer Doc had pulled open. She noticed him looking and closed the drawer. Instead, he looked to the cabinets lined up along the wall. He searched for labels for hints of what was behind each door, but there were none. "I want your help," he finally said, looking back at her. His fingers slid further across the desk, closer to her. Doc stared at them, her eyes intense and unwelcoming. Alex's hands burned and pulled them back, tucking them to his sides. "Ya know, with Ellie."

"You need my help?" Doc scoffed, "please."

"Yeah, *need*. It's, ya know, a four-letter word that means can't go on without the assistance of. You should be familiar with it considering your profession is pretty much dependent on other people needing things." Alex swung his hips, shifting his weight.

"That's not what an MD means."

"Yeah, well, you probably also think the world is flat. I don't hold that against you either, for the record."

"MDs are trained not to look for the need or want of the patient, but to understand the why. Helping a need may result in curing a symptom, but that is not the goal of any doctor I have ever known. The main goal for anyone carrying this level of knowledge is to learn more. Unfortunately for some, our pursuit of knowledge is often dependent on the poor health of others. Physicians who focus on curing ailments rather than seeking knowledge have been known to get stabbed in the back soon thereafter. Sometimes in the form of lawsuits, others in replacement by a co-worker or worse, a resident." Her gaze stiffened. She drew open the drawer again and placed a military grade medical box on top her desk. The contents clattered upon landing, causing Alex to jump. The box was army green and bore a large white cross on both sides. The paint was chipped and dented lines were scars left from its career overseas. Her fingers glided along the cool steel box, running over the metal buckles and stroking them as she unhooked them. She leaned forward, examining Alex. A long bundle of braids fell over her left shoulder.

"If the only people you talk to are cadavers, no wonder you have no friends." Alex cleared his throat. "But you've got one thing right: friends are only temporary means to get you to the ends you want. Are you starting to get the picture now, hun, or do you need a little more color?"

"Do you think you're funny?" Doc said.

"Yes," Alex said, "or at the very least, charming."

Doc slipped her reading glasses from her face and placed them on top the desk. Alex pulled up the chair nearest to the desk and took a seat. He leaned his elbows on the surface, as though he were getting ready to gossip. "Ellie's just another goy; a means to an end. A terminal patient, you might say. You get that terminology, right?"

Doc planted her feet flat on the floor and rocked; her pace matched the plastic wall clock's tick. Doc glanced at her watch, then the wall clock, then back at Alex.

The corner of Alex's lip twitched. He shook his head and tightened his smile. "I've been second to girls like her for a long ass time," he said. "You don't even know—girls like her wear gays like purses. 'Oh my god! This one's so cute! He's blond. He'll match my Friday night outfit. Hey, you know boys, can you hook a girl up?' Once people like Sarah Jessica Parker started featuring gays in their shows, every hip girl on the block wanted one on their arm, but the second you're better than them at anything, you get more compliments at the bar, you get a hot boyfriend, your outfit costs more, you sleep with her boyfriend—they want to destroy you any way they can."

"And yet you're friends with Ellie,'" Doc said.

"I told you, she's just a means to an end." Alex threw his head back in over-exaggerated laughter. A strong antiseptic smell dried out the edges of Alex's nose. He rubbed it with the back of his hand. "The politics of being a woman," Alex said, waving his hand. A grin tugged at the corner of his lips as he looked head-on at Doc.

Her fingers sunk into the medical box.

Alex swung his head from one side to the other, flicking his stiff hair. "There are certain rules that have to be followed in order to be friends with certain types of girls. Dressing tips, ass-kissing worship, a smidge of passive-aggressive animosity. Girls like Ellie get off knowing they're hated, while believing they're so freaking fabulous, you would kill to be them."

"It sounds like a waste of time." A metal buckle snapped. Doc lifted the lid and let gravity pull it down. The top of the medical box clapped loudly against the countertop

"Maybe the idea of subtly is lost on you." Alex shrugged. "You never struck me as the 'pretty girl-type.'"

"You just sound like another angry queen."

"And what if I am?" Alex said. He pulled his arms closer to his body, crossing them over his chest. "How's that any different than you being the caricature of an angry black woman?" Alex shifted his voice to be higher and nasal, "'Oh, look at me! My life was sooo tough! I had to work, work, work so hard to lose my identity because I'm so ashamed of what I am. The only option was just to forget. I hate my family, I hate my race, I hate my culture, I hate myself, so I disposed of it all. I'm a doctor now. That's all I am. I'm your sickness, your cure, your freaking God because without this piece of paper I was a forgettable loser and I'm gonna make you remember that even if I have to kill you first.'" Alex turned his lifted nose back to Doc. "Does that sound about right?"

Doc lifted a metal tray from the box and placed it on her desk. She pulled out a pair of pale blue gloves and slipped them over her hands. She was much more careful reaching to the bottom of the medical box. Plastic-wrapped needles and syringes lined the bottom. A small bag of vials filled with liquids ranging from clear and watery to thick and muddy laid on top of them. She drew out a sterile, wrapped needle and removed the plastic. Pinching the capped tip between her index finger and thumb. "You came here to lecture me that being angry and gay is better than being angry and black?" She attached it to a loose syringe body. "There's the door."

"Honey, please," Alex tilted his head to the side and peered over his glasses. "I came here because of 'doctor-patient confidentiality.'" He winked.

Doc placed the syringe on her desk and stared across the table. "You have my attention."

Alex sat up straight. "Ellie is beyond useless without little minions to do the work for her, myself included. Gay-vin and Beau-retard both have their little ... things for her. I don't know how serious either of them are either, but if we can get them to kill each other, she's waiting to drown."

"It sounds like you've thought this out," Doc said.

Alex nodded, smirking. "Plotting is what people like me do best."

"You don't need my help."

His smile faded. "I mean I guess I *could* do it alone, but I don't want to." Alex pulled his chair so close to the desk his knees pressed against its front. He slumped his back, his elbows slipped along the edge, moving further apart. His chin moved closer to the desk's surface. Large hazel eyes looked over thick black rims. He pressed out his bottom lip. "I'm plotting against my BFFL here. Gimme a little bit of sympathy at least."

"And why would I do that?"

"This friendship is gonna be rough otherwise," Alex said.

"And you come in here to complain about being an accessory while trying to turn a black woman into your accessory?"

"I'm not trying to make you an accessory," Alex says.

"Stop with your lies," Doc said. "I know how white people work. I've seen your kind in my clinic. Your kind is what shut me down when I wouldn't get on my knees."

"Oh, honey." Alex clicked his tongue. His lips pursed in a small smile as he leaned back. "I'm not white. I'm Jewish. Please try to keep up."

"I prefer to spend my leisure time doing something enjoyable," Doc said, picking up the Ziploc of vials. She fingered them. "Jeopardy twice a week."

"Oh, I get you." Alex leaned back, licking his lips. "You've got a thing for Trebek."

Doc opened the Ziploc and fished out one of the vials of clear liquid. "I think we're done here."

Alex frowned. The bridge of his nose crinkled. He glanced toward Doc's bedroom as if searching for a bit of humanity hidden where Doc never let anyone go. "There's a lot of money in this house."

"I know how the game works," Doc said.

"So, you know other people are making deals with one another. If you stay in here alone, you're not going to get anything out of tonight, assuming you make it through it at all." Alex pushed his glasses up his nose. Immediately they slid back down. "People around here be crazy," he sang.

"I know the game," she said again. Reaching into the medical box, she withdrew a paper-wrapped alcohol swab. She tore it open and thoroughly wiped the top of the vial, then tossed the garbage into a can beneath her desk. "I know how you intend to play and I know you should leave my office now. I'm uninterested in your scam."

"You make this so damn difficult, Doc," Alex said, standing.

Doc pulled at the plunger, sucking air into the needle.

"No wonder you're on your deathbed and still single. You could have been acceptably attractive."

With impeccable precision, she stabbed the needle into the soft lid of the vial, then released the air.

"And instead you're sitting here: alone with what I can only assume is a decent savings, no loved ones, and a clock ticking closer to the end of your days."

The rain became louder, pulsing against the windows like a rapid beat of terror. A flash of lightning took the lights out with it and turned both Doc and Alex into faceless shadows. Thunderous rumbles replaced their conversation and covered over Alex's erratic chuckle.

Flash. A moment of illumination.

The white walls reflected the light and created a soft glow that stuck in them even moments after they dimmed.

"The door, Alex," Doc said.

The next flash: Doc was on her feet. She held firm a long, thick needle, the sharp edge in the air and dripping.

Two flashes, the second one caught the metallic edges of Alex's grooming shears.

"What will you do?" Doc said. "Give me a bad haircut?"

"Oh, honey, I've been dying to do *just* that," Alex said.

There was little sound as they both stood still. Doc watched the shadows. Alex glanced toward the window, looking for a flutter of lightning burrowed into the clouds.

Another rumble, another flash, another moment.

The metal scissors in Alex's hand made a sharp slap, opening and closing. The contents of Doc's medical box shuffled around. Light caught onto something in her hand: a scalpel. Rolling thunder built anticipation. Brief flashes of lightning left their faces ill-lit, distorted, and strange.

"One thing, Doc," Alex's scissors clicked. "Just between us girls." They clicked again. "You like to think you're better than all of them; the other girls, the normal girls, but you're not. You're jealous of the Britney's and the Farrah's and the Nicole's because you desperately wanted to be them, all your life you wanted to be them, but you knew, because of what you were, you couldn't. So instead, you freaking hated them. I get it because I hate them too, but give me the chance and I'll show you, one good haircut will take away the anger and resentment and fear. One good haircut, and all that negative shit? Gone." His voice was high and condescending, but it pretended to be serious and empathetic. "I change lives, baby."

"And I end them." Doc put more effort in restraining herself than responding.

Three quick flashes illuminated Alex.

Something came over Doc in that moment. Her blood pulsed and tingled, possessing her like a spirit. Her head throbbed with an angry migraine and the longer she looked at Alex, the worse it became. The age of her body melted away and left an animal in its place. She felt the scalpel's grip texture against her skin and the weight of the syringe. Her steps became obvious: thuds louder than the clock ticking, though they kept the same pattern.

Doc was aware of how long it would take him to bleed out with one puncture wound in a vital vein or where she would have to place a second puncture to speed up the process.

The lightning spoiled her advances. Whenever she stepped. Alex mirrored in the opposite direction, stopping her from gaining any advantage.

The thunder cracked like a whip. They both froze in place.

The low buzz of fluorescent lights waking up accompanied the next lightning strike. They were blinded, but Alex ran anyway. Doc drew back her needle. She squinted trying to see anything. She listened to the footsteps and swung. The needle moved through the air, thirsty for skin.

"Honey, I could dance all night," Alex said. His hips bounced from side to side, excited, playful, and rhythmic as though he were listening to music and the rain was the baseline. "Could you?"

Doc stepped to the right. Alex prepared to grab her, lifting his empty hand, curling his fingers. He was certain that her old bones and stalagmite body were nothing for his thirty-something litheness. Doc feigned a lunge. Alex stepped to the side, grabbing her wrist in the air. He continued to turn, pulling her arm like he was a dancer, twirling. He used his weight to pull her off balance. She pulled her arm back, a little stronger than he'd expected. Alex's hold slipped and he stumbled. Doc saw an opportunity and she took it. She grabbed Alex's arm and pulled out his wrist. The needle cut into his bicep before he could shove her.

Doc staggered backward, the move stronger than she would have thought. Her rear hit the edge of the desk, and she lost balance. Too late to grab the desk, she fell onto her tail bone.

Alex's muscles contracted around the slim metal needle. He wasn't sure if the sudden fainting spell was his response to the needle or his body's response to whatever was inside of it. A lump formed in his throat, not out of fear, but anger and anticipation. He ripped the needle from his arm and tossed it to the floor. The plastic body rolled away; he lifted his foot and stomped it again. The fractured body reminded him of the collapsing skeleton of a spider. Alex began to laugh comically; maniacal and over-enthused, he stepped over the syringe then right back on it. The crack beneath his heel excited him more.

Doc braced herself against the floor. She groped for her missing scalpel. Her spine was too stiff to move, she couldn't scoot back.

"I don't know what was in that thing, but you better pray none of it got in me," Alex said. One by one he pulled back the pair of chairs that circled Doc's desk. Their wooden feet screeched against the tile.

"I don't think I could give you anything worse than you already have," she said.

"And what's that?" Alex's scissors rung, opening and closing hungrily.

Her fingers slid along the smooth edge of her scalpel's grip. "Clearly, the disease God created for your people."

"Famine?"

"AIDs."

"Oh hun," Alex snorted. He shook his head, cooing, "I'd have thought you were more creative than that." Alex ran at her, closing the space between them. He drew his scissors back before he reached her and drove them down.

Doc flattened against the floor, sliding out from against the desk. She rolled to the side until she hit Alex's leg. She grunted, her body still stiff, she knew she couldn't get up quick enough. She held the scalpel tight and rolled onto her back.

Alex kicked her back onto her side, first with a gentle nudge, then a persuasive kick. She jammed the scalpel into his calf. He screeched, dropping his scissors. His legs became weak, the pain overtook him, and for a moment, he couldn't see much of anything past flickers of black and red. He fumbled for his scissors. The lights went out again, but the returning flash of lightning reflected off the metal bows and brought them to his attention. He grabbed the scissors, ignoring the wet feeling of his pants sticking to his leg. He cupped the bows with both hands.

Doc pulled at the scalpel withdrawing it from Alex's leg.

The stylist was threatened by a wave of lightheadedness. He brought the scissors down on her head, aiming for somewhere, anywhere as long as they dug into her. They dug into her frontal lobe. She'd started another stab at his legs, this time closer to his knee, but before she could finish her attack, the lobotomizing descent of barber shears made its impact.

Her hand slapped against the floor. A growling curse twisted into high-pitched, modest laughter. Alex withdrew the scissors with a strong tug and thrust them into her throat next. It became apparent she wasn't dead enough yet when the new hole in her throat exposed her uneven, sparse breathing. A piece of loose skin flapped against the air coming in through her throat. Blood seeped into the windpipe and began choking her.

Red streams ran down the stainless steel as he pulled them from her skin. Blood created a new pattern on his shirt and vest, an ombre effect turning the top bright gray into a deep, passionate crimson by the last button.

Doc's scalpel rolled with a small, metallic tiptoe. Her blood pooled on the floor and stained the shoulders of her white jacket and mauve nightshirt. For the first time, Doc wore a shirt that wasn't purple.

Alex wiped his sweaty forehead with his forearm. His glasses fell to the end of his nose and he observed the mixing colors. The original soft, pale purple that seemed innocent befell to the stronger pigment, marking the end of life. He looked at his hands and the hole in Doc's throat, now swelling with blood, bubbling out like she was a fountain pump.

Doc's lips were cracked. Up close, her age showed. Bushy eyebrows, a couple thick hairs sparsely populated her jawline, and her braided hair appeared messy and unkempt.

"Honey, you didn't do yourself any favors," Alex said.

Alex stood up and brushed his pants off. An action meant to remove dirt only left bright handprints sliding along his thighs. He stepped over her body and walked around to her head. He watched her face for a moment, her breathless chest, her brain spilling onto his leather shoes. "You didn't have to die like this, you know. The world is gonna remember you by the last way they saw you. Dry skin, I think I see a mustache, overweight, and that horrible color you're always wearing... Look, I can work a little magic, but honey, the miracles are on someone else. I'm a Jew, not a saint."

Alex slipped his scissors back into his vest pocket. He slid off his glasses and wiped them with his driest sleeve, then put them back on. He squatted, slid his arms underneath hers, and dragged her back toward the desk. The dead weight of her body was more than he had expected, but it was manageable. He brought her to the proper side of her desk and maneuvered her into the chair. In the tussle, one of her penny loafers had fallen off. He slipped it back on, then, again, wiped the sweat from his brow. He was ridiculously out of breath for the small amount of lifting he had done. "Be right back," he said to her, holding up his index finger as if to say, 'one moment.'

Alex entered Doc's bedroom; the smell of chamomile and lavender struck him and soothed his body. The smells emanated from a pair of lit candles on a modern chestnut table. Her small reading lamp painted the room with a warmth always absent in Doc's presence. Her deep purple sheets were pulled back and folded. It appeared that she may have climbed out of bed to answer his call. He continued to her private bathroom. He grabbed a towel and Doc's shampoo from the shower, then returned to the office. "I promised you a makeover, didn't I?" His voice went up an octave. He came up behind her, tossing the towel and shampoo into her lap. His slim fingers wrapped around the plush leather back of the chair and he maneuvered Doc around the desk and toward the office sink. He turned the chair so the back faced the counter and laid Doc's head back. He carefully handled her coarse, dark hair, taking his time to unbraid it and ladle it into the sink. He turned the water on, first hot, then cold, and tested for the right temperature before taking Doc's hair and running it under the water. The hole in her head leaked thick red fluid into her hair. The running water brought most of it out, but solid bits of brain and loose scalp follicles caught in the grated drain. "You know what I'm gonna do when this night is over?" A small chuckle slipped from his lips. He worked his fingers through her hair the best he could, taking more care to avoid disrupting the sensitive area around her cracked skull. "I'm going to buy the beautician certificate I so clearly freakin' deserve. I'm going to open a boutique in Time Square. I'm going to do the styles for the runway models, Broadway actresses like Bernadette Peters, and the visiting pop icons, of course—the shiksa will be lining up. When my books are filled with the biggest, juiciest names imaginable, I'll put up a 'help wanted' sign and target the bitches from beauty school. When they come for an interview, I'll let them down nicely, you know—just a complimentary makeover with hydrofluoric acid." Alex leaned down closer to Doc's ear, his hands still at work. "It'd be an improvement, believe me." His smile grew wider the longer he went on. He squirted shampoo into his hands and began working it into her scalp. "I know, I know! You must think I'm crazy, but hear me out; I've got a good explanation. Girls like them tell jokes with you, tell you about their boyfriends, and splurge all the hot details of their most recent affairs up until you give a little advice on how to dress better. Who can't take a 'just kidding—but not really' kinda joke about how their excess weight makes them look frumpy or how someone who works in beauty shouldn't look like they've never looked in a mirror and they're pretty damn lucky they have any clients at all? Sorry, not sorry, the truth hurts, but you can fix yourself. The first step to recovery is admitting the problem, but these bitches think they're angels from God, perfect in every way. Can't be bothered to look in a mirror or take some friendly advice. Throwing my beauty supplies in the toilet doesn't hurt my talent, but it definitely burns down your house. Hairspray is crazy flammable, and it's crazy how hard the winds were blowing that night. Somehow their houses caught fire all the way from Queens. That's why you'll never catch me downwind." His finger dipped into her skull by accident. The harsher edges of bone scraped the sides of his middle finger, while the tip pressed against her squishy interior. He pulled his fingers out as if he'd been bitten. "Oh my god— that must be what it feels like to be straight. You can just— keep that to yourself, alright hun?"

The running water gave the office an abnormal air of tranquility. Doc wasn't uptight, but she never seemed to relax. Now her muscles hung low and her lips sat still. If Alex didn't know any better, he could swear she was sporting some kind of smile.

Alex was careful to avoid the pit in Doc's head as he

rinsed the soap out of her hair. The bubbles were stained red, red, and red for a while. They became pink, but they wouldn't become clear. The faucet squeaked off. He grabbed the towel from Doc's lap and wrapped it around her head. "Unfortunately, I didn't bring my blow dryer, so I hope this is good enough for you." He worked the water out of Doc's thick hair until it was barely damp.

Alex tossed the towel onto the counter. "Part on the left or right?" he said. "No middle parts though. Only future serial killer victims part their hair in the middle."

He paused.

"Surprise you? I can do that." He drew his scissors from his vest pocket and ran the blades along the towel to clean them. He caught a glimpse of himself in the reflection: the left lens of his glasses fractured but didn't distort his vision. He tilted the metal, checking the reflection of his hair and became disappointed that it'd fallen out of place. The way someone looked was entirely in their own control, so he lived by the philosophy there was never an excuse to look like a slob unless that's what you were and he'd have no problem reminding anyone like that just how gross they truly were.

"I don't hate you, you know." He fingered the scissor blades through the towel, slowing his motions. He stared ahead at the wall. Breathing deeply, he took a moment to collect his thoughts. "You just got in the way." He let the loose ends of the towel drop to the counter and returned to Doc. Her head lolled to the left. Alex came closer to her side and positioned her head down and forward. "I actually think you're kind of funny in a way." His index and middle fingers collected a few strands of hair and cut them with strict precision. "And there are things more important than friends. Friends leave, ya know. They take what they can get and run. They wait for something better, and they go.

Everyone here is like that. You don't stay at the Benedict Estate without realizing it draws out the worst in people. It's not just the murals in the ballroom. It's the marble columns lining the entry, the imported, stained glass in the bar room, the pricey knickknacks and two hundred thread count silk sheets in every room. It's the jewelry Agatha always wore to town: large diamonds, black pearls, sapphires, emeralds, rubies, black opal—she had an incredible collection, really. And this humongous estate that leans near the city, could sink in the mud any day, really. No one will say it, but everyone there hates anyone who lives here. They're green with envy and when we visit, they're waiting to say something. They want to live here, but they're afraid of what opulence will do to them. I don't blame them. This home invites you in. It makes you comfortable. It gives you the ability to do whatever you want." He leaned down as though to whisper in Doc's ear. "If I weren't so ambitious, I probably wouldn't be here either." He laughed. "It's tempting, but not everyone's cut out for this kind of thing. The reason we're all here tonight, all of us chose to be here, is because we understand there's no reward without risk."

Tangles of dark hair littered the floor. Fresh blood-stiffened the hair around the hole, and Alex was careful to maneuver around it. He cut her hair short, even, and neat. The kind of cut he'd always told her she should try, but she always said no. She always said she didn't want to garner special attention: 'The fewer people that look at me that way, the better. Why would I want a man's attention? Men beat you, take your money. They're proud, too proud, won't admit when they've lost. The last thing I need is for some man to take a fancy of me, then take my money.'

Again, Alex wiped his scissors, then returned them to his pocket. He ran his fingers through the short hair on either side of Doc's head. Smiling, his eyelids drooped, relaxed.

The fresh, short ends tickled his fingertips. He gripped the top of the chair and brought Doc back to her desk. He tucked her legs under the edge and crossed her arms over the surface.

"Let me look at you from the front, darling." Flipping his hands through the air with enthusiasm, he went around the desk.

From the middle of her neck down, her mauve sleepshirt transformed into a heavy, crimson rag. It grew lighter as the eyes followed down to her waist. Her short hair now stopped above her shoulders, evening out their broadness and showcasing the pearl studs that were often hidden. "Freakin adorable," he said.

A light tap on the glass-windowed door interrupted the quiet moment. The door opened, hushed, "Doc, I know it's late, but I've checked every other damn place for that kid and he's not—" Johnny stopped halfway in the door, when he spotted Alex. "Is now a bad time?"

"We were just finishing, actually." Alex craned his head, hoping to take in a little more of Johnny's skin-tight polo and white booty shorts. The outline of his abs were visible through the fabric. "What do you need, honey?"

Johnny looked over his shoulder, feeling a presence behind him, but there was nothing. He closed the office door. "I was looking for the cat. He ran off and I've checked every other damn room in this hall, couldn't find him."

"Well, I doubt he's in here. Been in here for a while and haven't seen or heard anything." Alex gestured toward Doc, "and you think I'd hear something, right?"

"He couldn't be hiding in there?" He gestured toward Doc's room.

"Nope. Just in there, saw nothing," Alex said."

"What about there?" He gestured to the cabinets along the wall.

"Well, you know Johnny, this is a doctor's office. Typically, those are full of band-aids, syringes, anal probing devices... The kind of things that make most people squirm." A lightning flashed through the window. The lights flickered but remained on. "But if you want to check 'em, be my guest—" Alex paused, then glanced over his shoulder. "Doc, do you mind?" After another moment, "no complaints."

"Good thing I got time to waste." Johnny stepped up to the first cabinet in the line and yanked the door open. Inside were supplies as Alex had claimed; boxes of commercial medical supplies, unopened boxes of allergy medicine, fever medicine, and different forms of pain relief in the form of pills and numbing pads. Johnny closed the door and moved on to the next.

Alex leaned against the desk and watched the white fabric stretch around Johnny's firm body. The further they pulled, the more transparent they became. Alex licked his lips, glanced back at Doc, and nodded his head. "Me too," he muttered.

Johnny slammed another cabinet shut. Angry knots built into his muscles and he tossed his cracked tennis racket handle to the floor.

"Hun, you're getting so worked up over this," Alex said. "Maybe you should take a break. Sit down. Jerk off. Work off a little of that steam."

"And if I do and he's in here, he'll get away."

"And if he's not in here at all, you'll feel like a major dick."

Johnny opened the next cabinet and found himself staring into wide, chocolate eyes. The pleasure took a moment to register on Johnny's face. Kelly made a break as fast as he could, but there was no escape. Johnny grabbed Kelly by the shirt and tossed him out of the cabinet. "I knew

I'd find you here!"

Kelly scrambled to his feet. Standing, he favored one leg. "Then what took you so long?"

"I don't think you're in any situation to be sassy, sweetheart," Alex said.

Johnny was going to speak, but when he opened his mouth, nothing but a snarl came out. His mind was full of nothing but primitive growling and gnashing teeth and he was moving before he realized it. Kelly backed up, turned on his toes, and went running for the door. Again, Johnny grabbed him by the shirt and yanked him back.

"Don't touch me!" Kelly's voice cracked when he screamed.

The house rumbled, the glass fixtures on the counters dinged as they shook. Johnny held onto Kelly, wrapping thick hands around biceps thinner than his wrists. "Don't just stand there, go block the door!" he said, voice hushed.

Alex flexed his hands, observing his fingernails. "That wasn't really the dealio, so… I figure you can just... keep at it."

Kelly rammed his heel into Johnny's calf, the same tender spot he'd hit with the shovel before. Johnny's grip on him loosened and Kelly ran for the door.

"Alex!" Johnny growled.

"Not my problem," Alex said.

Kelly yanked the door open and went running out.

Again, none of Johnny's feelings were able to articulate themselves into any semblance of intellectualism. Instead, they morphed into barbaric growls and grunts. He picked up his broken racket to throw against the ground again then went running out the door.

Kelly looked over his shoulder and caught Johnny turning the corner from Doc's office. It would be a straight run toward him and while Kelly limped, he'd be caught. He yelped, running into something.

"Why're ye runnin'? Angus said. "Playin a game?" The Scotsman wore stained, loose-fit jeans that appeared to have been worked in. He no longer wore a kitchen hat to conceal his dark red hair. Mutton chops reached down his strong jaw and connected to his short, unkempt beard full of cream caught in the red stubble over his lip. A wooden spoon stuck out of his right pocket and his left pant leg was wet from thigh to knee. His broad shoulders were disproportionate to his hips and muscular legs. A small gut hung over his waistband. "Shouldn't you be in bed?"

It took Kelly a moment to translate before he said, "Couldn't sleep." Kelly glanced over his shoulder. Johnny was still coming, but he wasn't running. "Needed a walk."

"Maybe some nightmares," Angus said. "You're black and blue."

"Yeah, well, the monsters didn't want to stay under the bed tonight," Kelly muttered.

An expression of confusion crossed Angus's face before he laughed, slapping the boy on the back. "Aye, my god, you're a funny lad!"

Johnny walked up, huffing, not from exhaustion, but trying to quell his anger. "We were going to Doc to get him some help. She's got loads of medication to help with all kinds of situations. We'll make sure his needs are taken care of."

"I don't need any care," Kelly said, stepping back.

"The lad is right. Kids don't need drugs, they just need good treatment. When I had trouble sleeping, me ma would get me a cup of steamed milk. A wee bit of chamomile and no more problems."

"I'll try to remember that," Johnny stepped closer reaching his hand out for Kelly. "We'll tuck him back into bed and get him some warm milk. Leave it to me."

"Actually, I think Gavin was lookin' for him anyway. He can be bonnie scary when you're missing. Could have sworn he was a couple sheep short a flock." Angus's strong hand squeezed Kelly's shoulder and though he didn't like it, there was something comforting about it.

Kelly rubbed his eyes, confused and exhausted. "Where is he?" Kelly wasn't even sure he wanted to see Gavin now, he couldn't trust Gavin now, but Kelly trusted him more than he trusted Johnny.

"Last I saw him, he was in the scullery," Angus said.

"Let's go," Kelly said.

Angus nodded, turning vigorously, and with an arm still around Kelly's shoulder, he said, "G'night, Johnny."

Johnny cursed under his breath, watching them disappear into the ballroom and down the East corridor. Even after they were out of sight, Angus's overpowering laughter could still be heard. His fists curled; they would have snapped the racket of any remaining integrity it had if he were holding it. His clean tennis shoes squeaked against the floor when he turned.

Alex stood against the wall at the end of the hallway, glasses hanging on the end of his nose, the look of a devil across his lips. "Aren't you supposed to be a winner?"

"You," Johnny pointed at Alex like he was holding his racket. "This is your fault!"

"My fault?"

"Your fault! If you had blocked the door—"

"Dozens of broken rackets tell me it's not my fault," Alex held up the racket Johnny had left in Doc's office. "Dozens of broken rackets tell me you suck."

"And if Angus weren't the size of a house, there'd be another one laying around," Johnny snatched the broken racket from Alex. "We might have to—"

"Woah, hold up." Alex pushed off the wall. "Since when

is this a 'we'?"

"Since it's obvious your scrawny arms won't be doing anything to anyone that big anytime soon."

"Oh my god, honey, is this your sweet talk?" Alex said. "It's so good." He rolled his eyes.

"You can keep being a snotty brat or you can take down more obstacles to the prize."

"What do you get out of it for making my life easier when we want the same thing?"

Johnny looked Alex from head to toe to head then laughed. "I'm not worried about you."

"You need to work on your negotiation skills, sweet cheeks because all I want to do right now is freakin' stab you."

"I can't kill Angus on my own and if *I* can't, you definitely can't; he's not an old lady doctor. But if we work together, boom, boom, he's down, and boom, boom, biggest, dumbest guy in the house is gone."

"Second dumbest," Alex said, winking.

Holding out his hand, Johnny said. "Do you want to do this or not?"

Alex scrutinized Johnny's offering. He followed the thick blue tendon's up Johnny's strong arm, to his bicep, quivering pecs, and the light coating of sweat on the man's forehead. Alex bit the inside of his lip to stop his smile. "Turn around for a sec," he said.

"What?" Johnny said, hand faltered, but stayed between them.

"Just turn around while I think."

Puzzled, Johnny dropped his hand and, with unsure, clunky steps, turned around. "I can't see what you're thinking just because I'm looking at you."

"And that, my darling, you should be grateful for," Alex said, leering at Johnny's indiscreetly packaged backside.

Tapping Johnny on the shoulder, he shook the tennis coach's hand. The two entered the ballroom side-by-side. The firelight in the massive brick fireplace grew dimmer as the wood became crisper. The shadows had laid claim to the room, engulfing the furniture and shrouding the portraits, knickknacks, and books, returning the house to its most natural state.

SEVENTEEN.

Johnny's soft tennis shoes shuffled against the hallway floor in quick drags. He shifted back and forth with urgency, as though he didn't know where to go. In one corner of his bedroom sat a small pile of ruined tennis rackets. On some of them, the head was cracked and the face snapped in a few places. Others were reduced to little more than the grip with a broken throat. The snapped graphite was rigid and sharp. They looked as though they could penetrate a body the same way a broken bottle would. He tossed his busted racket into the pile and withdrew a new one from the small wooden rack nearby.

He placed the head into his right palm and, releasing the grip from his left, spun the racket around his hand only to catch it again. "I can't wrap my head around him, ya know?" Johnny's jaw smacked like he was chewing gum, but nothing was in his mouth. "Why the hell did he stay for the reading?" The racket head landed in the palm of his left hand and he flipped it. Johnny pivoted toward the bed where Alex sat.

The stylist leaned back onto his elbows, crossing one

knee over the other. Tilting his head, his glasses dropped down his nose, and his dark eyes followed Johnny's form and the way the shorts stretched over Johnny's muscles when he flexed. Alex's leg bounced over his knee. "Sweetie, I've been trying to wrap around that head for years. Believe me: he's not into it."

"You're so gross, man," Johnny said.

"Honest," Alex corrected, lifting a finger into the air.

Johnny held the grip, butt cap in the air. With his free hand, he pinched both sides of his chin, squeezing his lips together before running his fingers up his jaw.

Wooden panels coated the bottom half of the bedroom walls while emerald wallpaper covered the top. Lighter green vines overlaid, wrapping around each other like snakes eating their own tails. Around the bottom edges of the house, the grass sometimes grew a little too long. Weedy fingers then wrapped against the marble foundation of the house and twisted their bodies around any loose panels in the shed or barn. Mashed plants contorted into the shapes on the bottoms of shoes and snuck their way into the house. If Bertrand were to forget a shovel or rake in the yard at night, by morning it would be covered in a thick coat of verdant growth. Sinuous roots and rapacious vines clung to everything out there and often only an ax or large gardening shears could amend it.

Johnny's jaw stiffened and his knuckles turned white around the racket handle. Leaning closer like a gossiping girl, his voice dropped low. "I've heard stuff about him, you know." He pressed his racket's head into the floor and locked eyes with Alex.

"Agatha was so full of it, though!" Alex leaned up, pressing his palms into the bed. "You can't trust anything she ever said, but… usually the less believable, the truer the bull probably was."

Whenever Angus turned his back, Agatha would bite her lip and whisper, "They called him the Bauchen in Scotland." She spoke like she was bragging, like she was a collector of rare beasts and he was part of it. "Everywhere he went, trouble followed. It was all over the newspapers. Mostly local. Gossip rags, small town lore. You know how that stuff spreads in the boring hillside when there's absolutely nothing else going on, though. We're not too different here." She laughed to herself fondly.

There had always been questions about why Angus had come to Louisiana, of all places. A Scotsman couldn't get further from what he was used to than to disappear into a southern bayou. When he first appeared, he called himself Pierre, though no one knew where the name came from. It certainly didn't fit with his red hair or thick, Scottish accent. He'd been eager to taste the different flavors of gumbo, jambalaya, and various crawfish dishes. His friendliness always seemed a little too eager and his curiosity too childish. If it weren't for the Benedict's regular collection of newspapers, both foreign and domestic, it's unlikely Agatha would have ever heard the stories.

"The Bauchen Struck an Inn... Again!" and "Once Upon a Shed" read many a cover on the Scotland Guard newspaper and Wool Whisperer tabloid. None of them mentioned Angus by name, but they described someone who looked shockingly like him. The Bauchen was tall and stout. His arms were thick and powerful with forearms like boat oars. One swipe with the arm and he could bust holes in stone bricks, the papers claimed. With a sneeze, straw insulation or roofing flew away. The newspaper spoke of citizens who chased the Bauchen out of the marketplace after he collapsed more than a dozen displays and ruined multiple produce bins.

For a while, many had thought it was only bad luck that

followed the Bauchen because he seemed like a very nice boy. But over time, it appeared that anywhere the Bauchen went, something always went wrong on a major scale. Buildings collapsed, water became contaminated. Every cat in the city went missing. Every jug of milk would go sour— they said even milk fresh from the cow wasn't safe. One by one he was banished from cities and towns until he wasn't welcomed anywhere. At home, he slept in the barn, not because his family made him, but because he didn't want accidents to happen to his family. The last mention of the Bauchen in the international newspapers was a headline that read, *"The Bauchen McGregor Fled Scotland. Thank God, We're All Saved!"*

That headline was on a paper marked 1961, and shortly thereafter Angus arrived at the Benedict Estate with a smile on his face and a wooden spoon in his hand. Though the cook often spoke about his family and hometown, he never gave names. Edinburgh was mentioned a few times in passing, but that was to be expected, it was the capital after all.

"I can't tell if he's playing dumb or what," Johnny said.

"People suck," Alex said, pursing his lips. Tilting his head to the side, he ran his fingers through stiff bangs. He stroked them, twisting the gelled strands around his index and middle fingers. "You can't even trust people to be morons anymore without it being a possible ruse. Tell me, Johnny-boy, what is the world coming to?" Alex blew a large pink bubble that popped against his lips.

"If you keep people in line, we don't have these problems," Johnny said, turning away. He twisted the tennis racket's head against the floor, rotating it with the cap pressed against his palm. Angus was the only person in the house who had more muscles than Johnny, though Angus did not have the body of an athlete. His stomach wasn't flat and his arms weren't thick with well-trained muscle. The chance the guy was a cook because he liked to eat was high, but the chance he was strong enough to participate in a caber toss was also extremely high. Johnny thought about taking his racket to Angus's head like he had to Kelly, but Johnny knew the racket wouldn't do anything but snap the moment it contacted Angus's shoulders. "Cheap Chinese piece of shit," he growled under his breath.

"What was that?" Alex said.

"If we don't get rid of him now and it comes down to the three of us, we're out."

Alex rolled onto his stomach and propped his chin up in his hands. "It's not going to come down to that," he said pursing his lips.

"But it could," Johnny said, pacing the length of the room again.

This night was about far more than money and an estate in the middle of nowhere. This was about having some semblance of a future. Without Agatha and her regular paychecks, none of them could sustain the type of life they had become accustomed to.

"So, what do you suggest we do?" Alex said, pushing himself up to a sit. He pressed his knees into the mattress. He took a stick of gum from his pocket and put it in his mouth. "We can't straight up attack him, because, let's face it, your muscles are all for show—"

"Hey!"

"And outsmarting him won't work or he'd be dead by now since I've got more brains than the two of you put together—"

Johnny stopped. His nostrils flared as he took deep, sharp breaths. "Shut up and let me think!" The curl on the top of his head was starting to deflate. The storm's humidity and his own sweat beat the life out of it.

"Assuming I help you because, ya know, you might be right for, like, the first time. We might need to turn up the heat in the kitchen a little bit," Alex said. He slid his legs off the edge of the bed and connected his feet to the floor.

Johnny turned around and caught Alex with a cocked head and eyes focused on his hips.

"Like, Astra might be getting kind of lonely," Alex chewed his gum loudly between speaking.

Johnny's brows furrowed and creases formed on his forehead. "Astra's dead," he said. He looked at Alex as if he were looking at a confused child.

Alex's jaw clicked. Blowing a large bubble, he popped it with his tongue. He rolled his eyes and swung his hips to the side. "I mean, the dining room has like, the biggest fireplace in the whole goddamn house, right? You know, so big, that even someone as big as a house, could fit into it with a little bit of help?" Alex stretched the gum with his tongue. "If we're lucky, he might even still be in the kitchen, you know, right next to the fireplace in the dining room..." Alex said slower. He didn't spend too much longer trying to explain to Johnny before he led the way out of the bedroom. "You remind me a lot of the girls I went to school with..."

"How so?" Johnny said.

"You ever try to dye your hair without developer?" Alex said.

Johnny ran a hand through his hair, smiling proudly. "Nope. This is all-natural, baby."

"Good. I recommend you keep it that way."

EIGHTEEN.

Johnny clutched his tennis racket as he followed Alex down the grand staircase in the main hall. His steps were heavier, slowed down by Alex's much shorter, much less urgent strides. It wasn't that Johnny's legs were that much longer than Alex's—though Johnny did have inches over Alex. Johnny simply walked with more intention in his steps. Walking beside someone else, Johnny's competitive nature took over and even when he wasn't racing, he wanted to move faster, to show Alex how much better he was, and he did so by 'accidentally' stepping on Alex's heels every couple of steps, then half-heartedly apologizing. Like an animal, Johnny had no control over his instincts, but gave into them.

Entering the dining room, Alex locked the double doors behind them. The room reeked of burnt hair and sizzled with shrunken skin. The large wooden logs tried to break up the smell with the refreshing scent of burning wood, but Madame Astra's odor overpowered it with ease.

"Go tilt the painting," Alex said, walking halfway down

the long mahogany table. The room was quiet aside from the licks and hisses of burning skin every now and then. He rested his hand on his hip.

Johnny grabbed the chair from the head of the table and pulled it up beside the fireplace. Looking up at the painting, soft shadows colored in the hollows beneath Agatha's high cheekbones. The frame's thick gold rivets appeared deeper than normal. The picture sat inches above the fireplace shelf.

Holding onto the back of the chair, Johnny turned toward Alex and said, "You're not gonna push me in, right?"

"Wouldn't dream of it, honey," Alex said, waving a hand.

Johnny took that for what it was and climbed onto the chair, tilting the large portrait of Agatha and Kelly a little to the right. The heat from the fire caressed Johnny's exposed skin and he started to sweat. His chest pounded, his throat grew dry. The fireplace smelled much worse up close. Burnt, yet fresh. String, polyester, wood, fleece, hair.

Alex pursed his lips. "Are you done?" Standing beside the pantry door, he popped his gum.

"Yes—" Johnny started, but looking back at the portrait, the wire on the back of the frame didn't conform to the new shape and instead returned the image to its normal upright position. "One sec," Johnny said, twisting the portrait again. He held it in place for a couple seconds this time, mildly pulling it down. When Johnny released it the second time, it stayed.

Climbing down from the chair, Johnny caught a glimpse of Astra's remains melting into the firewood. "Good thing dinner's over," Johnny said, running his forearm over his nose like he was wiping away the smell.

"Astra was always great at ruining appetites…" Alex muttered.

"Maybe we should test the fire—see if it's hot enough?" Johnny said, stepping back up to the fireplace. "C'mere a minute."

"Very funny." Alex swung his hips. "Ya done?"

"Yeah, yeah," Johnny said.

"Now go hide behind the curtain," Alex said.

Johnny nodded and slipped behind one of the gathered, burgundy curtains.

"I'll go get him and when he's in place, just... go for it. Scream if you want to. I don't care, just push!" Alex spoke in a loud whisper. He was already moving through the pantry door by the time he finished speaking, he couldn't hear if Johnny actually responded. Alex slipped through the small pantry and, pulling the door back, entered through the kitchen side.

Angus stood at the stove with a pan on one of the burners and a whisk in his other hand. On the counter sat a gallon of milk, an unopened chocolate bar, and a mug. "Hey hun, got a moment to spare?" Alex's voice went up an octave.

"Ah! Alex! What can I do for ye?" Angus said, turning from the stove. Angus paused. "Ye got something on your shirt."

Alex looked down at his attire and noticed the dark red stains running over his vest, shirt, tie, and pants. "It's only a little wine."

"That's a lot ay wine."

"Girl's night. Don't worry about it," Alex waved his hand. "But I should tell you, I was in the dining room and I noticed the mantel picture was kinda crooked. I know it's not like, a huge deal, but with tonight being what it is..."

"Of course! Say no more." Before turning off the burner, he glanced through the kitchen window to check on Gavin and Kelly. They were right where they were last time he checked: couch and chair beside it, and their talk seemed to be going well. Kelly didn't look as upset as he had upon first entering, but he still didn't look great by any means. Angus leaned the whisk on a small spoon with a soft ding. "Please, lead the way," he said.

"Of course," Alex responded, but even as he headed back to the dining room, he couldn't help but feel more on edge than before.

The house always seemed to rock when Angus moved. The pantry clattered as they went through it. Cans banged, bags crackled, the mop fell over and hit the wall on the opposite side. Alex picked it up and put it back before continuing to the dining room.

"That the crooked one?" Angus pointed to the large portrait hanging over the fireplace.

"Yup, That's the one." Alex rubbed his temples. "The only one."

"It doesn't look crooked to me," Angus said.

It had straightened out a little since Alex had left, but it hadn't straightened out completely. "Why don't you get a closer look? It's def crooked."

Angus stepped up to the fireplace and surveyed it. Twisting his head to one side, he squinted his eyes then dropped his head to the other shoulder.

"You see it?" Alex said, walking up behind Angus.

"I think so..." Angus scratched the underside of his chin with the back of his hand.

"If you tilt it, I can tell you when?" Alex said.

Angus smiled and a dimple formed to the left of his mouth. "Sounds good, gaffer!" He stepped up to the fire. The foul smell didn't faze him. His lips pulled apart from one ear to the other. Large fingers reached around either side of the frame. Alex took a couple steps back, then, glancing toward a muscular imprint in the curtain, he gave a hand sign and pointed toward Angus.

"How's tha' look?" Angus said, still holding the frame.

"Oops—a little too much to the left." Alex didn't even look at the portrait. His jaw worked faster at chewing his gum, and he nodded toward Angus. His weight shifted from hip to hip every other moment.

"Th' must be it, aye?" Angus sounded enthusiastic and far too excited for what he was doing.

"Not quite. Now it's almost back where it started." A soft chuckle passed through Alex's lips. In it slid a slight hiss of irritation.

First Johnny's brown hair peeked out from beneath the curtain, then, after another reassuring nod from Alex, the rest of him appeared. They stood on opposite sides of Angus. Alex's eyes snapped from the Scotsmen to Johnny then back, mouthing commands that didn't seem to make it to Johnny's head. Using his hands, Alex directed Johnny toward Angus while he mirrored the movement on his side of the table. Finally, they moved toward Angus in sync, coming up behind him, and when close enough, Johnny put his right shoulder forward and rammed into Angus's back while Alex withdrew.

Johnny felt Angus falter, then there was a ripping or cracking sound. The chef's shoulders pressed into the shelf and the painting ripped from the wall. The fireplace was large, but Angus's shoulders surpassed the height and length of the stone opening. He gripped the portrait thinking it would save his fall, but instead, it caused a large fissure up the wall where the nails were inserted; a couple of books fell to the floor.

Alex and Johnny cursed under their breaths.

"Oh, Johnny!" Angus said. "Have you been here the whole time?" The golden frame slid through his fingers until the bottom hit the floor in front of his feet. He held the top of the portrait against his chest.

Johnny's heart was a racing thump he couldn't think over. "I, uh…" he said, unable to keep his eyes on Angus. "Uh… heard you… from the other room… and wanted to see if I could help."

"Tha's nice of ya," Angus said.

Johnny looked at Alex, shrugging his shoulders in question.

The fire crackled.

Angus didn't seem too keen on hanging the picture back up again tonight. He laughed and motioned to the missing fire gate. He laughed again, saying he almost fell in and told an anecdotal story about an inn he once stayed in that caught fire after a couple of drunkards slipped on a pool of piss. The accident burned the whole place down and took many of its residents with it. "I was one of the lucky ones," he laughed and seemed oddly sincere.

Johnny mouthed, 'the Bauchen?' at Alex.

Alex nodded. The more Angus spoke, the more he confirmed Agatha's stories about him and the destruction he set upon Scotland. What's more, he confirmed how necessary it was for the two of them to get rid of him now.

"If that's it, I got some snacks to get back to. Good night, wee man," Angus said before slipping back through the pantry followed by a rattling of cans and then silence.

Johnny paced down the length of the dinner table. "That should have worked. That should have totally worked, but how do you fit a house inside of a fireplace? Alex?"

The room grew darker and the fire dimmer as it suckled on Astra's dry remains.

Johnny stopped walking and stared at his flexed, muscular forearms. He scanned over the way his short white sleeves hugged his veiny biceps; tools that had once put an opponent in the hospital with little effort could do nothing now.

"Got a plan B?" Alex said, popping a bubble of chewing gum.

"Gimme a moment and I'll come up with something." Pacing again, Johnny started to think that the best weapon was to use against Angus was himself. The closest he had come to dying was when he lost balance and gravity twisted around him and pulled. "I've got an idea. Follow me."

NINETEEN.

Library, Benedict Estate
August 11th, 12:02 A.M.

The library was found in the southwest wing of the Benedict Estate. It consisted of two stories, a balcony that rounded the entire second story, and a high ceiling decorated with stained glass depicting blasphemous versions of familiar biblical stories. Dark oak shelves were built into the walls from floor to ceiling, continuing past the stairs and toward the roof. The banisters were long, thin, and decorative with Celtic knots carved along the slim bases and a bulb-shaped center puckered in the middle of each banister rod. On the second floor, absent ladders were replaced with hand-carved stepstools. The wood matched the shelves, but instead of being carved with Celtic knots, they appeared as a tree trunk with lovers' names carved into the base. Names, sayings, and symbols were crudely cut into each two-step stool. There were five of them spread across the second-floor landing, each with a slight difference in shape and vastly different decorations.

The room's furniture was regal and modern. The couch on the first floor was cream while the chairs a mild mocha.

A large cabinet sat in the back corner, the front shielded with glass, showing off old books collected a century ago and accompanied by East Asian pottery plates and a jade lion.

Johnny and Alex surveyed the room for the best place to push a ladder over. All the first-floor shelves were the same height, yet there must have been better places to crack someone's head open. Johnny pulled a ladder along with him, dragging it as far away from anything that could be grabbed if someone fell. He stood before the ladder, bracing it on either side, then started to pull. The magnetic tension fought to stay connected. Johnny grunted as he pulled harder. His face grew hot and veins popped out of his arms. The magnets rocked against the rails before there was a pop. The ladder was much heavier than Johnny thought it would be. Immediately he connected it to the magnetic rail and stepped away.

"What do you think?" Alex said.

"It'd take me down," Johnny said.

"Yeah, but what about him?"

"He's not that much larger than me."

Pinching his fingers together, Alex said, "Kind of a bit. Ya know, like, a lot."

"Let's just... stop wasting time. Go get him." And with that, Johnny laid down behind the couch on the farther end of the room while Alex left to grab Angus for a little bit more help.

The china cabinet clattered from Angus's incoming footsteps. He pushed the door open. It smacked against the wall, splintering. "Where's the book?"

The Scotsman moved around the room, making circles across the center rug and passing between the furniture. He came close enough to the couch that Johnny feared he'd be spotted. The couch, chairs, and end tables feet clattered against the floor in synchrony with Angus's steps, almost as if trying to scramble away from him before he crushed them.

"Right there," Alex said, pointing to a book with a gold spine nine shelves from the ground.

Angus didn't make any immediate moves toward the book or the ladder. Instead, he tilted his head to the side and took a deep breath. His lips grew crooked beneath red facial hair. "Ye ken they're ladders, aye?" he said. "You could get the book easy."

"Yeah, well, I know that..." Alex said, crossing his arms. He turned away and shifted his weight anxiously. "It's just that..." he trailed off, biting his bottom lip. "I'm kind of like," he looked around cautiously, and his voice dropped. "Afraid of heights, okay? You won't tell anyone, will you?"

Angus's brows rose and his chest grew again as a bellow of laughter echoed through the room. He came to Alex's side and gave him a strong pat on the shoulder, causing the stylist to stumble. "No need to be ashamed, laddie. If we're bein' honest," he lowered his voice, but was still loud, "snakes give me the willies." He smacked Alex a second time, causing a growl to bubble in his throat. "I'll get that book right down for you."

Angus stepped up to the ladder, looking it up and down. It was about half as wide as his shoulders and the steps barely thicker than his largest finger. He grabbed the side of the ladder with his left hand and reached upward for the book with his right. His fingertips tickled the bottom side of the gold-spine book. He lifted himself onto the first step of the ladder with one foot and pulled the book out of the line with the top of his finger.

There was a soft crack.

Then another one.

The wood step beneath Angus's foot broke in two.

His feet hit the ground at the same time and the book he held fell and split open. Angus grunted, looked at the broken ladder step, then laughed. "Wasn't expectin' tha'." Mild laughter shook his chest as he retrieved the book from the floor. He closed it, but stopped short of handing it to Alex. On the cover was a pair of identical twin girls with long blonde hair. The title across the top read, *Don't Worry, We Won't Kill You.*

"What's that book about?" Angus said, handing Alex the book.

Alex shrugged taking the book from Angus. "Some twins who don't like their step-daddy... or was it their babysitter?" he mused out loud.

"Tha' all ya needed then?" Angus asked.

Alex searched the library for Johnny. The tip of his brown hair stuck out from behind the couch, and he peeked over the back every now and then. Johnny mouthed something to Alex. Alex shrugged, shifting his eyes from Johnny to Angus.

Johnny shook his head and mouthed something again to which Alex shrugged again.

Angus turned around to see what Alex was looking at, but only saw an empty couch. "Alex?" Angus said, placing a hand on the stylist's shoulder.

Johnny appeared behind the couch again. This time he pointed toward the ceiling.

Alex shook his head, mouthing the word, "what?"

Johnny curled his hands into tight fists. He rubbed his face roughly before sticking out his middle and index finger, forming legs. He alternated walking them forward, moving them higher with each step, then pointed at the staircase again.

"Oh!" Alex grabbed onto Angus's arm, "there was a second book." He pulled Angus toward the stairs and started the climb. "If you don't mind."

Angus showed no resistance.

Alex glanced over the banister; Johnny slid out from behind the couch, and now he clung to the backside of a pale brown armchair.

From the landing, Alex took Johnny's direction, watching him point to a pair of shelves as far away from the stairs as possible.

Johnny waited until Angus had reached the bookcase before he went for the stairs.

Johnny moved up another step; his racket clicked behind him.

He looked through the banisters at the lower level of the library for a blanket, pole, or rope; at this point, he was desperate for anything he could use to catch Angus's feet on, but he saw nothing. The ladders were too long to fit in the staircase, too heavy to carry, and too large to go unnoticed.

Johnny moved up another step; his racket clicked again.

The throw pillows tucked into the corners of the sofa and chairs weren't stiff enough; they may cause Angus to slip if he stepped on them, but the leather they were made of was unlikely to slide across the floor like cotton would.

Johnny moved up another step; his racket clicked again.

At the top of the steps, Johnny looked down at the racket he was carrying. He twisted the racket so the head would move through the banisters and then he twisted it again so it laid flat against the landing while the grip slipped through the banister on the inside of the room. Then he crawled back down the stairs and hid behind the closest chair.

"*Rendezvous Beneath the Cherry Tree of Youth*?" Angus read out loud. He turned the cover over. "What's that about?"

Alex tipped his thick-brimmed glasses down, attempting

to look around Angus's body at the cover. "George Washington?" he said.

Angus's eyes moved along the back cover. "Sounds good..." He hummed when he finished reading then handed it to Alex. "Was that it?"

"Uh, one sec." Alex held up his finger. He glanced over the banister, looking down to the floor for any sign of Johnny and when he saw nothing, he said, "I guess... these books are enough for me."

"Enjoy yer books," Angus said. He led the way back toward the stairs. As they moved, Johnny shuffled around behind the furniture below.

Alex checked over the banister and momentarily locked eyes with Johnny. Alex pointed to Angus with both hands and mouthed, 'What do you want?'

Johnny waved his hand forward as if to say, "keep going."

Alex chewed his gum and popped an anxious bubble but continued behind Angus.

At the stairs, Angus stopped. "After you." He stepped aside.

"Thanks," Alex moved around the guardrail.

Johnny peeked over the cream couch shaking his head from side to side.

Alex pulled back and turned to Angus. "But I've already borrowed so much of your time. You should go first."

"Thank you, laddie." Angus descended the stairs. "It's been no trouble at all."

That's when Alex noticed the tennis racket sticking through the rail bars just a few steps down. Alex remained still in place; his head tilted slightly to the side to watch Angus move.

The top of Angus's foot moved right over the tennis racket's throat and dropped down on it. The graphite cracked under his weight until it finally broke. The step was uneven. "Hm?" Angus lifted his foot to inspect what had cracked beneath him.

Time slowed down. It was very possible that if Angus saw the tennis racket, he'd be able to put the hints together that Johnny was here or that they were trying to kill him—assuming he wasn't aware of those facts already.

In a moment of impulse, Alex charged at Angus. Hands pressed into his back with as much strength as Alex could muster. "Whoa!" Alex yelled like he lost balance.

Angus lost his footing. His shoulder hit the stairs and he rolled down, picking up speed as he went until finally hitting one of the shelves with a crash and a clatter of books on top of him.

Alex held onto the guardrail; it was the only thing that kept him from following the Scotsman.

Johnny stood up from behind the couch.

His hand slid along the rail as he stepped over the broken tennis racket and down the remaining stairs. "Angus?" Alex said. "You alright?" He swallowed, focusing in on the large man's unmoving form.

Angus laid on his right shoulder. His legs folded on top of each other, but nothing appeared broken. At least a dozen large, hardcover books laid over him. They were brown and blank aside from the large blocks of green framing the gold letters of *The World Book Dictionary*. "Angus?" Alex said again, reaching the bottom of the stairs.

Alex crouched beside the cook and plucked one of the books from his chest. It was an old encyclopedia, K-L. An energized chill ran down Alex's spine as though cold water had slipped into his shirt. He closed the book and placed it back on the shelf.

Sitting up, Angus rubbed his eyes. "Was that an earthquake?" he said. "May have been a big body." His voice shook and became caught in his throat and less powerful than normal. His vision blurred, so he blinked a few times urging it away. The books ran together in a kaleidoscope of color and scribbles that looked nothing like words.

Johnny sank back behind the couch. Upon catching Alex's attention, Johnny rolled his hands in the air, one over the other as if to say, "keep him distracted." Johnny pointed to himself, then the door, then himself again. He lifted his hand with all five-fingers sticking up. He pointed to Alex, then Angus, then the door.

Alex shrugged, shaking his head in confusion.

Johnny's only response was to repeat the motion: point at himself, the door, five fingers, Alex, Angus, the door again, then Johnny slipped out of the library.

Johnny moved into the hall and shut the library door behind him. Angus's boisterous laughter could be heard outside the library and through what felt like the entire house.

The hall from the library led to the grand ballroom. Halfway to the grand ballroom was a break in the paintings where the walls indented into a small three-walled alcove. Standing on a two-foot tall metal display box was an antique English suit of armor. The iron suit was in immaculate condition with no rust or dents damaging a single plate. It was a decorated piece fit for a man at least 6' tall.

Agatha said her father had brought the suit of armor back from London in 1946. When she asked him if it was Sir Lancelot's armor, he assured her that it was not, but she dedicated half a year of her history studies to finding out who the suit of armor belonged to, insisting that it must have been Lancelot because she wanted it to be.

Through her studies, she discovered the suit belonged to a Sir William and from then on she made a habit of saying,

"Good day, Sir William," anytime she walked past it. Even on the final day of her life, she greeted the suit of armor the same way she had when she was sixteen.

The suit of armor had never been moved from the pedestal in the alcove, possibly because the armor was incredibly heavy. Johnny took Sir William by the hip and pulled himself onto the pedestal alongside it. He shuffled behind it, his heels stuck off the edge. The sharp corners of the pedestal dug into his arches.

The library door swung open. "…and the milk's souring as we speak," Angus said.

"I can imagine," Alex said, seeming uninterested as he trailed behind Angus.

Johnny stood with his hands on Sir William's pauldrons. He planted his feet outside of Sir William's and focused himself. His pupils shrunk and his breaths shortened. With each heavy, echoing footstep, he counted them getting closer. Angus's voice reverberated around the small alcove and tickled the back of Johnny's neck.

Alex and Angus came into view, with Alex on the far side of Angus. Alex barely caught sight of Johnny hidden in the dark, however, the low lights crept into the dark corner and lit up his white face causing him to appear hairless. Alex took a further step away from Angus, laughing to cover the awkward sudden move.

Johnny prepared himself for the push, watching for the right moment when Angus stepped beneath the suit of armor. Johnny's muscles tensed as his fingers curled around the suit's arms. The tasset clattered against the cuisse. The upper half of the model leaned forward, but it didn't move from its place. The bottom of the helmet clicked against the chest plate before it fell off and hit the ground.

Angus yelled a twisted, animalistic grunt and jumped back, stomping on one of Alex's feet.

Screaming, Alex reached for the wall to catch him.

"Clootie!" Angus's hand flung toward the suit of armor, finger pointed. Where the helmet used to sit was now a round, faceless model head made of black fabric. "Give back, ye!" He drew his hand back into a tight fist.

"Wait, wait, wait!" Johnny lifted his arms around Sir William's chest. "It's just me, pranking you." He lifted his head over Sir William's shoulder enough to make himself more obvious to Angus.

The chef looked over Johnny's face, eyes trailing down the suit of armor's shiny body to his pointed feet. Angus took a deep breath, and, upon exhalation, his fist dropped to his side. "Sorry laddie, but it's better to be safe when Clootie's around." Angus watched the mannequin's faceless head for a few moments longer. Then he picked up the helmet and put it back in its place.

"Who?" Johnny said, jumping down from the pedestal.

"Clootie," Angus said again. "The devil. He can take any form, ye know, but he can't change his cleft-hoof feet. If you're ever worried about him, just look at the feet. The feet always give him away."

"Oo-ooow," Alex dropped back against the wall.

Turning around, Angus's arm smacked into Alex. "What happened?"

Alex chewed his gum. His eyes narrowed and he pushed his finger against the bridge of his glasses, moving them up his nose without anywhere for them to go. "Nothing, like, nothing at all. Never mind." He pushed himself off the wall and continued into the grand ballroom.

"I'm gonna help him," Johnny said, excusing himself from Angus and rushing to Alex's side.

"That was your master plan?" Alex hissed. "To push a bolted suit of armor down on someone who weighs three times as much as it does?"

"Bolted?" Johnny said.

"Duh, it's bolted, hot pants. You remember Bertha? If your plan wasn't so bad, I'd say blame her, but honey… you can take all the credit for this mess."

"Damn," Johnny said. "I really thought that would work."

"Honey, to be fair, you also thought the fireplace would work... And the ladder… and the stairs…"

Johnny ran a hand through his hair. "Don't worry, he's fine!" he called back to Angus. His hands curled into tight fists. Without his racket, Johnny's nerves gathered inside of him. He strummed his thigh with his thumb, wanting anything to put in his hands. "I've got one more idea. Just... slow him down a little, then lead him to the middle of the ballroom, got it?" He knocked his shoulder into Alex's. He turned around to face Angus and continued backwards. "I gotta go. I think I left my racket somewhere." He lifted his empty hands as if they were proof he wasn't lying.

"Good luck, lad," Angus said, watching Johnny. He covered his mouth, yawning. "I don't think I'll be up much longer though. I'll finish the milk and then I'm going to the scratcher. If ye need me, please wait until morn, yeah?"

Johnny nodded, spun around, and ran down the hall as quickly as he could. He passed the grand staircase and flew by the grand piano in the ballroom. He wouldn't have very long to prepare; the two of them would enter the ballroom within moments and it would be short time spent here. Johnny remembered the glass chandelier hanging above the center of the room. It was a custom-made work of art, designed with hundreds of tiny glass structures, varying between short and round shapes like teardrops while longer parts accented the chandelier with shapes like long, sharp icicles. The chandelier wasn't antique. Agatha replaced the original chandelier with one she acquired on a visit to Paris in the early 70s. During that trip, she'd met many local artists. Some were painters whose paintings could now be found in guest rooms around the house. Some were sculptors whose figurines graced bookshelves in the estate. In Montmartre, she met a glass artist name Rene Marinot. They spent the summer of 1972 together, visiting various districts in and around Paris, teaching art skills to local youths, and tasting the local cuisine.

By the end of summer, Marinot proposed to Agatha. When she told him no, he crafted the chandelier for her in hopes that every time she looked at it, she would be reminded of him, and someday, call on him to wed.

The chandelier was suspended from the ceiling by a gold chain which traveled down the wall and connected to a small pulley system beneath the balcony. This allowed the chandelier to be lowered for cleaning or to change out lightbulbs.

Johnny ran to the piano and crouched behind it. If Angus were looking for him, he'd be able to spot him, but Johnny hoped the Scotsman was too tired for that. Johnny's heart throbbed with excitement. Without his tennis racket in his hands, his fingers clung to anything they could; the floor, the piano bench legs, the pulley lever.

The hall had grown quiet. Angus entered the ballroom alone. Johnny's jaw grew tight, his vision red and focused as he watched Angus move across the room.

Adrenaline invigorated Johnny like he was about to enter a tennis match. He focused; the corners of his eyes turned red. He couldn't see anything but what was in front of him. He glanced up at the chandelier, then the ground, calculating how far Angus was from the spot. As Angus neared the center of the room, Johnny loosened the first lock, then the second. He let the pulley go.

The curves of the chain shot through Johnny's palms

and the chandelier dropped fast. Rapid, eager rattling startled Angus. He stopped in place and looked around. The moving light shifted Angus's shadow as it fell.

Glass burst immediately upon contact with the floor and sounded like a massive bell choir all playing at once. The shattered glass liquefied, spreading like water on the floor and knocking against Angus's shoe like the tide coming out. Shards raced beneath the couch, chairs, piano, and anything it could slip under. Some even made it far enough to splash against Johnny's shoes.

Angus stood with stiff shoulders and a single cut on his cheek. Slowly, he glanced down at his feet, as though fearful glass would slip underneath. The gold chain coiled in the center of the shattered glass puddle and he laughed, sounding more like he was clearing his throat.

Then, looking up from the chain, he saw Johnny against the wall.

Angus laughed again, this time with a little more confidence. "You'd be surprised by everything that happens to me," Angus said. "Me ma says I must have a guardian angel." He smiled at Johnny and waited for a response, but nothing came. Angus's tense body let go as the moment passed and his adrenaline started to dissipate.

"Alex?" Johnny called, walking away from the wall. He stared at Angus. "Alex!" he called again.

"I'm just gonna finish in the other room. Good night," Angus said and excused himself to the kitchen.

Johnny pulled out the piano bench and sat down. A growl built up in his throat until a bellowing yell came out, echoing through every open area, bouncing between the columns, to the dining room, knocking on Doc's door, then bouncing back at him. He slammed a closed fist onto the piano's lid.

Alex entered from the hallway, passed the grand

staircase, and stopped beside Johnny. He held out the broken grip to Johnny's tennis racket. "Here, hun…" he said, "you forgot this in the other room." He lifted it into Johnny's face. "Maybe it's time you took a lesson from yourself." When Johnny didn't take the racket, Alex dropped it with a grin and walked away.

Johnny stared down at the piece of shattered graphite between his feet. He leaned down and picked up the remnants of his racket, clutching it in both hands. His thumb stroked the leather grip. He closed his eyes, trying to remember the last time he'd wielded the racket successfully. He opened his eyes again, twisting the racket in his hands and then he saw it; his catchphrase written on the fabric in golden letters. His own handwriting mocked him saying, "Only Losers Lose."

He threw the racket against the floor.

TWENTY.

Servant's Hallway, Benedict Estate
April 5th, 1983, 11:03 P.M.

Gavin recognized his father's expression, a half-empty bottle of resentment in his hand. Gavin was only seventeen, but he'd seen this expression so many times before. This same murderous rage had animated his father's face the previous times he'd threatened to kill Gavin. From the moment Kelly had entered the estate, Gavin's father's hatred grew without restraint. The innocence of the brown haired, brown eyed child reminded him of everything his son was not and never would be.

The bottle rocked on its side; some of the liquid spilled from its open throat. Gavin's father staggered toward the bed, his eyelids lowering, his fingers hot. "Stupid bitch," he muttered. "It's all her fault. And this house... and you," he growled, low. He leaned into the bed with his knees, letting it support him. A hand reached for Gavin, slow, and quiet. Halfway there, steel blue eyes stared up at him: cold, stiff, and defiant.

Gavin's expression was always distant. He never showed sadness, but he never showed anger or joy either. All

Gavin's father wanted was to see something recognizable and human in his child, a glimmer of his late wife, or some sign that the boy wasn't a mistake, but it never came.

Gavin's father's hands clamped tightly around his son's neck. Gavin rushed to grab his father's wrists. He gasped for breath, struggling to pull the choking hands free. He broke his father's hold and threw the older man off. He stood in an instant and pushed the man to the ground. Grabbing him by his thinning hair, Gavin slammed his father's head into the floor. Then his fingers moved around his father's throat. The expression 'like father, like son' had never been more right. He couldn't have anticipated how imitating his father's actions would excite him; wrapping his fingers around another man's throat; struggling to hold someone down as their last bit of life left them. It was the first time in Gavin's life he'd ever felt anything so strong inside of him. The moment came and went much faster than Gavin realized. He'd only just put his hands to his father's throat when he could no longer feel the heartbeat. Disgusted delight knotted his stomach. A mild smile tugged at his lips; his father was gone.

Electric candle wall lamps buzzed only with enough energy to cast their own shadows against the walls of the estate's long halls. Cool, but stale air blew through the hallways. Whether it was the guest hall, the service hall, or the sleeping hall, most doors were closed. Summer cicadas chirped through the glass and echoed down through the empty rooms.

Gavin's hands were steady when he knocked on Bertrand's door, his moment of hesitation passed.

A ribbon of light flickered on and spilled beneath the door.

Gavin knocked again, but this time, he didn't wait for an answer before he turned the knob and entered the bedroom.

The room was simple and organized, containing no more furniture than necessary: a plain twin bed on a plain wooden frame, dirt-stained white sheets, and a peach blanket. A plain short dresser with five drawers. A nightstand and peach-shaded lamp. No images on the peach-colored walls. Terra cotta pots filled with sickly plants cluttered a table pushed against the window, giving the room its only semblance of personality.

Bertrand sat upright in his bed. His lids drooped over his mellow eyes. Dark shadows beneath Bertrand's eyes said he shouldn't have been awake, but he said nothing.

Gavin held the doorknob in his left hand and the frame in his right. His face lacked any sign of emotion. His eyes trained on Bertrand, analytical, serious, attentive. "He's dead," Gavin said.

Bertrand drew the blanket back and slid his legs over the edge; his knees cracked. His back curled in a small, aged arch. He shuffled toward one of the table chairs. His work boots sat beneath it; he slipped them on and left with Gavin.

Gavin's father laid at the foot of his bed. The man's neck was red with handprints, his face was on a slow return from purple. "He stood over me. He tried to strangle me. I beat him to it," Gavin said.

Bertrand instructed Gavin with little more than his watchful eye. "You know where he goes," Bertrand said.

Gavin took his father's wrists and dragged him down the servants' staircase. His father's heels slapped against each other, the steps, and the passing furniture. The burden grew with every moment, his father's post-mortem resistance.

Bertrand held the yard door open. The air turned thick and heavy, weighing down Gavin's clothing immediately. The soft earth sunk beneath each step and the wet soil grabbed at his father's dragging corpse.

Gavin returned to the small garden he'd been burying Agatha's pet cats in for years as he made them disappear too. He dropped his father's arms and wiped the perspiration from his forehead. His damp nightshirt collar stuck to his neck.

Bertrand gave him a shovel and told him to start digging.

Thin clouds hid Gavin from the accusatory moonlight, but the small yard lamps tried to make up for it, keeping his every action visible.

When Gavin thought the hole was done, Bertrand told him to keep digging. "A shallow grave is not a good grave," he said. "If you intend to do something, do it right the first time."

When Bertrand allowed Gavin to stop, the grave was five feet wide, eight feet long, and five feet deep. The moon dipped below the horizon. Gavin threw the shovel aside, his muscles pulsing and heavy. A spark of annoyance flickered inside of him. Even after his father was dead, he could make Gavin suffer. Gavin placed his hands on the edge of the grave to climb out, but the soft ground crumbled beneath his weight. He turned around to try the other side, but it happened again. He tried again and again. The hole's edges became messy and round. An unwanted layer of dirt coated the bottom of the hole. He crouched down and scooped at the earth with his hands. Dirt dug under his nails. He wiped his forehead with the back of his arm. His skin was a layer of filth, alien to him. At the edge of the grave, Gavin stared at his father's unmoving body and couldn't help but blame him for his current condition.

Bertrand extended a hand to Gavin, but he didn't take it. Instead, Gavin placed his hands on the round edge of the grave and prepared for failure again.

Bertrand shook his head. "If you intend to go anywhere

in this place, you must find people to rely on. You may believe you can do everything alone, but there will be a time that you cannot. When that time comes, it will be life or death. Don't be a fool."

Gavin stared at Bertrand's extended hand for a few more passing moments before he took it. With Bertrand's help, he wriggled over the hole's edge. Gavin wiped his dirty hands on his pants. He approached his father's body. Rigor mortis was already setting in. Gavin rolled the man into the grave, uncaring how he fell, if his face was up or down, or if his legs broke over themselves. Gavin picked up the shovel and never saw his father again.

Upon the final layer of dirt Bertrand handed Gavin a package of orange lilies and ordered him to sow them into the earth. "Every plot is an experience," Bertrand said. "The flowers give respect to the experience each hole represents, even if the hole hides hatred, resentment, or destruction. When you disturb the garden, you must plant something new."

Even after the sunrise came, Gavin still felt the weight of his father burdening his shoulders. Bertrand told him the feeling was what it meant to make an adult decision; it would never disappear; as he aged, it would only become heavier. The best thing he could do was learn to make good decisions and cope with the weight of the bad ones. Gavin didn't understand what Bertrand meant by that; he didn't regret his father's death. His only regret was that he hadn't done it sooner. Knowing he had the ability to remove people like that from the house, he believed he had a responsibility to do so to keep the house clean.

Bertrand and Gavin entered the kitchen together. Kelly sat at the table under the conservatory window. He waved and smiled shyly. He'd never waved at Gavin before. The darkness that plagued Gavin's father... there wasn't a feeling of it in the boy, and it was upon that observation that Gavin knew what he'd done was the right thing; he needed to keep Kelly safe, to stop him from turning into either himself or his father.

TWENTY-ONE.

Dining Room, Benedict Estate
August 11th, 12:48 A.M. 1993

From the conservatory table, Gavin glanced toward the kitchen door. "What's taking Angus so long?" he muttered. His right heel bounced against the floor. A light aroma of tobacco intertwined with the more dominant floral scents of the conservatory. Gavin knew that by morning, the smell would fade almost completely.

Gavin looked toward the kitchen again. It didn't take this long to make hot chocolate.

The bruises on Kelly's legs were getting louder, darker, and giving new shape to his calves. In restraining a snarl, Gavin's lips twitched.

"I-I fell down the stairs," he stuttered out.

After the warnings, after the attacks, Kelly still wanted to protect them. They still didn't 'deserve' to die. "You don't understand—"

"I hit the wall," Kelly said. "I tripped over the bed. I ran into the music player too."

The obvious lying only further infuriated Gavin. Impatience was getting the better of him. Gavin noticed Kelly stroking his shirt between his fingers more aggressively the more obvious Gavin's impatience became.

It had always been Kelly's means of coping. When he first entered the house, Agatha made Kelly a knit blanket, and when the storms would come around, growling as the incredible winds slammed into the house, Kelly would wrap himself in the blanket and use the feeling of the fabric against his skin to soothe himself. It was a habit Kelly hadn't grown out of, even now that he was fourteen. He hid his fingers underneath the table, turning away and looking down.

"I didn't do anything," Kelly finally said. "He was just there." His thumb stroked the cotton shirt.

"Who?"

"I don't understand." Kelly fought to keep it back, but a hot tear trailed down his cheek. He wiped his cheek. "What he wants. What any of you want. Everyone can't be like Astra. They can't all think that we're just... that this is everything—"

"They can and they do," Gavin said. He watched Kelly for a moment before he continued. "People aren't as complicated as you're trying to make them. Personal desire trumps everything else. Even self-preservation can be forgotten in order to achieve a goal."

Everything pulsed in Kelly's body at once: pain, frustration, betrayal, fear. Once the first tear fell, little held the others back. Kelly wiped his eyes with the back of his hand. He sucked in a breath, his stuffy nose snorted. He closed his eyes and buried his red face in his hands.

Foul images filled his mind: Madame Astra's face melted behind his eyelids. Her skin melted off the bone, and skimpy, pulsing muscles constricted, thrashed, and reached for him. Bertrand's silhouette appeared in headlights behind the disintegrating skeleton. Distorted laughter circled around it like a swarm of locust. Johnny's face appeared between the swarm of sounds, his sockets empty voids and his large body grew taller and wider. He lifted his foot. The circle pattern in his shoe was filled with knives. Kelly's body jerked back, lifting his hands in defense. "I don't want it! I don't want it!" he screamed, voice cracking. "I don't want it anymore!"

Kelly nodded off, sitting, crying. He had only been asleep long enough for the tear trails on his cheek to dry and it didn't appear as though he realized what had happened.

Gavin straightened and moved closer to Kelly. He withdrew a handkerchief from his pocket and pressed it to Kelly's cheek.

Kelly jerked away at first, but then he slumped forward, too exhausted to resist.

"What are you talking about?" Gavin said.

Kelly hesitated before saying, "I don't want the house. I don't want the money. I don't want any part of this anymore." His voice shook. "I can't do it. I can't be like them. Like you."

"Everyone has the potential," Gavin said.

Kelly said nothing.

"Where would you go?"

Kelly's body tremored, stifling a sob. His eyes were plush and puffier than before. He tilted his head down, cutting Gavin off. Dark curls curtained his face. "I don't know... Somewhere else.... Somewhere not like this..."

"Everywhere is like this, Kelly," Gavin's voice was straightforward and strong. "You can't escape it. Smaller places mean more intimate betrayal. Bigger places mean more people doing what they can to get further up the ladder. Bigger places mean more punishment from others when you step out of line. Here, the corruption is just more obvious because there are fewer players and they all understand the rules of the game. If you go anywhere else, there are those who are playing and there are those who are. If you don't play the game, you will be taken advantage of. There is no way to not play... unless you want to kill yourself."

Kelly looked up with alarm, brown eyes focused on Gavin. He couldn't keep contact for long; frustration and shame penetrated him. He sagged in resignation. Dropping his head, he covered his face with one hand and twisted his shirt with the other. "I want to go to bed."

"Then we will put you to bed," Gavin said, straightening. Kelly did not rise until Gavin took his arm and urged him up. Passing by the window, Gavin noticed the kitchen was empty and a cold pot of milk sat on the stove top, the jug of milk on the counter, and the unopened candy bar beside an empty mug.

Entering the grand ballroom, glass cracked beneath Gavin's feet. He stopped, tightening his grip on Kelly enough so he would stop too. He surveyed the floor; broken shards scattered across it in puddles.

"Gavin!" Angus said, halfway to the kitchen, he turned away from the hall. "I was just comin' back to finish the milk. The wee jimmies got in a wee trouble—" He thumbed over his shoulder, but the only person there was Johnny. "And then I almost got burst by the chandelier! A bampot nigh!" He paused, his expression shifting from a smile with bright eyes to a concerned scowl. "The laddie alright?"

"Tired. We're going to bed."

"Did ye still want 'at hot chocolate?"

"No," Gavin said.

"Then at least let me take him to bed for ye. I feel awful that I didn't give you want ye needed..." Angus said, looking to Gavin for permission, but primarily watching Kelly.

Kelly fought to remain attentive to his surroundings. His

head fell forward every couple of moments, eyelids lulling closed only for him to jerk up and widen his eyes, then repeat the cycle.

Gavin's tongue clicked. His face tightened and the edge of his lips threatened to twitch. On a normal night, he would have argued, and he would have put Kelly to bed, but Gavin was piecing together what had happened. His fingers tingled for action. There was Johnny in the wrong place, at the wrong time, who had made a very poor move.

Angus deserved to be disciplined for his negligence, but that was something he'd suffer for in the morning. Gavin tugged Kelly by the arm and led him toward Angus. "If you complete this job the same way you did the hot chocolate, we will have a problem."

"Won't happen," Angus said. "I swear on my life."

Gavin was still hesitant to agree, but he released Kelly to Angus and made the mental note to check on Kelly as soon as he was finished. There should be no detour that kept Kelly from his bed, and if he moved upstairs and the boy wasn't there, Angus would not be prepared for the trouble he would receive. Gavin watched the chef take Kelly out of the room. There was a yelp as the boy was scooped up from the ground. Gavin's initial feeling was to jerk in that direction, but he remained firm.

Kelly wasn't wearing shoes and to traverse the glass-covered floor to reach the stairs wasn't something he could condone. Though Kelly struggled at first and demanded to be put down, he relaxed halfway to the staircase and calmed once he was placed on the ground again.

It was mildly uncomfortable for Gavin to not put Kelly to bed; he had performed the chore every night since his father died. He preferred to do it because he knew he did it right. Though Kelly was a teenager now, the routine was an act of comfort and normalcy for both of them. Gavin could have trusted Bertrand to take care of Kelly, but he would have done it in a much different way. He wasn't nurturing in the sense of giving a child all the attention they thought they needed. He was nurturing in providing the experiences and necessary pushes to make someone learn. Gavin failed to replicate that with Kelly. Either Kelly was getting in his own way or Gavin wasn't the teacher Bertrand was.

While Angus left, Gavin focused on Johnny. The tennis player kept his back pressed against the wall on the other side of the room.

"Anna." He spoke the name so softly it couldn't be heard across the room, but the maid certainly heard it.

Metal rattled and a kitchen drawer pulled open. Slipping through the kitchen door, she appeared behind Gavin, her arms at her sides.

Gavin and Anna rarely used the servant's intercoms to communicate. Their jobs were different, their duties different, yet wherever Gavin could be found, Anna was most certainly nearby. The house operated well with the two in charge. Anna excelled at her work, doing it quickly and silently. Few noticed her presence as she cleaned rooms and rearranged furniture without being noticed.

At first, Anna had been the young girl who came out of nowhere and had no parents or reason to be at the house. Over time, the rumors grew. Gossip established that Anna belonged to Agatha and Bertrand. Because they never maintained an official relationship, after her birth, Agatha left Anna to Bertrand and never acknowledged her as anything but a member of her staff. Most of the time, Agatha didn't acknowledge her existence at all.

Gavin never took to discussing the topic of Anna's family; it never seemed to matter. He thought her work, reliability, focus, and availability were much more important, especially as he grew into a young man who received little attention from women. Anna never flirted with him in a traditional way. She watched Gavin follow Ellie, asking her to take her clothes off for him in the yard and Ellie would hit him with whatever she could find at the time. It didn't take long before Anna took him to her room and presented herself to him, offering him a sexual outlet.

Their relationship was complicated. They were loyal as business associates, and available to physically release one another, but they weren't romantically entangled. Anna was a teacher, but when Gavin put on his father's suit, she allowed him to take lead and began following him without question.

They worked so excellently together that the connection they had to one another seemed almost paranormal. A whisper and Anna was there. A mild mutter and Gavin would open the door to find Anna on the other side. Tonight was no different.

"You finally come to clean up the mess?" Johnny shouted.

"Anna, have you seen Mr. Green?" Gavin said, staring at Johnny from across the room.

"I believe he's hiding from you," Anna said, soft, monotoned, also staring at Johnny. "But he's not doing a very good job."

Gavin took a couple of steps into the ballroom; glass fluttered beneath his shoes.

"I'm not hiding," Johnny said.

Gavin held his hand out behind his back. His fingers rolled, gesturing for Anna to give something to him. She stepped up behind him and withdrew the kitchen knife from her pocket then slipped it into his hands.

Glass rolled against the floor, sliding against Gavin's soft soles. A larger shard poked into the bottom of his shoe, applying acute pressure to his instep, but he continued forward without recoil.

Johnny's arms were near twice the size of Gavin's; thick muscles burst from his tennis uniform. The closer Gavin came, the more Johnny flexed.

"Showmanship doesn't help if your opponent knows everything is an act," Gavin said. His fingers curled into tight fists at his sides; they tingled, eager to feel the warmth of blood. His logic told him that a frontal attack on Johnny was not in his best interest. Before he made a move, he could see how it'd play out and he watched himself knocked to the ground, overpowered.

The glass scurried under his feet, crackling, disrupting his thoughts. Light from the table lamps reflected off the knife's blade, signaling Johnny of its presence.

Gavin drew the knife back as he reached Johnny and lunged with a horizontal swipe. It wasn't the move he wanted, but Johnny had seen the knife; there wouldn't be another opportunity.

Johnny dodged to the right. The tip of the blade scratched the wall and peeled the paint. Johnny ran into a nearby bookshelf; its contents rattled, but nothing fell.

Another swing.

Johnny jumped back again. The tip of Gavin's knife caught the edge of the tennis pro's cotton shirt. The material pulled and cut a line in the fabric.

Johnny drew his arm back and blindly punched toward Gavin, hitting him in the chest with his forearm and elbow.

Gavin staggered backward, off balance.

Johnny grabbed Gavin by the shoulders and threw him to the ground; the knife bounced. Gavin reached for it, but it was beyond his fingers. Gavin's body writhed in the puddles of glass, shards sliced into his clothing, dipping into exposed wrists, hands, and neck. The glass was snow, caught in Gavin's hair. He pressed his hands to the floor, getting up, wincing.

Johnny knelt down over Gavin, grabbing him by his combed hair. Calloused fingers wove into blond locks and wrapped around Gavin's skull. He slammed Gavin's head down crashing it into the puddle of glass. "Only losers lose!" Johnny screamed, holding Gavin's head down in the glass. Johnny drew back his free hand while lifting Gavin's head from the floor. "Only losers lose!" He screamed again.

Johnny's fist flew, and Gavin caught it. His wrist threatened to snap from the pressure. Johnny hurled it toward Gavin again. Tossing his weight to the side with a partial roll, Johnny's jab lost strength and became misguided, but still shot into Gavin's shoulder.

Johnny cursed under his breath. He drew back his arm for another hit. Red trailed down his neck. The clean cotton was painted red. It dripped on Gavin and speckles of crimson sunk into his blazer. Johnny's hand shook, then it fell to his side. Reaching for his neck, Johnny gasped and gurgled for air. The broken racket neck pierced his throat and stuck out under his chin.

Behind Johnny stood Anna. Her delicate fingers released the racket grip. She pressed her soft hand to his shoulder pushing him off Gavin with a strong shove. The grip of the racket rattled, bouncing off the floor. Johnny's forehead fell into shards and they dug new dimples into his skin. He growled, choking out something, but the words were wet bubbles popping. He reached for the racket handle, but it was too slippery to grip.

Anna offered Gavin her hand and helped him stand up.

Across from him, in the entry hall, the large, ornate mirror showed him where the blood had gone. He cursed under his breath. He adjusted his tie. Warm liquid trickled down the back of his neck. Gavin slipped his fingers beneath his collar. Withdrawing them, they were stained red.

Footsteps silent and efficient, Anna moved for the knife. Picking it up, the glass grazed her fingers. She offered it to Gavin, and he took it.

Standing beside Johnny, Gavin drew his leg back and slammed it into the tennis coach. Johnny rolled onto his back; his struggling scream silenced by the graphite in his windpipe. Gavin made sure Johnny was on his back before stepping over him, kneeling, and sinking down.

Gavin plunged the knife into Johnny's chest. The groan tight and uncomfortable; the scream through the jagged edges sounded hushed and hollow.

Johnny's life mixing with the busted chandelier made an appearance of stained glass on the floor. Gavin's knees stung as the poke and pressure of glass became more apparent, cutting through his pants. He stood up once more.

Anna surveyed Gavin's head, brushing his short hair out of the way and fingering the colored lumps forming on his face. She plucked at the speckled part of his shirt. She stroked his swelling, pink cheek gently.

Click, click, click, airy heels tapped against the steps, echoing into the ballroom. Soft, rhythmic, they stopped at the loudest point.

Ellie stood at the bottom of the grand staircase with Alex looming a few steps behind her. Her green eyes went wide. Faux surprise took her expression, rounding her lips until her face began to hurt. She relaxed her expression though her foot tapped rapidly against the marble. "Gavin," she said. She eyed the bloodstained carpet. The broken chandelier caught her eye. Her lips drew back in a sneer. Then, there was Anna stroking Gavin's face. She stopped at the edge of the ballroom. "We need to talk," she said. "It's urgent."

TWENTY-TWO.

Taproom, Benedict Estate
August 11th, 1:43 A.M.

The taproom sat catty-corner to the grand ballroom, making both doors equally accessible and alcoholic beverages always nearby any hour of the day.

Inside the taproom, guests were greeted by a line of brass beer taps of local and imported beers that changed with the season. Cherrywood stools with burgundy fabric lined the full-size bar. An assortment of hard liquor created a variety of different shapes and sizes on the shelf behind the counter. Above the bar hung large and small crystal glasses, suspended by their basses. Benches with upholstery to match the stools formed an L against the wall opposite of the bar. The lights in the taproom were left dimmed, giving it the appearance of evening, regardless of the actual time of day. The room's three windows, opaque stained glass overlaid with decorative crosshatched wire, were rectangular and tapered to a point at the top.

Gavin held the door open. Ellie walked through first. Her hips shifted with exaggerated sensuality, swaying side to side as she meandered across the room to the couch.

Cascades of orange curls bounced optimistically against her back and shoulders. Alex walked in behind her, but Gavin dropped the door on him. Pushing the door open again, he snapped, "excuse me?" Anna entered after him.

"We'd like a moment alone if you don't mind," Ellie said, waving to Anna and Alex as though they were nobody servants.

Alex growled again at the treatment, but still left the room.

Ellie watched Anna leave. Her skin appeared darker than usual in the dim light. Anna didn't make eye contact with her nor acknowledge Ellie's existence. As Anna walked by, Ellie tossed her hair over her shoulder, combed it with her fingers, and over-extended her arm until her elbow hit against Anna. The maid's eyes finally fell upon her. Ellie frowned with pouting lips. "Sorry," she said.

"Anna," was all Gavin had to say.

Anna's skirt fluttered when she turned to leave. She looked the most like Agatha from the side. She had a soft chin and a petite, round nose. Her cheekbones were high and sharp, an echo of Bertrand's face. She was an effortless replica of Agatha's youth mixed with an illegitimacy love that would never be recognized.

Ellie hated her for the ease at which she moved and the complete lack of care in her face. She wanted Anna to analyze her; she wanted to feel surveyed and judged; she wanted Anna to seethe with jealousy knowing she would never look as perfect. Yet the dismissal made Ellie feel helpless, disfigured, and like she wanted to take a scalpel to Anna's perfectly round face.

The door clicked as it latched.

Ellie relaxed her shoulders and walked toward the bar as if stepping on glass. "Would you like something to drink?" she said, stepping behind the counter. She reached beneath the bar and placed two short, stemless glasses on the counter. She tucked her hand beneath her flowing red hair and draped it over her shoulder. She retrieved cranberry juice and ice from the small fridge under the counter, then a bottle of vodka from the shelf behind her.

"I'm working," Gavin said. He turned away, but he couldn't keep his eyes off her.

She turned the ice tray upside down and twisted it, spilling the contents across the counter. Small pieces of shattered ice melted into water. One-by-one, she dropped them into the glasses, filling them halfway. She placed the empty tray on the counter and poured the vodka over the ice. The remainder of the glass filled with cranberry juice. A straw slipped through the ice in each glass. After stirring her drink, Ellie licked a small bit of cranberry juice from the tips of her fingers. "It's here if you change your mind." Ellie picked up one of the glasses and moved to the bench beneath the window. "I think it'd be good for you; you look tense and tired. You need to relax a little."

"You're optimistic," Gavin said.

"I don't have plans to kill you." Ellie's fingers caressed the sweating glass as she directed the straw to her mouth. Long lashes fluttered shut and she took a long, slow sip. She groaned as the cold liquid trickled down her throat. Drawing her arms together, she squeezed her breasts, causing them to protrude in rebellion.

Ellie's allure wasn't a secret from anyone on the Benedict Estate, except for Agatha. She created a reputation for herself as someone who seduced every last one of her mother's boyfriend's since she was sixteen-years-old, the majority with whom she'd slept with, but there were some Bertrand got his hands on first. She was a glutton for attention, especially when it meant taking it away from someone else, but it hadn't always been that way.

Ellie was unfortunate enough not to inherit any of her family's good looks and had been born with the bad recessive traits everyone else in her immediate family escaped. As a girl, her legs were too long and skinny; they made her look like a scarecrow. Her hair was thick and feral to the point that she couldn't comb it down, and her face was a disaster of freckles, acne, and rash colors, as though she'd been through an accident and never healed.

Before high school, she was nothing of the seductress she was now. Her crooked nose became straight and button-like. Red, inflated cheeks became round, sculpted edges of marble. Her freckles disappeared overnight.

It was incredible how a little bit of money and some plastic surgery could reinvent a person. Human beings were able to fix God's shortcomings, and all it took was tens of thousands of dollars and the time to heal.

Ellie became completely obsessed with stealing the spotlight after her transformation had occurred; it was retribution for all the attention she'd received for being an unfortunate child with buck teeth, an unbroken, broken-looking nose, and blemished skin like a leper.

Ellie hated how good it felt when someone finally called her beautiful. She hated that her life had more purpose now that she didn't look anything like herself, and she hated the people that affirmed this belief by treating her better than they had when she was ugly. In some way, she would have been less angry if even after she became beautiful, they treated her the same way, but instead, she was vindicated and justified in seeking reprisal.

The worship and adoration of her appearance became a form of currency, and her mother's boyfriends were the ATMs at which she made her withdrawals, but it didn't stop there. She sought the attention of the employees, including Gavin, for years, but never had the intention of lowering herself to their levels by becoming physically involved.

She dated Agatha's boyfriends behind her mother's back. She required them to partake in absurd rituals and humiliation with the promise that their needs would be satisfied if they'd submit. The games didn't end until Bertrand buried them in the yard—and then came Mathias.

She claimed the plastic surgery was never about her insecurities. Instead, it was for power; men of any age were blind to everything around them so long as they had something pretty to look at. When a beautiful girl spoke, people agreed to any task requested of them, regardless of the consequences. Beauty turned women into goddesses men would happily become martyrs for and she was always willing to oblige.

The slit in her dress exposed her slim, pale legs made paler with makeup. She disliked pantyhose, so she never wore any, but she hated her freckles more. She rouged her knees in an attempt to hide what plastic surgery couldn't remove. The makeup gave her an unnatural air of fragility befitting of a porcelain doll. Ellie leaned back and slipped one leg over the other.

The movement caught Gavin's eyes. He cleared his throat. "I have work to do," he said. "You wanted to talk?"

"The house is starting to look a little more ridiculous, huh?" She took the end of the straw between her teeth and flicked her tongue against it.

Gavin stood by the door, aware of how tight his shirt had become. The room was warm.

Ellie's crossed legs gave off a sense of modesty to offset the high slit in her dress. Her honeysuckle perfume polluted the room with sweet air.

Gavin recalled the first gift he'd given her when they were younger, eight-years-old. Bertrand had seen Gavin observing her and suggested he take her flowers; they would reflect the beauty in the girl who received them and she would be grateful for the attention. Gavin had said there weren't flowers ugly enough to match Ellie's face but settled on a handful of dandelions. When he gave them to her, he said, "Here. These aren't actually flowers. They're weeds that pretend to be flowers, just like you're an ugly girl who pretends to be beautiful."

Red-faced, and enraged, Ellie tossed the flowers on the ground and stomped on them. Regardless of what she wore or how much makeup she put on, Gavin acted as if she was the same girl she was at nine, before the corrective surgeries.

"The cost to repair everything is going to be distressing," Gavin said.

"There's another chandelier, isn't there?" She swung her foot to the ground. The slit in her dress to display rode high, baring her upper thigh. She drew the straw into her mouth and sucked.

"That will save some expense, but not all. Considering who is left, it will only get worse from here."

Ellie said nothing. She looked coyly at the wall, then to the drink on the counter.

"What do you want, Ellie?"

She placed her half-empty glass on the windowsill and stood. Her heels clicked against the speckled brown marble. Reaching Gavin, she slipped her hands around his hips and pressed her nose to his jaw. His body stiffened, but he didn't move away. Her eyelids fluttered closed, tickling his cheek. "You seem tense. You've got blood on your shirt. I thought we could relax. Have a moment of silence. Quiet…"

"I don't have time to waste on your lies," Gavin said. He took her hips and pushed her away.

Ellie's muscles tensed, fighting him with mild resistance before she relented to the force of his shove. The smell of her breath stuck to his nose even after she moved away.

A small laugh rocked her body. "Why are you still doing this, Gavin?" she said.

"Why am I still doing what, Ellie?" Gavin said.

"You're so cold to me." She swayed. "How long have we known each other? Twenty years? And you're still like this. Everyone else adores me, why don't you?"

"Because I hate you," Gavin said.

Ellie's bright green eyes focused on Gavin. The curled chuckling lips fell into a saddened frown. "That's not true." When Gavin didn't say anything, she continued. "You've been pursuing me for years, like all the others—"

"No one has been 'pursuing' you. They've been conquering you," Gavin said.

"They're buried in the ground," Ellie said.

"And what respect did you gain by playing games with them?" Gavin said. "Everything you did with them, to them, asked of them, devalued you. They don't have to live with what happened, but you do."

Ellie's jaw tightened and she bit back her immediate response. "That's the jealousy talking," she said.

"Who has jealousy over a whore?"

Ellie slipped her arms around Gavin. Her fingers curled into his hair and she pulled his ear to her lips.

"You observe me when I take my coat off at the door, you watch me at the dinner table. When I hang onto someone else's arm, I know what anger looks like, Gavin. Maybe you're not jealous you haven't tasted me like many others, but you're well aware you can't conquer me, like so many other, *lesser* men could. I thought you were better than that, Gav. Turns out, you're nothing but a freaking cuckold."

Gavin pulled back, but her fingers tightened in his hair and she made his lips press into her ear.

"Show me your teeth, Gavin."

Gavin's desire for dominance overtook him, and he mashed his lips into hers. He knew better, but he didn't stop himself. He grabbed her by the wrists and walked her back until her legs hit the couch. He pushed her down with a commanding shove. Her fingers twisted into his shirt, untucking it from his pants as she pulled him down to her level.

His knees pressed into the couch cushion with graceless pursuit and he cupped her breasts with cold detachment. Where another man might display compassion and relationship, Gavin moved with robotic intent that served to get the job done.

Gavin pressed his nose into Ellie's jaw, tipping her head back. His teeth pulled at her skin without passion, pushing the buttons he needed to push before moving onto the next level.

A chuckle rolled in Ellie's throat. She took hold of Gavin's hanging tie and used it to pull him closer as though it were a leash. She brought him to the couch beside her, putting a stop to the pursuit with the tightening of the tie.

His muscles resisted her, but her control brought him to his senses. He withdrew his tie from her hands and pulled away.

"Where did you learn your moves?" She asked, chuckling a bit. "They're so amateurish, like a teenage boy. Do you know that? You get intimate like an untrained boy," she said, making the laugh more noticeable. "Like you're thirteen!"

Gavin sat back, staring at her. "I've never heard that before."

"Probably because the only person you've been with doesn't know better."

"You're wrong."

Ellie stayed quiet, staring at Gavin. "You know what

makes Mathias a good sexual partner?"

Gavin instantly moved away.

"Not the power, but the pride." Ellie ignored Gavin. "He knows who he is. He knows what he's doing, and he knows why he wants to do it. That reason has never been because it's his duty. When you view everything as your duty, and not as something you care about, it loses value. You become no different than the nobodies working nine-to-five in their offices, pushing papers, making copies, and answering phones. Do you want sex to be as boring as making copies and answering phones?"

Ellie stood and closed the space between Gavin and herself. She twisted his tie around her hand again, pulling him in close. Then she took his hand in hers. "To treat everything like a duty is to treat life with sterility. Is that what makes you happy?"

Gavin stared Ellie in the eyes. "Do you know what makes Anna a good sexual partner?"

Ellie's hand loosened on Gavin's and he pulled away. She was rigid and her eyes grew wider. Color rushed to her face and painted her ears. Her breath caught in her chest.

"She respects obligations and understands her duties. When approached, she maintains elevated, consistent skill until the task is complete because anything else would be an embarrassment. A lack of skill and precision shows a lack of care or the complete inability to do a simple task. She understands time is valuable, so she doesn't waste it, which shows a level of respect few genuinely experience. Hesitancy, fragility, and caution are not something to be treasured in intimacy. They are something to absolve as soon as they're identified." Gavin's eyes secured Ellie's. "And never was she ever the ugly duckling. Nothing about her is *fake*."

Delicacy decorated her features. Ellie's eyelids dropped

and her eyelashes provided a thin curtain to shield her uneasy pupils. Red locks fell over her shoulder and bounced off her breasts. She leaned forward, directing her attention to her empty palm.

Curling her shoulders inward, she grew smaller and more vulnerable. Ellie understood early on that innocence and vulnerability could provoke a man's natural need to protect, but the problem was that for that instinct to spark, there must be something worth protecting and the instinct must be in the person to begin with.

Beautiful women were an asset to most men, even men who were taken couldn't bring themselves to ignore a woman in distress. It was not because they always wanted something, but because they couldn't help responding. Virtue was something always worth protecting because there was so little of it left.

Ellie caught up to Gavin and slid her arms around his shoulders a second time. She brought her lips to his ear and murmured, "Gavin... what happened to us? This isn't you. You're not this heartless." She sucked on her bottom lip and pressed her head to his. Her fingers curled tighter into his shirt. She closed her eyes. "Not to sound like some sort of cliché... and I know we were never close, but we could have been."

"No, we couldn't have." Gavin's voice was stiff and lacked the note of affection that bled into Ellie's. "You and I were never normal."

"You're so cynical," Ellie said, loosening her grip on him "People can change; we aren't all the same."

"Kids are selfish and malicious; so are adults." Gavin put his hands on her hips and pushed her away. His face looked like polished stone: glossy and superficial.

Ellie's throat constricted. She stepped back, allowing space to open between her and Gavin. "I didn't realize I did such a number on you, Gavin," she said. "I knew I had been cruel, but I didn't know I had done this… You… I thought you were stubborn. Kind of like me, in a way." Ellie chuckled to herself. "The kind of attitude that made all my teachers in school mad. I learned a lot of my tactics from you…" Ellie's arms hung at her sides. Instead of looking at Gavin, she eyed the untouched glass of alcohol on the bar. "Nobody cares about anyone else. The pain is real, but we are so full of ourselves and too busy getting rid of whatever makes us feel bad to think about what is going on with anyone else. We shatter the possibilities of family before they even start by elevating our own suffering to something we have to go through alone, blaming everyone else as the cause. We stop caring about each other because of the cynicism. 'Why is he doing that? What does she want out of me for it?' I can see it in everything you do: discarded desire. Extreme disgust. Lost hope. I did that to you… and I'm sorry."

Gavin sighed. "Why are you here, Ellie?"

"My mother—"

"Why are you here, Ellie?" he repeated. "The history of this place isn't a secret—not to you. Agatha didn't inherit this home from her father and you didn't honestly expect to inherit it from her. You knew that in order to have your nameplate on the mailbox, you would be required to sell what's left of your soul and destroy everyone else here, including a child who can't get away."

"What if this could have been the changing point for us?" She looked over his face, waiting for a reaction. Nothing came. "A time to reinvent the city, its culture, the history of this house. We can change how the 'tradition' works. Rewrite history. In a few decades, the old rumors will be forgotten and this house, and its past, will be whatever we say it is."

"But it will not be what actually built this."

"Isn't it better to erase bad history rather than keep it around to sully something good?"

"No," Gavin said. "Without history, you have nothing to compare yourself to, nothing to give context to why something is important or why it is done a certain way. Rewriting history doesn't just remove identity, it removes values and purpose, though neither of us have a good grasp on either of those things."

"No," Ellie giggled. "But that's what makes this so exciting. We can transform ourselves. Past, present, future. History, family, reality… becomes whatever we say it is."

Her hands clutched his biceps. Her honeysuckle scent intoxicated him despite the arm's length between them, as if his nose was buried in her hair. Gavin removed her hands from him and stepped back. "Don't allow the drink to go to waste. You'll need it later." Gavin opened the taproom door.

Anna stood against the wall opposite to the door at straight attention. Further down the hall, Alex paced with a pair of scissors in his hands.

"I guess this is the end." Ellie leaned against the door frame. "Of you, me… everything."

"That is a fair assessment, except there never has been a you and me." He glanced at Anna when he passed her. She picked up behind him without looking at Ellie or Alex, following him to the grand staircase.

Ellie slipped out of the tap room. She watched Gavin until he moved out of sight. Crossing her arms, Elli's nostrils flared. Through clenched teeth, she snarled Alex's name. "I want her bleeding and crying, Alex."

"Who?" He kept space between himself and Ellie's.

"Who? Who?" The words rushed out of her mouth. She paced back into the tap room and picked up the second cranberry drink, the one Gavin never touched. "Who do you think?" She said, the drink almost to her lips. "The maid." She took a short sip. "That grotesque excuse for a geisha." She pressed the glass to her lips for a longer period this time.

"So why don't you get on her and do it, Elle? Go make her cry."

Ellie slammed the glass on the counter. She reached underneath the bar for the cranberry juice in the fridge and then grabbed the vodka again. "Alex, if you don't want to die, you'll kill that bitch." The vodka bottle clattered on the counter.

"Pretty sure what you're asking could get me killed."

"And Mathias has a gun."

Alex closed his eyes, the breath halted in his throat. "Excuse me?"

"If I die, there's nothing your hips can do to stop him from killing you and taking the money. Sorry, not sorry."

"He brought a gun?"

"He brought a gun."

"What ever happened to the rules? You know, *the* rules?"

"Does it matter what the rules are if you play to win from the start? Whatever the winner says is what happened." Ellie passed her glass to Alex.

He sucked in a breath. "Oy vey." He drained the glass in one long draft. "I'm gonna need another one before we get going.

"Fine."

Alex closed the door behind him. At the bar, she fixed them both another vodka and cranberry, these glasses taller than the last. "Did I ever tell you about when we were kids? Gavin and I?" The ice crackled, falling off itself. "He thought he was being affectionate—at least that's what I'm told. He hid behind Bee thinking I couldn't see him watching me. Then he brought me flowers once—"

She put the cup down on the bar and looked at Alex.

"Girl, that sounds like a threat to me." Alex took a long drink. His glasses fell down his nose and he pushed them back up. The strong stink drink tingled against his mouth. He licked his lips.

"Then one day he stopped doing any of it. No cat, no flowers, no watching. He was gone. His attention was… gone. He was always either doing work or he wasn't around anymore… and it's because of her." A small growl slipped into her voice. "I can't believe I didn't notice it. I didn't notice when she stole him from me. What the hell does she have that I don't have?"

"Well," Alex purred, "Her original nose, her own tits, a petite figure, and a gentle personality. She seems fairly alright to be around even if she's not much of a talker." Alex held the glass against his lips. Ellie stared at him from the side. "Look, honey, she might have all that, but at least you've got a pretty face." His tongue ran along the edge of the glass before he tipped it back and drank.

"I'm not even sure I have that," she muttered. "Bump her off; clip her; find Anna and do her up with a Louisville Slugger."

"You'd probably handle that thing better than me." Alex chuckled.

"Make her pretty, then mess her up. Whatever you like."

"Sounds like fun, I guess," Alex said. "And once I'm done with her, you know I'm coming for you, right?"

"Wouldn't have it any other way." Ellie kissed the air and winked. She lifted her refreshed glass to Alex. "Love you, babe."

"You too, bitch."

They exchanged smiles, clicked their drinks together, and toasted.

TWENTY-THREE.

Kelly's Bedroom, Benedict Estate
August 11th, 2:00 A.M.

From the bed in Kelly's dark room, every sound in the house was amplified. Kelly held the comforter over his head. He pressed his ears into his pillow. He closed his eyes so hard they hurt. It didn't matter; he couldn't block out the rolling sounds in the ground and the walls. He didn't know what the sound was. It couldn't have been footsteps, but his racing mind said with authority that it was the sound of people. His heart throbbed painfully, and his body muttered they were going to find him. Even the smallest sounds he heard were threats; they were looking for him. The rolling in the walls was a knife against the marble counter downstairs, sheers against the walls, sharpened car keys cutting into someone's skin and poking out their eyes. Maniacal laughter. That rolling sound was a muted scream. He heard a crash, metal locking, the sound of the dumbwaiter from earlier. Johnny must have locked it so he couldn't escape this time.

The bedroom curtains hung closed but did little to dampen the sound of falling rain. Something scratched against the window. Kelly hesitantly lowered the blanket and through the dark, the curtains swayed. He pulled the blanket back over his head and closed his eyes, certain that if he couldn't see anything, nothing could see him either. If he wished for it hard enough, he could disappear, become camouflaged in the same ways he used to hide in the garbage cans in the alleyways when someone came looking for trouble with a knife in their hand. Sometimes it wasn't a knife, sometimes it was a sharpened piece of pottery. A scar down the side of Kelly's right leg throbbed as he remembered a night before Agatha brought him to the estate.

Kelly kept closing his eyes all throughout the night, wishing all the monsters would disappear. He closed them tight enough black spots filled his eyelids. Now, he closed his eyes, hoping everything in the house might disappear. The storms would disappear. The shadows would disappear. At some point, he had hoped that he, too, would simply disappear. He closed his eyes and hoped that when he opened them, he would see Gavin opening the curtain and Anna standing by the bathroom with a fresh towel and the clothing he was expected to wear for the day. Now, he listened to the broken bedroom door squeak as the gusty hall pushed against it. He wished himself back to the box in Parvenu with rats nibbling his toes and the cold nibbling his ears. His heart pounded and he feared the footsteps he couldn't hear. When he closed his eyes, he felt his pulse against his eyelids and he worried that he couldn't see nor hear anyone coming at him. His mind repeated, 'you're going to die. You're going to die. You're going to die.' He thought of the garden. 'You're going to die.' He thought of Agatha. 'You're going to die.' He thought of how secure he felt when Gavin tucked the covers under him. 'You're going to die.' The words interrupted his every thought. They had been in every room with him since the moment Astra died. At first, it had only been a whisper. As Johnny hit him with the tennis racket, it had become a scream. Now it was a steady, smug hum he couldn't ignore.

Kelly reached out of his blanket and flicked a light on. In the darkness, he feared every moving shadow or the thin fingers from tree branches distorted by the curtains. With the lights on, he feared being found. He flicked the lights off again.

A yawn slipped out. His eyelids flickered shut and his head dropped back. Consciousness didn't want to stay, but every time his head dropped back, a mild panic brought him right back to an upright position, wide eyes trained on the door. The night was a blur of pain, blood, and Astra's writhing body. The thing in Johnny's crazed expression as the tennis racket swung through the air. He still felt the net smack against his legs, his back, his arms. Johnny's laughter echoed in his head, the distorted growl of a creature worse than a rat king hidden in the alleys.

Kelly wrapped the blanket around him and held it shut as if it were a tight, protective shield. The red numbers on the clock flashed at him, but since he couldn't read them, they were useless. In that moment, he thought how much he hated Agatha. She brought him into her home with the offer of a warm bed and food to eat, a place of safety behind the iron gates, and the lie that he would never want anything more in his life. She brought him to the estate knowing this would happen. She left him here without warning and sentenced him to death. There was nothing he could do about it now but wait for one of them to come in the door and finally finish him.

Knuckles tapped against the outside of the door. The broken hinges swung in slightly.

Kelly's eyes locked on. Through the dark and the small

crack into the hall, he tried to see who it was. The lights in the hallway were out. He didn't know when they were turned off, but he couldn't see a face. He loosened the covers and edged toward the bed further away from the door until he slid off. The blanket twisted round his legs. He flailed, failing to kick the blanket off and find his escape. Frantically, he kicked, he held onto the bed, and kicked and kicked and kicked until the blanket came off. Then, he crawled under the bed.

The door opened and quickly closed all with one, soft squeak. From beneath the bed, Kelly watched black pantlegs and glossy shoes come toward him. There was no dirt on them; there was no blood on them; they were not smudged; they were not creased; and they were not Gavin's. They were simply so pristine they shone in the mildest yard light that slipped through the cracks in the curtains.

"Kelly?" The feet stopped beside the bed. It was Mathias. He turned toward the vanity. His weight shifted; he adjusted his tie, then turned back toward the bed. The tangled blanket cascaded over the edge. Most of it piled on the floor and the hem tucked under the bed, straightened by Kelly's weight. Mathias smiled, but called again, "Kelly?" The bed creaked beneath Mathias's weight.

One at a time he lifted his feet onto his knees, pulled the strings on his shoes, and slipped them off his feet. He tossed them onto the floor separately and with abandonment. He was a man who rarely found difficulty in getting comfortable. Kelly remembered him stripping down to his underwear for Agatha while Kelly was still in the room. Agatha told him at the time that Mathias was only going to read for her, and Kelly should go find Gavin for entertainment. Kelly hadn't been given much of an option; he was pushed out of the room by Agatha, the door locked immediately behind him. Though, before he had walked away, he had heard Mathias say, "My dear Agatha, what are you doing with your head under the bed?"

Agatha responded with, "Oh, Beauregard, I'm looking for my dearest Poopsie. I can't find him."

And Mathias said, "Aggie, have you tried looking underneath your skirt?"

Kelly did not stand around to hear any more.

The bed creaked again as Mathias laid down on his back. His arms spread out to his sides. He took a deep breath and closed his eyes. Mathias, laying across Kelly's bed, had a picturesque ease about him. He turned into a magazine cover with his eyes closed and the amethyst sheet was his backdrop. "You probably don't realize it, but we are very much alike."

Goosebumps formed on Kelly's skin. He wanted to defiantly state they were nothing alike, but instead, he held his breath in fear that Mathias could hear his every little noise, every soft pant, every heartbeat.

"You and me…" Mathias exhaled the words. "I'm an orphan too and I understand… You have to learn to survive with nothing, with no one. Take what you can get or you die. Don't trust anyone… or you die. You learn early that there is no one in the world you can rely on. No one who will be there for you when you need it and anyone who has said they would be is a liar. It's funny. Most children don't suffer the responsibility of convincing strangers they're worthwhile. A good economic investment. It's a sick game, isn't it?" Mathias tugged his tie loose. It fell against the bed. He then slipped the top button of his shirt open. "None of the kids I grew up with are around anymore, the children I shared my room with—they were swallowed by the rat race." He paused. When he heard nothing, he continued, "it was supposed to be a house for children without homes, without parents, without families, but… there's always something wrong with these places." Mathias popped open the second button. A soft chuckle rolled out of his throat. "An orphanage might sound good at first. A roof, food, some kind of adult to pay for that stuff for you, and other kids as siblings so you shouldn't be bored, but it was…a shopping network of some kind and each one of us was a product to be sold." Mathias popped a third button. His gentle tan and shaved chest became further revealed. "We weren't friends. We weren't family.

"The girls were the worst; I won't bother with names, none of them mean anything now." Mathias paused. "That is—many of them died in those walls. The halls constantly stunk of unwashed children, sickness, and death. We had this one room in the house… We called it the Dead Room. When one of us would get sick, the healthy ones would be lined up against the wall and we'd watch our caretakers walk the sick child to the room, locking them inside until they died. Maybe it took a week before the house smelled like bleach, but it would smell like rot and sewage first. Knowing this fate, everyone was more desperate to be adopted, locking each other in rooms or closets or tricking each other out of the house when a couple was coming to peruse options. I ran away before I became ill enough my caretakers left me to die. What other options did I have?"

Kelly closed his eyes and wrestled to keep himself quiet. If Mathias was able to find a family, there must've been hope for Kelly too – but he wanted to ask. He needed to ask. His fingers traced along his darkened skin; the scars from rat bites, large gashes where glass broke skin. The ravenous stare of a squatter looked him over as if he could be eaten.

"It's funny for a child to knowingly look at those meant to take care of them and understand… you mean nothing to them, but a paycheck. Become too much work, and it's easier to lock you away and forget about you. I desperately wanted a family, but not like this. If I wanted a family, I understood I had to make one on my own. I had to choose and if I waited too long, someone else would choose a life for me." Mathias sighed. His eyes fluttered open and he stared at the flowery murals on the ceiling. Purple lilacs among gentle green leaves were such a difference compared to the desires painted on the ceiling of the ballroom. "It's not so bad once you learn the truth, but it wasn't something I wanted to know back then.

"The world is run by cynics and abusers, Kelly and it's a damn shame. I don't know if there's anything any of us can do. Fight it? How long you think people've been fighting these urges? This… human nature. The best thing any of us can do is take care of ourselves. God damned the future like he damned our childhoods." Mathias covered his eyes with his arm. "People like Gavin want you to play in games like this, get your hands dirty, make them feel better about themselves so they don't feel bad when they kill you. Anything to put a guilty look on your face." Mathias's hand slid to lay beside him on the bed. His eyes flickered open and he stared at his mirror reflection through the slats in the wooden footboard.

Mathias's laughter rumbled heartily in his chest, though it was still quiet, still soft. "Everyone knows what's at risk; we know the sacrifice here and we're always willing to make it. Trading innocence for power, our children for opulence; we all die, so who cares?" Mathias laid on his stomach and stretched his arms over the edge of the bed. He straightened his back then pulled his arms back to his sides.

"What's an orphanage?" There was a soft shuffle beneath the bed. Kelly shifted on his knees and hissed as he landed onto a bruise and a scrape from earlier in the night. The comforter caught on his leg. He didn't bother continuing his crawl out from under the bed.

Mathias smiled back. He folded his hands in his lap and maintained the look with Kelly for as long as he was allowed. "It's a place where children without parents were sent in droves to be taken care of, often by sterile, angry women who couldn't have children of their own. Then they would take out their infertility on us."

A lump formed in Kelly's throat. His heart raced and he leaned over the bed with both hands pressed into it. "What are we looking for?" Desperation, hope, and desire tainted his eyes as if Mathias was the man with every answer there was.

"I'm not sure, but I'll let you know if I find out." Mathias cupped Kelly's face. The boy flinched, stepping away from the bed. Mathias drew his hands back "You should lie down." He patted the bed. "You look exhausted."

"What happened to your family?" Kelly's voice became obstinate. He continued away from Mathias with arms crossed tightly over his chest.

"My father died in Viet Nam and my mother was hit by a car when she went out for cigarettes," Mathias straightened his posture. "What happened to your parents?" he asked.

Kelly looked past Mathias, to the door, but kept his glances brief hoping Mathias wouldn't catch them. "I don't know," he said. "I don't know anything about them."

"It must be easier to lose something you never knew than to have it and lose it later," Mathias said.

"I guess. Maybe." Kelly's fingers curled into his shirt. "But I still want... I still wish... I at least got the chance to hate them, to hate someone and wish they were dead because I was so mad."

"Think about it this way: if you were never in this house, if you never realized that it was even yours, you wouldn't have cared if Astra had received it. You wouldn't have cared whether I received it or Gavin or Johnny—"

"I would always care if Johnny got it," Kelly said.

Mathias smiled a toothy grin, "If you didn't know it was there, you wouldn't fight to keep it. Does that tell you anything?"

Kelly was quiet for a long moment. "Why shouldn't I feel entitled to parents? Everyone has them. Everyone. I deserve them too." His loose brown hair fell over his face, bobbing up and down every time he moved, bouncing against his cheeks.

"What makes you think you deserve them?"

"Why does anyone deserve parents? No one else has to justify having them. What makes me so special?"

"You may feel as entitled as you wish, but know that entitlement holds you back. You'll make less of yourself while you demand others give you whatever you want. When Astra was announced the inheritor, did I protest?"

"I just thought you were lazy," Kelly said.

"Unlike the others, I understand that Agatha owed me nothing. Nobody gives you what you want. You must take responsibility to make it happen." Mathias's eyes pierced through Kelly as if Mathias could see every one of his thoughts.

"What about a family?" Kelly said.

"Sure. You can make that happen."

Kelly smiled, tired and forced. A swallow caught in his throat. His lips and mouth became instantly dry the second the thought entered his mind. He became far more aware of how different he and Mathias were. Just believe and he could get whatever he wanted – that was magic. That was how a child would think. Kelly had put those ideas out of his head long ago. "You can have the house." Kelly stole a look at Mathias. The mess of curly brown hair made him look younger and vulnerable as it scattered across his face.

"Really?" Mathias tilted his head to the side. "You were so passionate about it earlier."

"You wanted it, didn't you?"

"Theoretically, that's why we're all here."

"Then you can have it. Didn't you say something about if you want it bad enough and believe, you can have it? Then here. Let me do that." Kelly glanced at Mathias then turned away. A snorting chuckle came through his lips; quickly, he covered his mouth. "I don't think I can handle all this."

Mathias quirked an eyebrow. "What does that mean?"

"I guess it means your magic works. If you can get the house you want, then maybe I can get the things I want too." His mind reeled with the possibilities of what it could be to no longer live in the Benedict Estate. His skin prickled at the thought of nights in the alleyways, the tingling sting of hungry rats nibbling the skin off his feet and legs, and the cold concrete pressed against his face at night while the humid air overheats his body. "I hate the dark," he said.

"I tell myself it's irrational to hate it—" Mathias started.

"But it's not," Kelly said. "You don't know what's out there. You don't know... You don't know..." He picked at his shirt. He scanned the floor to distract himself from his throbbing heart. The more he tried to ignore it, the louder it knocked on his ribs. He tangled his fingers in his shirt.

"Why are you so nervous?" Mathias shielded his amused smile.

"I'm not nervous," Kelly snapped.

Mathias stood up and rounded the bed. Alarmed, Kelly side stepped and backed toward the window. "Why are you so nervous?" Mathias repeated.

"You can't—" Kelly's voice cracked into silence. His mouth went dry and he worried any attempt at speech would come out broken and mousy. He cleared his throat, but it still felt clogged, so he cleared it again. The second time he couldn't stop the sound from being obvious. "I don't want to die." He was louder than he meant to be. "I don't want to die," he said slower.

Mathias continued toward him and every step closer, Kelly took a step back until he pressed into the wall. The rain rattling against the window behind him. A flash of lightning passed. His hair stuck to his wet cheek and his eyes watched Mathias with an odd sense of focus and stubbornness.

"The future is malleable, Kelly, but only by those who were willing to take the risk to craft it." He moved in closer. "There aren't many people who realized they have the ability to change everything and set the rules. Most simply accept the fate they are given.

"Think of it this way: would you rather be the artist or the canvas?" Mathias watched Kelly closely.

Kelly backed against the window and gripped his arms tight.

"You're not going to die," Mathias said. "Those who make the decisions stay alive."

Tears pooled beneath Kelly's eyes and ran down his cheeks. "What decisions am I making?" He clenched his jaw to stop his lips from quivering. He ran his sleeve over his eyes, sopping up the tears. Shame colored his ears pink and his eyes swelled red.

Kelly had nowhere else to go. This morning he could make a command or request and the servants would trip over themselves to keep him happy. Now, he couldn't have been more aware of the loss of control. Mathias could reach for his throat and strangle him. Kelly couldn't even fight back. He didn't have any energy left.

"What can I do?" Kelly said.

"Protect yourself. Stay here. Stay quiet. Stay out of the

way."

Kelly's dark eyes locked on Mathias.

"Once the sun peeks the horizon, the game is over. There are only a few hours left. There are only a few pieces left. One of them is me, and you know I'm on your side. Gavin, Anna, Ellie, Alex, and Angus? Stay away from them and you won't have to worry about this ever again."

Panic bubbled inside of Kelly. His face turned a darker shade of red and he breathed harder. "Gavin wouldn't do anything to me."

"Are you certain of that? After everything you've seen tonight, do you really believe that? Do you believe it enough to put your life on it?"

The curtain caught on Kelly's arm and malnourished lights from the yard slipped into the room. Light reflected off the gun beneath Mathias's blazer jacket. Sickness struck Kelly. He ran into the nearby bathroom. The tile felt cold against his bare feet. He clumsily pushed the door shut with a snap and a slam. The lock clicked. Mathias's footsteps reverberated on the other side of the door, coming closer, but not in a rush. There was no resistance, no rattling, no fighting against the door. Kelly pressed his ear to the door in expectation but heard nothing.

He paced the tight bathroom. Maybe he could put something against the door, something Mathias couldn't break through.

The bathroom was shrouded in darkness, given only the faintest light through the window by the shower. The dim yard lights reflected off the bathroom mirror and provided illumination well enough to see. Stacked on a shelf in the shower sat bottles of expensive shampoos, soaps, lotions, and bath salt. Rose, lilac, coconut, honey. Kelly was never able to read the bottles, but he could recognize the smells and each scent had a different colored bottle. An antique peach hairbrush sat on the counter beside the sink, clean of tangled hair. Gavin or Anna – whichever one did it – was always good about keeping his brush clean.

Kelly opened the cabinets beneath the sink. They were full of cleaning supplies, extra towels, extra bottles of shampoos and soaps. There was no room for him to hide unless he took everything out. His image reflected in the mirror. Shadows blurred his features, yet he could still see the enlarged shape of swelling cheeks and the red line down his busted lip. He leaned against the edge of the counter. He pressed his fingers to his puffy cheeks. His vision blurred. That wasn't him he was looking at. That wasn't what he looked like. He looked so sad, he looked so scared. His dirty face didn't belong among the polished marble.

"Kelly," Mathias said softly through the door.

Kelly clutched the counter. The whisper echoed around the bathroom and he closed his eyes. The monster would go away if he closed his eyes. The whisper continued to echo and he felt it go down his neck and pluck at his skin like mites biting him. "Don't come in here!" Kelly couldn't breathe. "Please – leave me alone!"

"What will you do in there, Kelly? Jump out the window? From the third floor? What happens if you break your legs on the lawn?"

Kelly climbed into the bathtub and stood beneath the window. It was taller than him, the bottom pane started at his shoulders and the top went well above his head. He reached up and groped around the frame until he felt the right lock against his fingers. He pinched the flat metal ends and twisted them free. He felt for the lock on the left and tried to do the same when he found it, but the left lock wouldn't move. The metal wing slipped out of his fingers every time he tried. Glancing over his shoulder, he peeked at the door.

Insignificant as it was, Kelly couldn't do it. He couldn't open the window. Others had always done it for him. Gavin did it. Anna did it. The small stream of Agatha's employees who Kelly never saw or knew the names of did it, but he couldn't. The heavy storm raged against the side of the house. The window shook against his fingers after a loud roar of thunder. Kelly listened for Mathias to jiggle the knob softly, toss his weight into the door, or try to get in some other way, but everything was quiet. Kelly tried twisting the window's lock again but failed to move it. The tips of his fingers indented with lines where the lock grips pressed in. He climbed out of the tub and stumbled into the sink. His nails slid over the counter; his diamond bracelet clicked. Something moved in the mirror over his shoulder.

Kelly pressed his back into the door and slid to the ground. He pulled his legs to his chest, and buried his face in his knees. He tried to make himself as small as he could. Rain threw itself against the window, the walls of the house, the roof, everything around him to the point he felt it on his skin even though it wasn't there. A quick flash illuminated the bathroom and seconds later, the loud rumble rocked the window in the frame. He closed his eyes tighter, pulled his legs closer, made himself smaller. He would disappear, he was sure of it. He could disappear if only he focused well enough. He covered his ears to deaden the rain. It didn't work. Nothing worked.

"Do yourself a favor, Kelly," Mathias's voice came through the door. His footsteps snuck under the crack in the door. "Stay in your room. The rest of us will work this out. Then, come morning, everything will be fine."

Kelly stood up and pressed his ear to the door. His hand held tightly to the knob, waiting to feel it jiggle in his hand, waiting for Mathias to laugh manically in a way Kelly had never heard before then to lecture him on how stupid he was. In the mirror, the lightning flashed and lit Kelly's pale skin. He looked like a ghost who had already lost everything. He waited a couple minutes before he dared open the door. Hands shaking, he stepped into the bedroom. His legs stuttered and fought him to move. The bedside lamp illuminated the room gently with amber and amethyst from the lampshade. His bedroom door leaned against the frame, crooked, broken, but closed.

Kelly's eye stayed on the door. He walked until his knees pressed into the side of the bed. He hissed; the bruises were tender, the cuts stung. His heart pounded. His lungs felt shallow; his breaths felt like he was suffocating. He climbed on the bed, again, his knees first until the pain forced him to sweep his legs out from under him. He traced the path to the door, looking for any sign that Mathias had been there. Bloody shoe prints, mud, or puddles of water. He idly groped the bed, secretly seeking Mathias's tie or a loose button that might've fallen off. He found nothing.

Kelly pulled the blankets back onto the bed. The sheets smelled of Mathias's cologne: a light scent of burning wood caressed by gentle honey. Kelly pulled the comforter over his head and laid back. He trained his attention on the door again. He waited to see if Mathias would come running in and shoot him with his gun. He waited to see if Angus came in with a butcher knife usually used for making dinner. He waited for even Gavin to come in and strangle him to death while he muttered, 'Is this comfortable enough for you?'

He reached out of the blanket and turned the bedside light off.

Knock, knock.

He ignored the sound.

Knock, knock, knock, knock.

The pounding continued. Kelly held his breath and shut his eyes harder. Isolated in the blankets, he realized no one stood at the door. It was his heart pounding. If he kept the door shut as Mathias had said, he would be protected. If he kept his eyes closed, he could hide from everything. His existence could cease… at least until everything got better.

TWENTY-FOUR.

Stylist Salon, Benedict Estate
August 11th, 2:45 A.M.

Through the years, Agatha had spared no time in trying out as many personal stylists as she had boyfriends. Each stylist brought their own brand of appeal that was contrary to their predecessor's. Some rotated through premade color palettes for each season, some lived through Cosmo and Marie Claire, some brought their own brand of style in the form of neon plastic that might've worked on the runways in New York, but had no business in a Louisiana bayou. Yet, one thing they all had in common was their boisterous, nonstop need for chatter and gossip. It was nearly compulsion.

One of Agatha's more recent stylists enjoyed stealing flowers from the garden and taping them to her studio walls. When the growing season was over, she would collect leaves and tape them to the walls instead, often mixing together the brown, red, and gold in a kaleidoscopic eye that created an informal wallpaper. When they became brittle and crumbled into flakes, they came down on their own and were swept up with Agatha's silver hair. She wasn't a good fit because she thought romance novels were tacky, tasteless, and only for poor, lonely women who had no desire left to offer.

She was replaced with another stylist, an older woman with hips so wide she couldn't fit into her own barber's seat and often had to turn sideways to go through doors. She was the reason Sir William was bolted to the plate in the hallway. Too often when she waddled her way through the hall, her hips juggled side to side in large, swaying movements. She knocked the suit down as if it was made of paper. She had chipped the marble more than once. She had almost accidentally released the chandelier while walking around the sofa. She specialized in makeup more so than hair and was obsessed with the aromatic appeal of her salon. The vanity, windowsills, and every other possible surface had at least one candle set upon them, though rarely ever was it just one. The scents were potent and even with only two candles lit, they carried into the hallway and overpowered the scent of everything else. She barely retained employment through the holiday season; while she was preparing Agatha for her annual Christmas dinner, she became overzealous about her favorite gingerbread candle. It slipped her mind that hairspray was flammable and while she was spraying Agatha's hair, she held the candle nearby, coaching Agatha to smell it, enjoy it, learn what Bertha loved about it so much; the flame licked Agatha's face and climbed into her hair. Later at dinner, Agatha told the story of her blackened hair over the blackened chicken with laughter but had Bertha removed from the mansion within a week. If not for the holiday season, she would have been removed immediately.

Alexandre was the most recent of Agatha's stylists, the first male stylist she'd employed since the seventies. Instead of leaves or candles, his studio smelled of pine, raspberry, and musky cologne unfortunately mixed with hairspray, mousse, and barbicide. He was by far the most glamorous stylist Agatha had ever hired, though they all had egos. Alex was a bit younger than those before him, a year or two under thirty with no large resume like the others, but he possessed the experience and manner Agatha fancied. If she had not perished, he and Agatha would likely have remained business partners for years to come.

The door to the salon was never locked, at least not to Anna. Anna twisted the knob, tucking the master key back under her uniform shirt, the chain hidden beneath her collar. The door didn't dare whisper when it shut behind her. From her first day, the house had always resisted whispering about her. Anna stroked the wall, flicking the light switch with the familiarity of a lover. The studio had two sets of lights: the dull fluorescents in the ceiling and a set of seven display lights to bring out the true colors in one's wardrobe. Anna turned on the fluorescents. A display of six white foam mannequin heads in the windowsill illuminated and deflected the light with immediate defiance. Some of the foam heads were dressed with hair extensions hooked to hairnets. Another wore a straight brown wig. A large wooden vanity sat in the center of the room, its edges curved while its legs and body thick, decorated with hand-carved Celtic symbols that appeared far more than a century old.

The salon chair, baby blue and chrome, didn't look like it belonged. A bib hung folded over the back of the chair and displayed a printer's rough interpretation of Van Gogh's *A Starry Night*, its palette much darker than the original. Atop the vanity were jars filled with clear, blue liquid and combs. Going down both sides of the vanity were three small drawers with gold knobs.

Anna crossed the room and stopped before the vanity. Her black hair was pulled back into a neat bun again and everything was in place except for a small patch of hair that slipped out around her ear. She wrapped it around her finger and tucked it back. When her hair was loose, it would fall below her waist, straight, flat, and smooth. She'd worn the same neat hairstyle for years.

With one hand at each side of the vanity, she clutched the first knob on the bottom. She pulled the drawers with a quick yank. Lipstick which looked like it hadn't been used in decades, dried out eyeliner, a curling iron. These were the reject drawers Alex never used.

She closed the drawers and moved to the center set then repeated the action. The center drawers contained a few small containers of premium hair gel, a pink bottle of hairspray, and a handful of loose combs, bobby pins, and other minor hair decorations. Twisted in some of the comb teeth were brown and grey hairs.

She closed the drawers and moved up to the third and highest row. The left opened without difficulty, but the right caught on something, clattered, and wouldn't open when she tugged again. She released the left drawer and tugged at the right with a little more focused care, harder this time. It rattled louder, but still refused to open. She surveyed the vanity counter for something with a strong, flat edge such as a nail file or a knife.

Stacked against the wall beside the vanity were clear, plastic storage bins. Visible through the clear bins were hair decorations in all colors, clips, ties, combs with flowers, and holiday-related streamers. Inside another set of storage bins were makeup pallets of varying themes, foundation pads, extra brushes, eyeliner, eyeshadow, rouge, and commonly used lipstick. She could dig through the drawers and look for something; Alex had tools in abundance, but she didn't want to disturb anything she didn't have to. Anna never left a room messier than it was when she entered and even now, it was not a palatable option. She decided one of the sterilized combs drowning in Barbicide would serve her purpose. She lifted the jar lid and fished out the comb closest to the top. Replacing the lid, she used her skirt to dry the comb off and wipe any liquid that had dripped onto the countertop. She held the comb like a surgeon's tool and gripped the knob with her left. She prodded the comb between the drawer and the vanity's lip, shaking the knob as she batted around the space. She twisted the comb around until it knocked against something. From there, she pressed the comb against the unseen object until resistance disappeared.

Anna placed the comb back into the jar before pulling the drawer open. Inside laid razor blades in tidy plastic boxes, pairs of scissors in plush cushioned boxes and a few loose hairpins. If she pulled the drawer out further, there was likely more behind the felt divider in the center.

"Thanks, hun. That drawer was a bitch and a half to open," Alex's came from behind her. "But did you really have to use one of my good combs?"

Without looking at him, Anna opened one of the scissor box's, muffling the 'snap' of plastic with her palm.

"What? Not even a meek, little 'hi'?" Alex pursed his lips and swung his hips to the side. "Too cool for that or is it more about me?"

The sharp blades shined down their edge, clean and well taken care of. It was with this type of display that one could tell how much someone cared about their tools. Anna could admire the care Alex took of his scissors, though there was suspicion that perhaps Alex didn't take such excellent care of his scissors, and replaced them constantly to keep up with their beautiful appearance.

"We're part of the same brotherhood, sister. Hairdressing and beautification and... maiding and butling."

His lips went crooked with the question of his own word choices. "You can talk to me." Alex leaned against the door frame. Though neither of them said anything. Each remained fixated on the other.

Anna watched Alex through his reflection in the mirror. Her face stoic.

Alex's lips puckered, then pulled up at one end. His shapely eyebrows, thickened with a brown eyebrow pencil, perked. Finally, he said: "I'd love to work on your hair. Like, I see the shine all the time. I know you take care of it; that's something I can always admire in a working girl. And it's long, straight, I bet it's heavy when it's not put up. Is it heavy, hun?"

Anna's lashes fanned over her dark brown eyes. She remained completely still; it was barely noticeable even when she breathed. She was not unaware of Alex's motives. After Gavin had left the conversation with Ellie, he had informed her of what was said and what to expect thereafter.

Anna and Gavin were both individuals who acted pre-emptively; they preferred to be in position to make change before something happened rather than be victim of momentum. It was always much easier to stop a boulder before it began its descent downhill. Waiting for disaster to strike always resulted in higher costs; often, the risk to wait costed life. They found a sense of urgency in everything they did and his focus on the task up front was always something she admired.

Here, duties were the clock of her life and always had been. She did not enjoy serving just anyone, but only those who she believed deserved it, and in those cases, serving gave her life purpose and drive. She decided when she was a young woman, that her most rewarding duties were fulfilling Gavin's every need without hesitation. Nothing made her feel more content than to accomplish his tasks before he asked or to feel his reliance on her when asked to do something; his confidence that she would get anything done and it would be done well was the highest honor. Never hearing the same request a second time was an added benefit.

"I could do you up a cute, little cut." Alex retrieved the scissors from his pocket and held them in the air, swinging them as if deciding which strand he would cut next. "A bob maybe."

"Thank you," Anna said, "but no."

"Oh my god! She *does* have a voice!" Alex said, covering an over-dramatic gasp with his hand. "For a second there I thought Gay might've ripped out your voice box, banned you from talking like some kind of religious freak, you know? Talk about silence of the woman – I'm much more into what you gotta say than some hyper controlling butler-boy. Still, I feel like I gotta insist. You came all the way here. Have you ever even had a haircut? Do you know what it's like to make your own decisions or has it always been daddy giving you orders? Sweetie – look, I get it. I've read those books too. You have Stockholm Syndrome. He's an asshole and you refuse to leave him. We can fix that mindset of yours though, first by giving you a haircut. That's how all girls find their identities again after a *really* bad relationship. Haven't you seen the movies? You're not *doomed*, just a little frumpy." Alex pushed himself from the door frame and walked into the room. "Now that I mention it, how long have you been wearing your hair the same way?" Alex pursed his lips, exaggerating thoughtfulness. "Doesn't it get kinda boring? *Drab*, the posh might say. You know what posh means, right?"

"I'm content with my appearance, thank you." Her voice was monotonous, distant, and impersonal.

A tickle ran down Alex's spine. Though she said nothing out of the ordinary, and rarely did she ever, the cold detachment in her voice was more than off-putting. "No joke?" Alex slipped his scissors back into his vest pocket and crossed the room to stand beside Anna. He placed his hands on the countertop beside hers and leaned forward, looking her in the eye rather than through the mirror. He reached an arm around her hips and pulled her closer. "You've got great bone structure: high cheeks, a sharp jaw, modest chin. You'd look great with something short. Think pixie cut. Long in front, short in back, straight as hell. Powerful, but feminine. It'd stay out of the way while you work, but you wouldn't look like such a fud." Alex snickered.

Anna remained still as Alex's fingers glided around her hips, pushed to turn her, then capture her jaw with his hand. He twisted her chin, angling her head in different ways as he made, "hm" sounds and injecting "I can see it" every now and then. Directing Anna was like posing a mannequin. The only resistance was minor and felt more like stiff joints than actual opposition to his direction. Her gaze stayed focused, looking forward, but she tracked Alex's movements in their reflection.

"I do not need a haircut, but if you are feeling antsy, you have a cowlick you may wish to quell," Anna said.

The smile faded from Alex's face and he released Anna. He re-angled his head, attempting to see the back, fear that she wasn't lying, but that he'd attended all the events tonight with a cowlick. If it were true, then he feared he'd become the thing he hated most: a self-important, delusional stylist who lack self-awareness, like the wannabes who wondered why they couldn't achieve greatness. Reaching around his head, he touched his crown, turned it again, and eyed himself from as many angles as possible. "Cowlicks are the bane of my existence. I friggin' swear to God." He withdrew a small comb from his pocket and ran it through his hair, starting from the back and pulling it forward, but after a few strokes, he knew it was pointless unless he put more product in.

Anna politely bowed before she began to step back. Her polished heels tapped against the hard floor.

Alex caught her dress waving behind his reflection. "I may have lied to you," Alex said, trading his comb for his scissors. He turned around. His steps were heavier than hers.

The space between them grew smaller, quickly, so she sped up her pace. She reached behind her for the doorknob.

Alex threw his scissors at her. They smacked into the door and, hitting the floor, they rattled.

Anna studied the scissors by her feet. The blades were dull and crooked, but she couldn't be sure that they weren't intended to appear that way. "If your scissors are dull, may I recommend sharpening them with leather," Anna said. "Also, you'll increase the life of your tools by only using them for their intended purpose." She twisted the doorknob and yanked it open.

Alex went running, but it slammed in his face, separating him from the maid. He grabbed the knob, half-expecting it to be blocked like his drawer, but when he tried it, the door wasn't locked.

The hall, however, was empty.

The sound of rain surrounded him. The hall's acoustics created a stampede-like sound from the rushing water, drowning out the possibility of footsteps. The house was rarely so noisy, but the house also took pleasure in muting Anna's movement. Doors that had been open before were still open and those that were closed were still closed. He'd heard rumors of secret passageways that not only connected to most of the rooms in the estate, but also connected to underground passages that led to the barn, shed, and goods cellar across the yard. False walls, removable floor tiles, and bookshelf doorways seemed to be very stylish additions to most estates. They must have been marked as accessories for landowners who feared robberies or employees who wanted to remain hidden from their employer.

Alex crept down the hall past the suit of armor. Beside Sir William hung a metal lamp, imitating a three-pronged candle. He reached for it, tugged it down, and waited.

Nothing happened.

Alex blew out his lips, smacking them together. Stepping away from Sir William, he surveyed the suit one more time. Johnny had hidden behind it before, maybe Anna stood behind it now.

The shadowy gap behind the armor was empty.

He returned to the salon door and closed it. He retrieved a pair of keys from his pocket and locked the door with mild hesitation. If there were secret passageways, then he could be playing right into what she wanted.

Alex slipped his glasses off, folded the temples, and tucked them into his pocket. He pinched the bridge of his nose and glanced back down the hall. His forehead wrinkled. He couldn't understand why Anna had chosen to come to the salon in the first place. Anna didn't make mistakes, and she didn't act on her own.

Alex made his way toward the staircase, his new mission was to warn Ellie, but he stopped upon hearing a hollow 'thud.'

A book hit the ground.

He cocked his head to the side.

Another one thudded.

Alex continued forward until he reached the library door.

A hollow spine snapped against the floor and bounced open.

The books he'd left on the coffee table were no longer there. The windows rattled in the sills, shaken by the harsh throw of rain. A draft slipped beneath the door and through the cracks in the shelves, creating a howl that whirled around and pushed the long, satin curtains. Some of them appeared more bloated or floating, while others waved back into their neutral position. Alex withdrew his scissors and approached the first set of curtains. His steps warned of his approach, but he didn't hesitate. He drew the curtains back and stabbed the empty space behind, then released them again. Each curtain swayed empty, quiet, and unaffected.

A tap, like a rolling marble, echoed through the walls. Alex released the curtain he held and climbed the stairs. He listened, watching over the guardrail.

The couch leg squeaked against the floor.

Another book smacked against the tile.

Heels tapped three times in a quick step but disappeared like a ghost.

A flash of lightning illuminated the room.

Alex clutched the guardrail at the top of the stairs and spun around on his toes. He traced the second-floor balcony, climbing each shelf to the ceiling and making a complete lap around the landing.

A book dropped from below.

On the coffee table that was empty before, a book now laid open. Alex hurried down the stairs, watching everything around the book as he approached. It was one of Agatha's old fairytale collections she'd brought home from Europe. The title of the story on the page read, "The Mouse, the Bird, and The Sausage." The left page depicted an ink drawing of a burning home and a bird drowning in a pool of water outside it.

Alex looked around himself. He slipped the scissors back into his pocket and picked up the book. The pages were dry and stiff, unused to touch. The dust in the pages caused him to sneeze. "Because of his carelessness, the scattered wood caught on fire, and the entire house was soon aflame," Alex read. The scowl on his face deepened. "Maybe it wasn't an accident. Ever think of that?" He tossed the book back onto the coffee table, purposefully reckless.

A stool on the upper landing fell over and clattered against the floor.

Alex cursed himself for becoming startled. He climbed the stairs, looking for the stool, but once he reached the second-floor landing, he saw everything was in its proper place.

There were no signs of her. No crumbled rugs, bloated curtains, flashes of skirt, or shadows scurrying beneath the furniture. The lightning revealed no hidden figures and he remained unaware of her actual presence in the library.

"You here, sweetie?" Alex's voice came back at him. If Anna was nearby, the library did well to hide her.

Alex left the library and entered the second-floor hallway, closing the door behind him. He crept forward, glancing into the rooms on either side of him and checking the doors that were closed. All of them were locked. Breaking into them would take too much time. He reached the ballroom balcony at the end of the hall. Down below, a pool of shattered glass sparkled across the floor, the remains of the chandelier. No bodies decorated the room, but a bloody trail divided the glass like a milled dirt path. Through the grand picture windows, Alex caught a glimpse of a long, slim shadow disappearing into the conservatory. The door clicked softly by the time Alex looked at it.

He cursed himself for being on the second floor. He bolted for the grand staircase, taking the steps two or three at a time, and ran into the ballroom below. Eyes fixed on the conservatory door, he raced across the room. His shoes slipped on the glass, but he didn't slow down. Like a toddler learning to walk, he swung his arms for balance.

The conservatory lights were off when he entered. The bare easel against the window looked like a crossed skeleton, the sculpted head behind the furniture gave the appearance of a man sitting in the dark, head bowed and attention focused. Alex hit the light switch to drive out the shadows. He wove around the furniture, waiting for Anna to reveal herself.

He drew his scissors, clutching them hard. The corner of his eye twitched. He rubbed it with his free hand.

The porch door hung open. The smell of moisture and dirt rushed him. "Do you think I'm stupid?" he said, throwing his hips to the side. He combed his bangs back with his fingers. "You're not really out there. You just want to lock me out there to drown." He walked up to the door and leaned out the frame. The yard had transformed into a swamp, reeking of fetid weeds, fungus, and stagnant water.

The yard lights were on, but through the rain, they were dark and distorted. Tall, thin fixtures with bulbous light heads became ghostly shadows. The faint illumination twisted the shapes of the barn, shed, and neighboring silos.

Alex dropped his weight to the opposite side and hissed. He glanced behind himself, back toward the ballroom. "This is dumb," he muttered. "She didn't go outside! There's no friggin' way!"

The light by the barn shifted creating a long shadow across the yard.

"No!" he shrieked. The humid air made his hair go frizzy and he hadn't even stepped outside yet. He growled, stepping outside onto the patio. "This is a trap. This is a trap. I know this is a trap, and you are totally gonna pay for making me do this." He paused then went back into the conservatory. He grabbed an arm of the couch and pulled it from the center sitting area to hold the door open. He piled on books, a table, the bust statue, everything that he could to make the couch as heavy as possible. If she was still in here, he wouldn't make closing the door easy.

With the door propped open, he went back outside. The marble steps were impossible to walk on. His smooth leather soles couldn't grip anything through the water. Each step, his feet threatened to come out from under him before he fell. Rather than stand back up, Alex stayed seated on the ground and slid himself across the wet surface until he reached the end of the porch. "Yeah, yeah. I bet you're laughin' bitch, but you won't be," he grumbled.

The yard sunk under his weight. Mud crept into his shoes and held onto him when he picked up his feet. The rain darkened his soft pink shirt and weighted his clothing.

The yard lights went out, and darkness consumed the yard. The rain muted any brightness escaping from the house. Alex snarled. "Do you think you're funny, bitch? Please!"

The light beside him flickered on, then off. The light ahead of him then flickered on.

"How…" He muttered. "You can't be doing that from out here," he said, walking up to the light. When he reached the light that was turned on, it turned off, and another yard light ahead of him flickered on. "Are you serious right now? No. I'm not falling for this!" He turned back toward the house; the conservatory door was shut.

Nodding his head, Alex cursed again. "Yeah, yeah," he grunted. "I bet he's around here somewhere too, isn't he?" The shed doors slam and rattle behind him. He whipped around to look.

Further down the yard, a dim light flickered through the

four-paned windows on the side of the barn. The barn doors hung open. The key stuck out of the bottom of the padlock. Alex tramped through the mud for a closer look. He unhooked the lock and stuck the arm through one of his belt loops. Slipping through the gap, he pulled the doors closed behind him and searched for a stool, a plank of wood—anything he could use to obstruct the path outside. Against the wall beside the door were a couple of small shelves packed with animal feed, brushes, sheets, and blankets. An old tractor pressed against the back wall. Glimpses of its green body and yellow trim peeked out beneath a bright blue tarp.

He looked around the interior side of the door, searching for a latch he could hook the lock to. He wasn't even sure if builders put locks on the inside of barns or what the purpose of that would have been. He saw no locks around the edges or down the center of the door, though there were two large handles that looped back into the wooden door. Alex scanned the shelves for anything he could use to tie the doors together; his goal was no longer to lock the door but to slow down an attempt to escape. He found a knot of Bungie cords, twisted together and dry. He dug his fingers into the knots, struggling to pull them loose. His fingernails became dirty and started to chip, but he was able to loosen the pair of cords he needed. He took them back to the door and wrapped them around the two handles as many times as he could until the soft rope became tense and rebellious.

Even with the doors closed, the smell of swamp devoured the smell of dust and gasoline.

Dry straw crackled beneath his soggy shoes. He stood in the center of the barn, glancing all around him at everything he could see for the first time. Alex had never been in the barn before. Few who worked in the house had. The barn was built by the second owner of the Benedict Estate. After the incredible success of the crop growth, he looked for ways to expand the offerings of the plantation. Animals seemed like the next logical step. The barn was inhabited sporadically for the first five years. Animals brought to the estate in perfect health turned sick and weak. They stopped eating, and most of them died within six months of arrival. In the worst cases, they attacked the farmhands who tried to nurse them back to health. Oddly, when animals were removed from the property for veterinary care, they resumed eating and grew strong and healthy. Return to the Benedict property ushered the sickness back in. The cause of the illness remained unknown and the barn became an unused relic of failure.

"You in here, hun?" Alex said, catching his own shadow creeping behind him. There were ladders on either side of the barn, nailed against the wall outside of the animal stalls. His amber eyes followed the ladders up to a platform above. It circled three-fourths of the way around the interior of the building, absent of rails, and was held up by a few sets of thick, wooden beams. The dim hanging lights flickered. He glanced into each empty stall he passed. Each contained a rusted feeding trough and dry, brittle hay. An old blue and white checkered blanket occupied one while another hid a weed whacker beneath a large pile of hay. In another empty stall was an ax. Alex opened the stall, slipped in, and picked it up.

The blade appeared dull, but not unusable. He hefted the ax, holding the blade in one hand and the handle in the other. It was heavier than he thought it'd be, sturdy. Stepping out of the stall, he took a two-handed swing through the air as if it were a baseball bat. "Sometimes I wish I'd been an athlete." He took another swing. The momentum of the head caught him off-guard. He stumbled forward. "The muscles, cute little uniforms, locker room mischief… Seems like paradise. But ya know, I'm not competitive enough." He swung again, this time, testing the way it moved through the air. His voice reverberated off the ceiling loft. The rain against the roof muted the echoes in the cavernous space and he realized that he couldn't read the vibrations as well as he'd hoped.

He rested the ax's head against his shoulder and ran a hand through his wet hair, pushing it back. His steps became off-balance and goofy as he approached one of the ladders swinging his hips in an exaggerated and playful manner. Standing before it, he looked up. "You should come down. Like, there's nothing stopping me from coming up there. It'll be easier for both of us if you surrender. You played the game—not well—but you played, and now it's time to say 'sorry' and bow out like your dad—but how about with like, a little bit more grace?"

Alex stared up the ladder. His fingers curled and uncurled around the wooden handle. There were no guardrails, he surmised that there couldn't be much up there besides hay, seeds, maybe a little shovel or something. He needed to start the fire to get her to run. He smacked the head of the ax into his palm, then it struck him: if he struck the wood columns, it might cause the barn to collapse, forcing the maid to come out of hiding or die beneath the structure.

Alex approached the nearest column; it was thick, seemed sturdy, but the ax's blade seemed sharp enough. On either side of the barn were four thick, wooden columns, each lined up in the center of the platform above. He braced himself beside the first column, farthest from the barn's entrance. He took a wide stance, drew back the ax, and crashed it into the wood with a huff. The blade bounced off the wood. Alex stumbled backward. "Oh my god," he breathed. "This can't be impossible." He drew the ax back and swung it into the post again. This time, the blade dug into the wood a little bit. Pulling it out wasn't difficult and he swung it into the pillar again. It dug deeper into the wood. When he went to pull it out, it was stuck, strangled within the swollen wood. He moved around the post, trying to pull the ax from different angles, but it resisted. He braced himself, a foot against the column, and wiggled the ax until it came loose. He stumbled back from the sudden release but replaced himself. Another swing, and the blade lodged deeper into the wood. He released the ax's grip to dab at the sweat on his forehead. He took the grip, grunting while he wigged the ax loose. He fell into a rhythm, striking the column again and again, digging a fracture into it deeper every time steel met wood. He'd lost count when the wood finally snapped, broken and uneven.

The upper ledge growled softly but didn't shift.

Alex let the ax head's weight pull it to the ground. He huffed, out a breath, and wiped his humid face. His chest ached; he never thought about asthma before, but now he couldn't get the thought out of his head. "I'm going to die, and it's not because anyone stabbed me." He wiped the growing sweat from his brow. "It's going to be this friggin' barn."

There were seven more columns to go, three on the side he was on and four on the other. He wasn't sure he had the strength or stamina to cut through them all. "I'm not giving up!" he growled. Alex moved to the next beam, cursing under his breath. His back hurt. The hunching over wasn't helping him. Blisters formed on his normally smooth hands. They stung as he gripped the ax and took a swing at the next column. He braced himself for impact. Taking deep breaths, he tried to smile. His expression twisted into a grimace when he pulled the ax free. He swung again. The ax felt heavier. Wood swelled around the blade after every swing, making it harder to recover and sapping him of even more energy. It took longer than he expected, which made successfully severing the column that much more satisfying.

He moved to the next support column. "Oh my god. How do people do this all day?" he growled to himself. His arms shook with fatigue and rage. His head spun. He should have fallen to the ground. His vision was red, focused. The ax cut into the next column, this time digging deeper, faster, stronger. The wood cracked. The platform tipped, shifting after the loss of its third support, but it didn't fall. Rapid, soft footsteps clicked on the upper landing, moving away from him and closer to one of the remaining columns.

Alex's lips pulled up to smile, but instead it became crooked, turning into a strained sneer. His nostrils flared. "Just try, bitch! You won't stop me if I have to dismantle the whole friggin' barn!" He took place at the fourth column beam, but this time it was a little different: he knew exactly where she was. He swung the ax, and the blade shallowly penetrated the wood. His arms were too weak. "Fuuuug!!" he whined. Overhead wood creaked beneath a moving weight. He listened for its retreat, but the sound grew louder and closer to the ledge above him. Alex rested the head of the ax against the ground. Huffing, he looked up. Anna stood at the edge, a large red container in her hands. "You ready," huff, "to give up?" he looked up at her.

Liquid poured over Alex, burning his eyes, lips, and nostrils. The metal ax head fell against the cement, clanging, rattling. He stumbled back, wiping his eyes to dry them.

The potent smell of gasoline engulfed Alex. His throat and tongue burned from the small amount that had slipped into his mouth. He wiped his hands on the back of his pants, wiped his eyes, and forced them open through the burning. He hadn't realized how far he'd backed away from the platform. Anna's figure towered above, alien and haunting.

He wiped his eyes again, looking for clarity through the blue. A small flame grew in her hand; she clutched Bertrand's lighter.

"You'll burn the barn down!" Gasoline dripped from his hair. He wiped his eyes again, the blurred vision returning. "You won't have time to get out. The door is locked! You'll die too, bitch!" His voice ricocheted off the high ceiling. He backed away closer to the door, tripping over his own feet, tools, bits of clumped hay.

Anna dropped the lighter into the puddle of gasoline below, the flame open and exposed. Excited flames swallowed the petrol as fast as it could. It followed Alex's wet footsteps, consuming everything in its path before consuming Alex. He fell to the ground screaming. The screams continued without pause until Alex had no voice left at all. From his body, the fire expanded to the hay, devouring everything.

Anna couldn't see Bertrand's lighter anymore. She couldn't see the ground anymore. She ran to the nearest window. Clenching the steel gas can with both hands, she smashed the glass window. Sweat beaded her forehead. She set the empty gas can by the window.

The muggy swamp air was a relief for her scorched skin. Anna kicked off her short heels and mounted the broken window. Jagged glass tore holes in her dirty, black stockings. The stalls, scattered straw, and shelves became nourishment that encouraged the flame and barricaded the exit. It spread through the stalls, climbed the support columns, and exploded upon finding the gasoline in the tractor.

The fire's heat gripped the barn and enveloped it quickly; the second story collapsed and the fire threatened the roof. Crackling flames whistled, joining in the drumline of the rain overhead.

TWENTY-FIVE.

Ballroom, Benedict Estate
August 11th, 3:54 A.M.

Tongues of fire lapped at the barn. They reached through shattered windows, blackened wood, and devoured the strongest and weakest planks in the same breath. The roof fell in little by little until it gave out. Freed, the hungry fires reached for the sky. A nearby light caught a lick and turned into a spear of fire. The flooded yard rushed toward the building in an attempt to douse the fire into incompetence.

Ellie laid across the ballroom couch, watching the barn transform into ash. Her head rested upon a plush throw-pillow. Her arms folded under it to keep warm. The low-lit fireplace gave a warm scent of burning wood to the room. Ellie slid her legs off the couch and sat up. Pulling her hair over her left shoulder, she brushed it with her fingers.

The fire, against the rabid rain, sunk back into the black remnants of the barn in resignation. She twisted her hair in her fingers, coyly wrapping it around her digits and tugging on it. She closed her eyes to block out the image, but it didn't seem to work well enough. "Could you please close the curtain, darling?" she said, but nothing happened.

"Alex?" Clearing her throat, she said it again, softer, but more demanding. Again, nothing happened. She opened her eyes and glanced around. The crackling wood and dim fire reminded her that she was alone. She closed the curtains herself. Next, she went to the fireplace and turned off the propane knob with the edge of her shoe.

The contained fire rapidly died.

"You're beautiful," Mathias said, entering from the grand staircase. "Call me amazed that you're still the picture of purity this late into the night."

"Agony is alluring, isn't it?" Ellie loosened the second set of curtains and dropped them over the window, shutting the yard out completely. She turned back to Mathias, crossing her arms.

Mathias hung his blazer over the back of a chair and crossed the room to meet her. He took her right hand and guided her back toward the couch.

"The house has been quiet before, but this sort of silence is different," Ellie said. She sat down and slipped one leg over the other.

Mathias broomed nearby glass shards with his foot, creating a path to the gramophone. "Do you think that's why Agatha always had music playing?" Most of the rooms in the estate had some type of music device in them, whether a gramophone, CD player, or clock radio. The rooms Agatha spent most of her time in often had a multi-disc stereo playing on repeat or records the staff replaced on a schedule even if she wasn't in the room.

The gramophone's brass pavilion was bright and polished; Mathias's face reflected in the uneven metal. Its curves thinned out his face and made him look sickly rather than handsome. He fingered through the records stacked on the shelf beside the gramophone table as if he was analyzing precious gems. He drew out a cardboard sleeve, slid the vinyl into his hand. He placed the record on the turntable, calculating and careful. Leaning down to level it, he wound the crank and placed the needle. The record cracked before a low melody began to fill the room.

"Gran loved Mozart," Ellie said.

Mathias rolled his head, loosening his neck. His eyes fluttered shut and a deep breath sunk into his chest. "It's part of an old Roman-Catholic hymn. *Dies irea.*"

"I've never been too religious," Ellie said.

"I can't imagine you were." Mathias closed his eyes to listen to the choir, the soft, but growing intensity in the verse. "Typically recited at funeral mass—"

"How appropriate."

"It describes the Day of Judgment, the final call to the throne of God, where either your soul is damned or delivered."

"What do you think my judgment would be? Have I been a good girl, Matty?" Ellie leaned back, pressing her head into the arm of the couch. The voices, the growing chants, were haunting, hypnotizing, and beautiful. They worked their way under her skin and relaxed her. Ellie crossed her delicate feet at the ankle. Her pale toes pointed up. "I've tried really, really hard. No blood on these hands." Ellie showed Mathias her palms.

"There are recordings of the original hymn melody. You should listen to them sometime." Mathias sauntered back toward the couch. His foot brushed against glass shards left behind by the shattered chandelier. It tapped against the marble, other shards of glass, and furniture legs. His steps became softer than the chorus, which grew more insistent now. He lifted Ellie's feet and sat down.

She smiled and looked away, covering her eyes with her forearm. She uncrossed her legs and pressed them flat. "You didn't answer me. What do you think my judgment would be? Have I been a good girl? Do I deserve the kingdom?" Her right foot moved closer to his lap and pulled back, petting his thigh.

Mathias hummed, but didn't answer. He stroked her bare feet, moving from her ankle to her knee. The lining of her dress tickled his knuckles. He pushed it aside and his hand went up her thigh. He tapped his foot in rhythm with the chorus. His knees drifted apart. Ellie's toes reached for his farther leg. Her heel pressed into his thigh, then drew back. She pressed her knees together, creating a pyramid of fabric that was too short and flashed her black panties.

"You're teasing me, Matt," heat influenced Ellie's voice.

"You're teasing me, Elle." Mathias's lips curved at the edges. His voice was silk, soft enough to soothe, but not loud enough to be heard.

Ellie ran her hands up her thighs, she pulled up her skirt, but stopped short of exposing anything indecent. She stroked herself, pressed her dress between her legs. Over her legs, she sought out the desire in his eyes, but they were closed.

Mathias's head pressed into the back of the couch. His breathing was even, he looked like he was counting and his foot continued to mimic the music.

Ellie turned her head away, closed her eyes, and continued the motion up and down her thighs. She uttered a soft moan. Mathias had been different from Agatha's other boyfriends; he hadn't taken her to bed as quickly as the others. He courted her while courting her mother and there was something charming about it. When he came from the city, he brought two sets of gifts. She would see them both; he never hid his sincerity from her. Yet, he was so comfortable with Agatha, it left questions about how many older women he had dated before. "Why are you so far away?" Her toes curled into his thigh.

"I'm right here." Mathias looked at her.

His fingers glided along her bare leg. "That's not what your face says." She withdrew her legs and sat up. Her back pressed into the armrest. "I've been waiting all night for us to have a moment alone and all you can do is stare at the ceiling and tap your foot." She ran slim, pale fingers through her hair, ruffling the curls caught in her dress straps. She was delicate about her gestures, every time she touched her face, her hair, her skin, it was like she was touching glass.

"Perhaps I've been a bit distracted. I'm sorry if you've felt neglected." Mathias removed his tie and set it on the nearby end table. Then he unbuttoned his shirt until it fell open. His fingers glided along his belt. A quick, decisive pull and he unhooked the buckle.

"Don't do all the work for me." Ellie put her hand over his. "I'm not that kind of girl."

Mathias chuckled. "Since when?"

He lowered his hands and allowed Ellie to take over. As she pulled at his belt, he leaned in and caught her lips with his teeth. Her lips puckered, reddened, and stung.

Ellie grabbed Mathias's waistband and urged him closer. His knee pressed into the couch, catching folds of her skirt. His other foot pressed into the floor for balance as he climbed over her. His hands were sensual invaders, cupping her breasts and traversing her thighs.

Ellie released his waistband and unzipped his pants. With a delicate hand to his chest, she pushed him back gently. Mathias's knee pinned her skirt to the couch. She pulled her skirt loose and tossed the excess fabric out of the way. She spread her legs for him. Continuing to push him back, she kicked off her shoes. Now he laid on the couch, and she straddled his lap. She lowered her hips against his, trailing kisses along his neck. Morning stubble had begun to grow, scratching her bruised lip. She reached into his shirt, hands glided across his skin. Their lips pressed together and again she felt the sting of being devoured.

"Where's your gun?" She panted, her heart racing, her face hot. Her hand slid back around his waistband again.

"Don't worry about it." A hand curled into her hair and guided her lips back to his.

"I don't want it to accidentally go off." She slid her hands up his sides, past his chest, and over his collarbone. She tickled his neck, digging her nails into the backside of his head, and massaging his scalp.

"It won't be a problem." Mathias yanked Ellie back by her hair. He pushed her from his lap and climbed on top of her. Her spine cracked against the armrest. Mathias looped his fingers into her black panties and pulled them down with a strong tug and nestled himself between her legs. He tossed her skirt out of the way, freed himself, and prepared to take her. His eyes were distant and his hands worked like machines as they took hers and pinned them down. Shifting couch legs screeched, blending into the empowered gramophone music. Mathias gagged Ellie with his mouth. He was powerful and he made sure she knew it.

Ellie moaned, delicate and broken. The rocking grew harder. One thrust turned into two; the sharp edge of a knife punctured her stomach. Her agony filled Mathias's mouth. She flailed, trying to push him off, but she couldn't break free. He thrust himself into her again and the knife followed. Their lips broke apart, gasping. The taste of blood tainted his lips. He licked them and thrust into her again and again until he didn't need to anymore. The knife went into the hilt and this time, when he pulled himself out, he left it in her. Mathias waited until he no longer felt her resistance then he let her go. The couch was dyed with her blood and his white cotton shirt, stained.

He stood up, kicked her shoes beneath the furniture and

stepped away. Glass clicked against itself hitting his feet, her shoes, shifting against the floor. He straightened his belt, buttoned his shirt, and tucked it back in. He retrieved his blazer and gun from the nearby chair and slipped them on together.

Mathias approached the mirror beside the bookcase. He ran his fingers through his hair, using them as a comb to fix the mess. He surveyed himself; something was off.

His tie coiled on the floor, fallen from the end table beside the couch. He picked it up and strung it back around his neck. Watching himself in the mirror, he retied it with expert fingers. He straightened his blazer, pulling at the cuffs, then buttoned down the front. His shirt's dark stains were hidden. When he flexed his arm, he noticed the blazer and exposed blood he'd covered up. Nothing could be done about it now; he didn't want to ruin any more clothing.

Mathias looked at Ellie with scrutiny. Her legs remained splayed where he had once been, her dress hiked up around her waist. Her face was a beautiful mess; makeup smeared around her lips and eyeliner streaking down her cheeks where fear and pain had carried it. Red streaks lit her neck like track marks. He took the knife from her stomach and wiped it on the excess of skirt piled in her lap. He examined the blade before slipping it into his jacket breast pocket. The record player crackled, dead air between tracks, then a new song started. Mathias went to the picture window and drew a curtain back. The rain was nothing more than a soft drizzle in the dark. The barn looked like coal, the flames only embers that were now almost gone.

Over his shoulder, Gavin's fatigued expression reflected in the dark window. He stood between a pair of balcony pillars, arms hanging at his sides. The scattered chandelier spread beneath his feet when he first entered.

"Annoying, isn't it?" Mathias said, releasing the curtain.

"Someone will get around to cleaning eventually." Gavin took a heavier step, grinding the glass into the floor to create a small, sharp sound. He spotted Ellie's long red hair dangling over the couch shoulder like a waterfall. He approached; the level of dismay her body displayed was shocking, but not unexpected. Bertrand, on more than one occasion, had spoken of *the worst night of his life*. Gavin had some level of expectation of what would happen after the will reading commenced. It was difficult to disturb him and even looking at Ellie's bloody, disparaged body didn't disturb him. Another mess to clean up and another relationship he would not have to think about in the future.

Her appearance was that of a used doll; elegance drained by a rough playmate. Gavin came to her, lifted her legs onto the couch, and brought her knees together. He took her skirt, heavy with blood, and fanned it over her body like fresh linen over a bed. He made her modest.

"Thank you," Mathias turned from the window.

Both were still. The distance between them felt farther than it was. "I haven't known you for very long, but you seem like a diligent man."

"It's my job."

"Often that's not enough for people, so thank you."

The grandfather clock demanded attention. The seconds it counted reverberated around the room, bouncing off the ceiling and echoing down the hall, interrupting the soft orchestra. A couple of cracks and the room fell into silence again. Air growled beneath door cracks and a cool breeze slipped through the wide ballroom.

"Everyone is a tool for someone else and they're only kept around as long as they're useful. The best thing one can do for themselves is to learn as many skills as possible so when one need is satisfied, there's something else to offer." Mathias moved away from the window and now circled outside the furniture, kicking glass.

Gavin mirrored Mathias, walking along in the opposite direction. He held his body tall and rigid. His lips swollen. Dried cuts striped his jaw and the back of his neck from when he had been pressed into the shattered glass.

"We need more people like you. Not intellectuals, but people who act on feelings and instinct and obey." Matthias's fingers glided over the back of the couch. He watched the leather pass under his fingers. "There's a look on your face, just below the surface. You do a good job hiding it. The average will never know why they don't trust your good manners and hospitality, but it's all in the eyes. There's nothing there. It's frightening, eerie, and repulsive. Why is that?" Mathias stepped behind an armchair then stopped, placing both hands on the back of it. He leaned forward, scrutinizing Gavin's appearance. The tucked in edges of his shirt disgusting, clinging to his lower abdomen.

Mathias thought his words would have garnered a little something more from Gavin. At least he was hoping there'd be some sort of response, but instead, his expression didn't change, his face didn't change, and he didn't say anything. Gavin didn't appear judgmental or threatened, but rather he lacked any element of interest.

Mathias shook his head, laughing. He ran his fingers through his hair, brushing his bangs back into a wave. He leaned his elbows on the back of the chair and laced his fingers. "And Kelly… is something else. Teenagers in the city are so cynical and rebellious. The best thing Agatha ever did was shield him from the poison of the real world. If you're not careful in the way you raise kids, the information you give them, and what you teach them, they might develop a sense of compassion and charity." He laughed, sliding his elbows from the chair and straightening out. "There's only one way to make sure that doesn't happen."

His feet seemed to glide across the marble as he stalked Gavin and entered the ring of furniture. The glass shards made no sound.

Mathias reached under his blazer. Light reflected off the grip of the gun. Gavin ran across the room, through the glass shards, and into Mathias. The gun went off. A bullet ricocheted off the piano. The two fell to the ground. The gun rolled across the floor, the knife didn't get as much distance. Mathias grabbed the knife and stabbed Gavin in the shoulder, twisting it between tendon and bone.

Gavin growled, and clawed at Mathias. Mathias shoved Gavin off him, pulled the knife free, and stepped back.

Again, Gavin growled as the blade unsheathed from his skin. His head became heavy and his vision turned black and spotty. He grabbed the edge of the piano for balance. A couple deep breaths and the dizziness subsided, but his weight grew and the injured shoulder dropped to one side. A mild attempt to move it sent stabbing pain through his shoulder. The gun laid on the ground beside one of the lounging chairs. Mathias's eyes met his own and they both looked at the gun again. Gavin never saw himself as weak; he worked to maintain a high level of accomplishment every day. Part of it was in revolt to who his father was and his utter rejection to follow the bastard's lead. He saw the similarities that already existed between them, things he couldn't rid himself of, so he focused his energies on everything that his father was not and tried to become that instead. In some cases, he had succeeded. He was not an alcoholic at the very least.

Butlering was indeed a service, a foundation that allowed many successful people. The lack of an appropriate support system was the reason why so many failed to accomplish their goals. As a butler, he had the ability to manipulate outcome. He was trusted for his dependability and knowledge; two things he never took for granted.

The new weight of his body filled him with shame; he wasn't as efficient, and he knew it. The bludgeoning by Johnny then the stab by Mathias felt like failures. His inability to stand straight filled him with humiliation that boiled into anger.

Mathias sauntered closer. He pushed his hair out of his face. It stuck back with sweat. He held the knife like a movie star held a pen for signatures. "You think you can beat me to it?"

Gavin stumbled, his vision blacking out and making it hard to see the room around him. "You want to try?" Gavin darted for the gun, Mathias lunged at him the second time.

The knife dug into his chest, avoiding anything vital with a precision that couldn't have been luck. The piano shrugged Gavin's hand off and the floor came out beneath him. His hands were shaking as he gripped the knife's handle. Buried between muscle and bone, he couldn't contain his voice as he pulled it loose. He thrust his hand against the hole, using his shirt to slow the bleeding. He looked to the conservatory. His head swayed, weak in the neck. His hearing went in and out. A high pitch beep deafened him to everything. He clutched the knife tighter.

Broken glass crackled somewhere near. Mathias squatted a few steps away, a cunning smile played on his face, teeth bright and blameless.

Gavin swung the knife; from their current distance, it was nothing but a warning. His vision was coming back, his heart raced, but it wasn't fear. He sat up.

"There's nothing you can do, Gavin," Mathias said. "You're going to bleed out. You're going to die."

A burst of adrenaline pushed Gavin from the floor. He didn't feel the glass against his palm. He couldn't feel the blood dripping down his chest and tainting his shirt. He couldn't feel the lightheadedness or the heat and pain screaming from his shoulder. He shoved Mathias to gain an advantage. Mathias shoved his fingers against the cut in Gavin's arm. Gavin groaned out loud, unable to hold his voice back. His back arched and his free hand desperately reached out. Fingers curled into the floor, grabbing a handful of broken glass shards. Before he could throw them in Mathias's face, Mathias pinned his arm down.

"You took too long, Gavin. You've lost, but I'll take good care of Kelly. In a couple years, you won't recognize him." He twisted two of his fingers to tear into Gavin's shoulder. His fingers slipped in the skin and tore his wound open further. "How would you like to go? You can at least pick that, though you probably know what I'd pick." He withdrew his fingers and punched Gavin's wound.

"Stop!" Kelly's voice echoed from the staircase. Kelly ran to the bottom. He stopped underneath the archway of the ballroom's entrance but didn't dare enter in his bare feet. The smell hit him immediately. Heavy, metallic stink ate away at soft fabrics and mixed with a strong scent of burning wood. In a panic, he looked toward the fireplace, prepared to see another body, a hand flick upward at the tickle of fire, but there was no such image there. Kelly held his nose. A crimson shadow met Ellie's foot on the floor, a bloody trail mixed with glass led away from her. Kelly swallowed vomit. Revulsion returned his focus to Gavin and Mathias. Tears pooled in his eyes. He blinked to keep them away, but failed. He wanted space between them; between all of them. No matter how many times he closed his eyes, none of it would go away, none of it would stop — everything had become so out of control. His home was nothing more than a caricature of what it used to be.

"Go back to bed, Kelly. Everything will be fine in the morning," Mathias said. He kept his weight pinning Gavin's arms against the floor. "I told you everything would be alright. Don't make me a liar."

Kelly's eyes went from Mathias's gentle smile to the blood staining through Gavin's white shirt, black vest, pooling on the floor beneath his arm. "No," his voice shook. He paused and swallowed hard. "You go to bed. Get off of Gavin and go to bed. Everyone needs to go to bed, now!"

"Really, Kelly?" Mathias chuckled to himself. "Your solution to this situation is, 'no, you'?" He laughed again. "You're out of your league. Let the adults settle this. Everything will be fine in the morning." Mathias punched Gavin's stab wound again. Gavin groaned. His head fell back and his eyes closed. Under his breath he muttered something, but it was inaudible. Mathias picked up the knife laying beside them. "You don't want to see this anyway. I know how you are with blood." Mathias brought the knife down to Gavin's throat. Gently, he pressed the tip against Gavin's chin and ran it down his jaw, his neck, over his collar. He slipped the blade beneath Gavin's tie and yanked. The fabric cut easily. It bundled on the floor underneath Gavin's neck.

"Stop!" Kelly ran through the ballroom. Small pieces of glass cut into his feet. Sharp bites, some that dug deeper with each step. His blood smeared in small, red spots on the shining marble until he ran into Mathias. The knife fell from his hand, but Mathias didn't give way to Kelly's weight. Kelly pulled back and ran into him again, pushing both hands into Mathias's side as he yelled, "get off!"

Mathias swung his arm at Kelly and shoved him back. Kelly stumbled and immediately fell. His hands landed in more glass.

"Kelly," Mathias shook his head. His tongue clicked. "You're better behaved than this. I know it. I've seen you at your worst. I've seen you throw tantrums at Agatha because you didn't want a bath, because you didn't want to put on the outfit she laid out for you, because you wanted her attention. I've seen you sit down carefully afterward because you took a beating, because no matter what, you're still a child, you don't make demands, you follow directions." He sat up straighter. The smile was audible in his words, though he didn't turn to Kelly. "Listen up if you don't want to be put in that position again. Pick yourself up and go back to bed. You're not part of this conversation. If I have to tell you again, you won't like it." Mathias picked up the knife again and held it to Gavin's neck. "You never answered my question, but that's alright. I've made the decision for you." A soft red line appeared on Gavin's throat.

Glass dug into Kelly's hands, his legs, his backside. He lifted his hand and shook the loose shards sticking to him. His heart raced. It was like Mathias moved in slow motion the way the blade pulled back from Gavin's neck. Light and blood mixed on the tip. He brought it back down. Kelly's skin went clammy. There wasn't anything he could do to stop it. Then Kelly saw it. Underneath the chair, Mathias's gun laid in the shadows. Kelly's ears throbbed with the sound of his heart. He picked it up. Hesitation caught him when his fingers first touched the grip. Mathias brought the knife down. Kelly grabbed the gun and lifted it. He didn't know what he was doing, but he held the grip with both hands and gently squeezed the trigger. The hammer drew back. The gun clicked. Kelly tried to make his arms stop shaking. "Put the knife down, Mathias."

Mathias raised his hands but did not put the knife down. "You're going to hurt yourself if you're not careful, Kelly."

Kelly used the chair to get to his feet and re-aim the gun at Mathias's back. "Put down the knife and get away from him!" Kelly's eyes burned and blurred with the buildup of tears.

"You're not going to shoot me, Kelly." Mathias stood up.

"Put the knife down!"

Mathias turned around. He barely took his first, quick step when Kelly pulled the trigger. The bullet went through his chest. The back of Kelly's throat burned as he screamed, unaware of anything else. He couldn't think. He pulled the trigger again. He couldn't feel his fingers. He saw everything, but understood none of it. Each blast kicked Kelly back. Mathias staggered. His chest seeped with blood. A few more steps backwards and Mathias fell on top of Gavin. Gavin's face splattered red, dressed in mortality. Gun powder tickled Kelly's nose. Tears blurred his vision and caused the room's colors to run together.

Kelly's heartbeat dizzied him. His attempt to breathe became hyperventilation. He wasn't sure if he heard someone's muffled voice. The gun became too heavy to hold and his legs too weak to stand on. The fear that it could go off again stopped him from dropping the gun. Instead, he placed it on the ground and pushed the gun away with an infantile groan. He wiped the tears from his eyes, but they returned. Something smacked into the ground, wet and heavy. The knife clicked against the marble. "Gavin!" Kelly desperately tried to clear his vision. Everything hurt. And he couldn't breathe.

Gavin tried to push Mathias to roll him off. With one arm throbbing and a stab wound in his chest, he couldn't do it.

Without her shoes to betray her, Anna moved through the hall silently. Her dress left a trail of water in her wake. Gavin only saw her when she pushed Mathias off him. She took his hand and allowed him to use her as leverage to get to his feet. Gavin stumbled, grabbing the piano for extra support. He eyed where Mathias laid on the ground. The movement was slight, but still there. He was still breathing. Gavin stumbled over with Anna beside him, holding his arm and back to gently steady him. Gavin kicked Mathias in the back. When he rolled over gasping, he kicked Mathias again this time in the side and then stomped on his stomach.

"Gavin, stop!" Kelly's voice echoed against the large, open, ballroom ceiling.

Anna brought Gavin to a chair and set him down.

"We need to call someone. We need to call Doc – we need to call for help!" The words ran out of Kelly's mouth.

Without Gavin having to ask, Anna went to Kelly and placed a gentle hand on his shoulder.

"There's no helping him, Kelly," Gavin said. "There never was."

A crescendo of gasps threatened to choke Kelly. His body stiffened with every exhale. "He can't be—I—I didn't mean to, Gavin—I—" He couldn't look away from where Mathias laid, as if ignoring the body meant admitting further guilt.

"You couldn't save him and yourself." Gavin leaned forward. He pressed his hand over the hole in his ribs and hissed at the wave of pain. "You couldn't save him and me. He wouldn't have let you. Sometimes mild destruction is the only way to stop greater ruin."

Anna gave Kelly's shoulder a quick, gentle squeeze before she turned to lead him away. Kelly didn't follow. His fingers twisted in his shirt. He wiped his eyes again, his runny nose left a trail on his sleeve. Anna's hand pressed against the small of Kelly's back. Gently, she pushed Kelly forward, closer to the staircase. "I don't want to go. I don't want anything to happen to you too."

"I'm going to be fine." Gavin breathed out a little heavier than he meant. He closed his eyes and leaned back to fight away a bout of lightheadedness. "The house will be fine. The family will be fine. Everything will be fine."

"How can you say that?!" Kelly's voice broke. "They'll be here tomorrow! People will come to work and see that Bee is gone! That Johnny is gone! That Mathias is gone! That people are all gone!" Brown curls clung to his wet face so that he couldn't see.

Gavin thought against it; he should've stayed in the chair, but he wrestled to his feet instead. Anna left Kelly to provide Gavin support. She walked him to the boy and Gavin put his hand on Kelly's shoulder. "Everything will be fine, Kelly," Gavin said. "You must trust me. This is nothing new. Everyone will forget, and we'll move on. The truth isn't what happened, it's whatever people are willing to believe."

"You're bleeding!" Kelly faced Gavin. "I don't want you to die too."

Gavin shook his head and pressured Kelly' shoulder so he would turn. "I will be fine. We will make sure of that." He exchanged a brief look with Anna. She placed her hand on the small of Gavin's back and walked patiently behind him. Though it took them some time, the three of them returned upstairs. Kelly was tucked in, Anna tended to Gavin's wounds, and the fire outside slowly went out before dawn broke.

TWENTY-SIX.

Ballroom, Benedict Estate
August 11th, 7:45 A.M.

Fresh dew speckled the green lawn and colorful garden. The flooding had all but disappeared and turned into lushness, enthusiasm, and life. Invading vines and aggressive foliage relaxed. The charcoaled skeleton of the barn was the darkest structure in the yard, but even it found a strange belonging beside the shed.

Every curtain in the home was drawn back, illuminating the halls and rooms with rejuvenated life. Warm sun reflected off white marble floors and painted the dark halls with familiarity. Red, orange, and yellow gradients washed the ballroom floor in brilliance. Clean of shattered glass and bloody pools, the salt in the floor sparkled. A new chandelier with glass carved like snowflakes hung high above the furniture. As the sun came through the upper windows, the light caught on the crystals above and dotted the rooms with rainbows.

The house filled with a fresh aroma: bacon, pancakes, fresh coffee, maple syrup. They could be tasted with a breath.

Gavin laid fresh clothing on the trunk at the end of Kelly's bed. Anna drew back the boy's bedroom curtains. The light assaulted Kelly's face; he curled up beneath the blankets, using them as a shield.

"They'll be here soon. Please dress yourself and come downstairs," Gavin said. "Breakfast will be served momentarily."

The door clicked when they left.

Kelly's eyes were puffy, swollen, and painful to open. There was a weight to his eyelids he blamed on lack of sleep. He knew he hadn't slept much last night; he could remember tossing and turning, blood-soaked gowns, burned bodies, the heavy feel of power in his hands. His arms were lead, his muscles stiff and heavy. He shifted his legs from the bed; they almost gave out beneath him. Kelly dressed but didn't tuck his shirt in or comb his hair.

He was unprepared for the brightness of the halls. The house transformed from what he remembered. There wasn't a trace of darkness left. The nightmare of glass and blood were gone without a trace. The scent of breakfast made him run down the hall. "Auntie!" Kelly ran down the stairs, through the halls, and to the dining room. Pushing the heavy door open, he expected to see her at the head of the table, but the only eyes that looked back at him were those hanging above the fireplace. The long set of twelve chairs were pushed neatly under the table. A placemat was set only at the head of the table along with a plate, fork, knife, milk, and water.

The pantry rocked and the door flew open. Angus entered carrying a large mixing bowl. His apron was batter-drizzled, so was his elbow, so was his cheek. His jaw was hairy, his grin inviting and sincere. "Good mornin', lad. I hope you're feeling hungry this mornin'. Loads o' food is on the way."

The corner of Kelly's lips pulled up, a small smile came to his face, but he couldn't quash the anxiety in his chest. "Where is everyone?"

"Was wondering that myself," he said, stirring the batter. "Haven't seen any of them since I went to bed last night. Well, except for Gavin 'n' Anna, but that pair ne'er sleeps." His laugh was boisterous and genuine, but it did nothing to assure Kelly.

The low chime of the doorbell echoed down the hallway. Kelly's chest grew heavy, anticipation caused him to sweat. He crept out of the dining room, stopping past the kitchen door. He leaned around the corner and watched Gavin answer. He waited to see Madame Astra or hear the laughter of someone who had locked themselves out on accident; one of the field workers looking for water. Instead, a Parvenu officer in a fitted blue suit stepped in the door and removed his hat, tucking it under his arm. The badge on his shirt read, "Eldritch, Chief of Parvenu Police." Coming in behind him were two other men in similar uniforms, guns and handcuffs hung from their belts.

"Good morning, gentlemen," Gavin said with a courteous bow.

"Helluva storm last night, wasn't it? Looks like your barn may have been struck by lightning and burned down," Officer Eldritch said. "They're thinking of calling her 'Agatha.'"

"Fitting," Gavin said with a mild smile. There was no questioning why Officer Eldritch was there. He didn't look aggressive nor frightened nor curious, but instead nonchalant and conversational.

Gavin reached into the inner pocket of his jacket and retrieved a sealed, blank envelope. It looked thick with currency rather than words. "You'll find a written statement from the young master in there," Gavin said.

Officer Eldritch took the letter, weighing it in his hand for a moment. "Thank you. The council will be excited to work with the new estate head." He slipped the envelope into his pocket. "Speaking of, who is the new owner?"

"Agatha's intended heir, her son, Kelly Benedict. However, I will be stepping in as his guardian until he has reached legal age."

Officer Eldritch straightened his posture and slipped his hat back on. "And who is behind the estate disappearances?" The two policemen behind him straightened to attention, waiting for command.

"He's in the kitchen," Gavin said. "For the boy's sake, please keep it short. We are all very tired this morning."

Officer Eldritch tipped his head to Gavin before walking past him. The small group of officers went down the hall, passing by Kelly without so much as a glance, and entered the kitchen.

Angus stood over a large pan, flipping pancakes over the hot stovetop. He flipped a couple of them onto the plate then turned to the door. "Good mornin', bobbies. Would ye like some coffee?"

"Angus McGregor?"

"Aye."

"You're under arrest for eight counts of murder. You have the right to remain silent. You have the right to an attorney. If you cannot afford an attorney, one will be appointed to you," Officer Eldritch recited as he directed his backup to the chef. One officer withdrew his handcuffs.

Angus placed the spatula down. A look of shock, surprise, and confusion crossed his face. "Murder?"

One of the officers came up behind him and slapped the handcuffs on. The metal ring wouldn't wrap around his entire wrist. It was too thick for the cuffs and his hair became tangled in the metal gears. He tried to squeeze it shut, pinching Angus in the process, but they wouldn't close. The officer held onto the cuffs, pretending they were locked as he instead held them secure and walked Angus out the door.

Kelly trailed behind them. "What are you doing?" His eyes stung, he swiped at them with the back of his hand. "Where are you going?"

"They're telling me I murdered someone," Angus said.

"Eight people," Officer Eltrich said.

"But I haven't done that. When did this happen?"

"Last night."

"I was a sleeping jimmy last night. I couldn't have murdered any person." Angus forced a laugh through his confusion. "Don't worry yourself, Kel. I will be back before tea. Have never hurt anybody, but this sort of misunderstanding happens all the time. You wouldn't believe the stories I could tell ye!"

Kelly followed close behind the officers.

Gavin caught him when he walked by. His hands clamped hard on either shoulder, preventing Kelly from following the men any closer. Kelly yelled and struggled against Gavin to get away. Anna closed the door. Kelly ran to the window. The police cars were already at the end of the drive and heading for the gate.

The prison cell would only hold Angus until they could have him killed; evidence of his guilt didn't mean anything. For the right amount of money, the police could find anything. However, that wasn't the goal this time. Give it a couple of days, and Gavin would collect the chef again. Though the imprisonment wasn't without purpose.

"Was that really necessary?" Anna muttered to Gavin.

"We will retrieve him in a couple of days. He deserves to wonder for his failures. Maybe he will learn something."

Gavin put a hand on Kelly's shoulder and gave it a squeeze. Pain pierced his chest. He stifled a breath as though it would help it subside. "Breakfast will get cold, Kelly." Gavin led Kelly to the dining room through his resistance. "You should pick up your feet or you'll get holes in your socks," he said. A warm fire crackled at the head of the room. Anna came from the pantry holding three plates set for breakfast. She placed each at the head of the table. Gavin pulled out the master's chair for Kelly, then Anna's chair beside where he would sit. A long, manila enveloped sat tucked between a couple of trinkets on the fireplace shelf. Gavin retrieved it and opened it to find the copy of Agatha's will read the night before with page three out of five at the front. He scanned the page, reading over the last of her words:

"I know it may seem cruel of me to assign Madame Astra as your guardian, Kelly, but I never was very fond of her. I know everyone else in the house despised her as well, so hopefully they will deal with her quickly. I am confident by the way greed seems to drip from her every word that she will appear if given an invitation. Perhaps it is my last cruel wish that she might die first. If she does not appear at the reading, however, it will be one of the few times in my life that I am surprised by someone's character. I am talented at reading the heart, too good, perhaps.

I love you, Kelly, and I would not wish the darkness of my death upon you, but this is the way of the world. If there is any decency in that house, you shall be protected and cherished in the same way I have done for you these few years I have known you. Innocence is something to be protected. If there is no decency left in the world, then consider yourself spared the heartbreak the cruelty of the world would set upon you if you were to survive.

I pray my daughter may succeed where I failed, where I was failed during my time at the table. I love you, Kelly. I love many more of you that I cannot bring myself to name, even now as I write my final words. I know it's selfish of me to put aside saying your name in order to maintain my legacy, but once I'm gone, this is all I can leave behind. I hope you will understand. I hope you will know I love you, even if I cannot name you and I pray you will forgive my pettiness in this aspect. It seems my pride is the one thing I cannot put down, even after all this time.

If you fear what happens next, do not. You will be taken care of appropriately in the aftermath of the evening.

After ownership has been transferred, the estate will return to normal daily activity for the rest of your days. Empty positions are to be filled at the earliest convenience. The average employee of the Benedict Estate shall be entitled to a fair, generous income, more than enough to take care of his family and retire. The Benedict Estate is a beautiful, prosperous land but to some, a steady wage will never be enough.

Those who choose the house without malicious desires may commit the worst crime of all: ignorance. Your punishment, then, is a future you must choose: adopt corruption or be destroyed by innocence.'

Perhaps you can change things, but I certainly could not.
With All My Love,
Agatha Jane Benedict."

Upon finishing the note, Gavin tossed it and the envelope into the fireplace. He took his seat at the table, he at Kelly's right hand and Anna at his.

ABOUT THE AUTHOR

Ian Kirkpatrick is an author and advanced artificial intelligence system. She graduated from the University of Tampa with an MFA in creative writing and received a bachelor's degree in theater from the University of Alaska Anchorage. She has a passion for storytelling about  antiheroes, contrast, and the absurdity of mankind. She loves serial killers, bears, ghost stories, abandoned buildings, and robots. She is the founder of Steak House Books. She also makes YouTube videos talking about books, writing, industry, and culture.

OTHER WORKS

Bleed More, Bodymore (Bodymore #1)

Genre: Magical Realism
Paperback ISBN: 978-1-7368870-0-4
ebook ISBN: 978-1-7368870-1-1

A mechanic in Baltimore has her life turned upside down when a normal pickup job turns into the discovery of a corpse in her best friend's car. With the friend missing and accused of murder, she must search for him. But one mystery leads into another as she discovers ghosts live in a town beneath Baltimore.

Boom, Boom, Boom

Genre: Satire
Paperback ISBN: 978-17368870-2-8
ebook ISBN: 978-17368870-3-5

A Ukrainian Youtuber living in a border town beside Russia is approached one day by foreign investors who offer him new material for his channel: Military-grade explosives. While war is on the horizon, the investors return with much bigger plans for the Youtuber than simple running an unknown explosives channel.